VISIONS OF KINGS

The Seer's Blessing: Book 3

Jana Sun

CONTENTS

CHAPTER ONE

JACK

The clearing was quiet.

Diego was less than a foot away from me, but he felt farther. His smile played at the corners of his mouth instead of taking over his face, lighting up his eyes. There was a faint blush staining his cheeks and the bridge of his nose, creeping down the edges of his neck. The slight, barely-there wind rustled his hair and my chest went tight.

"I hope she doesn't regret staying here. I hope she doesn't regret choosing me," his thoughts echoed loudly around my mind. The tree sentinels worked their way back to the forest, trying to allow us some privacy even though I felt their roots beneath me, still listening.

He kept raising and dropping his hands, the heart link warming against my skin. Diego wanted to reach for me, but didn't. I searched his large, golden eyes, and saw uncertainty there. I was still getting used to that engulfing, pure gold—they were chocolatey brown on Earth. Warm and deep, little pools to get lost in. Here it was like staring into the suns. The more I stared at him, the deeper the blush became until his skin was splotchy from my attention.

I held my hand out for him to take. I remembered him in my house before it burned; how he moved like the walls would come crashing down around him if he existed too loudly or moved too quickly. He had that same air of caution, so I seized the moment, grabbed his hand and squeezed. The heart links pulsed a few times, little jolts of happiness and approval at the contact.

My staff bobbed happily beside me, floating and circling around us, breaking the moment and giving Diego a chance to breathe again. I caught him glancing at the crystal and I knew what he saw. There was one bright, emerald green spark floating within Harold's perfect crystal: Snapdragon. Her spirit had decayed past recognition; she was a fragment of a fragment. All that was left was her rage and fear, twisting her into something no one could recognize. The portal back to Earth flickered in and out, the magic finally fading even though Diego and I had dropped the spell ages ago. Magic was desperate to stay alive in Obius, but the portal knitted itself closed, until finally we were alone.

We'd won the battle–Arturo retreated, Snapdragon finally fell, and everyone else returned to Earth. Mari and Falcon were worse for wear; Mari swallowed Wildfire like she was a circus performer and Falcon took more hits than any man had a right to and remained standing. Their spirits were as battered as their bodies, but they were too far away now for me to help. I wanted Mari to release that horrid magic, but she just held on tighter. Peony and Sherwin vowed to get them back on their feet and work on everything earthside, but there was no one to make sure *they* were okay too. Peony had to be exhausted from the sheer amount of magic she cast, but that was another problem I couldn't solve.

All I could focus on was the man standing in front of me, with cautious eyes and loud thoughts.

And the souls that still needed to rest.

The link to Sanctum was still closed and like the rest of the souls here, there was no rest for her. I pulled Snapdragon into the crystal with the rest of the lost souls to give them someplace to go. Snapdragon's emerald magic bounced around in the crystal, floating gently and I hoped that she found some peace.

The suns had risen, and in the daylight, the clearing was much more desolate than I thought. The battle between Arturo's army and Mari was grisly. The ground still steamed from Mari's flames, and the fallen soldiers littered the field. My stomach twisted, and I forced myself to look away. Their souls were already calling for rest and I didn't have much to offer. Diego's gaze gave me goosebumps; the heat of his body next to mine warming the air between us.

"So," I said.

"So," Diego said. He tugged me a little closer, enveloping me in a hug. His arms wrapped around my shoulders, and the weight of him clung to me like a second skin. He smelled of sweat and sandalwood–always sandalwood–and I rubbed my face against his chest.

"Where do we even start?" I asked.

"Well, I think we should probably tend to those souls. I saw you looking at the soldiers." Diego stroked my hair, his fingers tangling in the knots and easily pulling them out. It reminded me how profoundly filthy I was and I almost felt bad for snuggling so close to him. Almost. He was also objectively gross, and I didn't mind in the least. Maybe he didn't either.

"My Blossom?"

"Hmm?"

"I can, um, hear your thoughts. Loudly," he stifled a small laugh, biting at his lips, making him utterly irresistible. And *here*, with me, standing under the brilliantly blue sky of Trellis.

Oh. Ohh. *Ohh.*

Diego laughed again, low and gruff, and brushed his nose against my temple. "You smell like jasmine flowers," his words tickled against my ear before he planted a small kiss on it. The hum of my staff drew our focus to the smoldering forest, and he let me go enough so he could really take in the sights of his homeland. It wasn't pretty. Wildfire had scarred the land and the flames seemed to have burned the soul of it too. I watched as he scanned the horizon; Diego stared into the distance, in the direction of the castle. The Trellian banner was limp, and no amount of wind seemed to bring it to life. It was a small white and green blip against the skyline, the castle just thin gray towers instead of the impressive stone that I knew it was.

He searched for the tree sentinels that slowly moved away from the clearing and back to their posts; quiet, ever-standing guardians. The flames didn't reach them, thank the Goddesses.

"The land feels..."

"Dead?" he finished. Diego knelt and ran his hands in the dirt. He scooped up clumps of it, and it fell like dust from his fingers.

"Scarred," I corrected. I felt the tremblings and rumblings of life deep below the ground under my feet, but it would take ages for that to bubble up to the surface again. Generations of time needed to pass before the trees would rise again. It was hard to picture; that much time passing without the Rainbow Forest for the Fae to live in.

"Arturo will need to answer for his madness," Diego said. He was using his King voice, commanding and clear, like even the bugs would take heed of his words. It made the hair on my arms stand up. Diego's jaw was set and the hard line of his mouth had erased any trace of a smile from just moments ago.

"Diego?"

"Hmm?"

A vision danced just at the edges of my eyes, not ready to fully reveal itself, and I dug my fingers into Diego's arm. Floating through the wind,

I saw feathers that were a bright, cerulean blue. The color of Kings. The color of Diego.

But these were far away. It didn't feel like Trellis; the world around them felt too *blue* to be Trellis. I saw Diego's lips moving, but his words had fallen away. I tried to focus on the falling feathers in my mind's eye. I turned to him and played with the feathers on his forearms. They had small bits of fuzz at the base like a hatchling bird. I plucked some of it away and he twitched.

"Sorry, did that hurt?"

"A little, it felt like you were pulling out a hair." Diego ruffled his feathers, stretching his arms and flexing the muscles to make them fan out. He smoothed them back down, almost like he was smoothing out a bunched-up jacket on his arms. "Are you sure this isn't too much?"

His mouth said the words, but his mind asked another question, ***"Am I too weird for you?"***

"I personally don't think many men can pull off feathers, but they really work on you." I grinned, trying to convey how little the feathers and horns meant to me. They were the missing pieces of him on Earth, and seeing him in Obius just reinforced how complete he looked now.

"Well, I do my best to be presentable, my Blossom."

This was the easy intimacy that I craved; the easy joking and easy smiles. Diego in Obius unlocked all the hidden pieces, and I loved each one. I prayed that it would always be this easy.

He tilted my chin up, forcing our eyes to meet. Staring into his eyes felt like scrying, and the magic pulled me away into the vision.

"Tell me what you see," he said, steadying his grip around my waist as the Seer's magic washed over me fully. The downy softness on his arms was a stark contrast to the strength of his grip, and it made it easier to stay latched into the present while I searched the vision.

More falling blue feathers. Blue waters. Bridges connecting small huts across the waterways. The huts were thatched and cozy; smoke tails coming from the chimneys, strong enough that I could smell them. Cooking fires, not the musky, heady smell of Wildfire. Then, a man dressed in black with golden eyes and black hair. His horns curled against his head and his hard eyes pierced through the vision. He stared at me, head cocked in confusion, but his lips were set in a thin line of determination that felt vaguely familiar. His energy was expansive and so green. A quick tug on the long black sleeve of his right arm drew my attention and I saw a blue feather.

"Diego, do you have any other family here?"

"Not that I know of, why?"

"I think our priorities have just shifted."

I saw the man's face in my mind again, and the more I focused on his features, the more I knew them. The cheekbones, the shape of his nose, and the fullness of his lips. He was the spitting image of Diego.

The throes of the vision left as quickly it came and I was eye to eye with Diego again. I took in all the lines of his face; the crow's feet around his eyes from what I prayed were years of smiles, the crook in his nose that made him feel like a real person, the sharpness of his cheekbones and where the scruff of his beard was shaved. His 5 o'clock shadow was less of a shadow and more scruff now. The man in my vision could be his twin.

"Shifted?" he asked.

Diego tugged on my hand to pull me down, and we sat on a large flat rock together. I wondered what this place was for; if this was a stage or just a rock, if it was meant for something more. The damage made it hard to discern what it looked like before the fire, but I could picture people gathering here. I wondered what Trellis was like when it was alive.

"I saw someone with blue feathers," I said. Diego scratched his nails against the rock, the noise only slightly louder than the light breeze. The suns heated up the stones, and the warmth seeped into my skin.

"I don't understand," he said. Diego's volume was a giveaway for his emotions. Loud and confident and happy. Quiet and careful and shy. His words were whispered, more to himself than to me, but the heart link pulsed again, letting me know his need for connection.

"I think you have a brother, Diego." I bumped my foot to his, and he took that as an invitation to lay us back on the rock. Eyes skyward, he opened an arm for me to curl against him.

"That... seems unlikely."

"Are clones a thing here?"

"No?" he laughed.

"Then you've got a brother. Cousin. Something. He looked just like you."

"Are you sure it wasn't me?"

"The timeline felt wrong for it to be you. It felt like I was watching something that was happening now. And he seemed far too serious to be you, which... is saying something, really."

Diego bumped my arm, tangling our fingers together again. He kept reaching for me, like I was the one that would disappear.

"I'm not that serious," he said, his tone a promise of mischief that gave me shivers.

With the portal closed, the land empty, and the sky stretching out forever, I felt very alone on this rock with Diego. Taking in the details of his horns and the hue of his feathers filled in the missing parts of him. I reached up to touch the hardened keratin of his horns. They had a very light fuzz, and the ridges of them reminded me of the texture of a tightly woven basket. The feathers twitched when I touched them.

"I think we need to find him," I said.

"You're right, but we have other work to do first." Diego's voice had lost its airiness just as quickly as it came as he nodded in the direction of the castle. "We're a good day's walk and I want to see if any of the smaller villages have survived the blaze. As much as I love the quiet, *this* quiet is unnatural. I'm afraid there's no life left in Trellis."

"The trees are still here," I said, feeling their roots beneath us.

"Yes, but there should be so much more life. Trellis buzzed. There were Fae folk everywhere, living in the trees, on the sides of mountains, in clearings, and around small lakes. This space is too wide and too silent. We need to look for the people that are still here," he said.

"I didn't burn that much of the forest, Deign was always so dramatic. Everything was grand and kingly. He hasn't changed," the words played through me and I turned, searching for the voice.

Snapdragon.

"I'm in the crystal, you dolt. Remember? You stuffed me in here."

"Jack, what's wrong? What do you see?" Diego's panicked expression made me realize that he wasn't hearing her. That she was just talking to me, from my crystal ball. The staff bobbed as if it was annoyed, and it had her *posture*, which was absurd; it's a staff, not a person. It had a slight tilt as it bobbed a little faster, like it was trying to tap a foot.

"Snapdragon," I said. It came out way more annoyed than I meant, and Diego was instantly on guard.

"What!"

"She's in my staff. And she's awake? Conscious? I don't know. She's talking to me."

"Can she hear me too?"

"Unfortunately," she hissed.

"Yep, but she isn't happy about it."

"Likewise," Diego mumbled, running his hand through his hair and once again forgetting about his horns. He bumped them, twitching a bit, before combing through his hair again. He was making the adorable mop of curls turn into a mess.

"He really hasn't changed. He's going to scratch his nose next because he's flustered. He did this all the time at court."

And then Diego scratched the side of his nose, and I groaned.

"We *are not* going to be co-pilots the entire time we're in Trellis," I said, grabbing my staff and shaking it a little. Her little green dot flew around the orb and satisfaction surged through me.

Don't be petty, I scolded myself.

"Is she speaking again?" Diego asked.

"Not anymore," I said. I glared at the crystal ball; not that she would be able to see it. I didn't think she had eyes anymore. She was just energy.

"Don't glare at me, human. Don't be angry at me because I know Deign's mannerisms better than both of you. You barely know him."

I stared at the suns in the sky, letting the light sear my eyes. This was going to be a long journey with Snapdragon narrating the whole way.

"You'll tell me what she says, yes?" Diego asked, touching my arm to jar me from my thoughts.

"She's not saying anything important. Maybe she needs a nap, or you know, being a restless spirit that couldn't let go of her own death," I said.

"I wish I was trapped underwater, drowning for an eternity instead of in this wretched crystal with you."

Likewise, sister.

"My Blossom, I think we should get going."

"We need to see to the soldiers first," I said quietly. Snapdragon had nothing to say to that, and I was thankful for the silence.

The souls of the soldiers were stirring; the energy came in waves, like they were summoning their strength for the call to rest. I placed my hands on the scorched ground and felt the loss of life. My lungs and throat closed up and my chest heaved from it. The emerald green of Snapdragon's spark caught my eye and I jumped.

"This part never gets easier," Snapdragon whispered.

I swallowed hard, the truth of her words echoing through me. Every soul I collected would feel like this. I wondered how much magic my staff could hold, how many souls, and if the links to Sanctum would ever be reopened. The magic flowed from my staff before I even started the words of the spell.

Two weeks ago, if someone told me that I would be standing in a razed field in Obius, the realm of magic, raising the spirits of the dead, I would have laughed. I would have thought them crazy, and yet...

My staff spun in wide circles as my hands moved on their own; my body knew the dance more than my memory. I stepped and twirled, dancing through the ancient spellwork, until the orbs started to rise from the ground. It made my knees quake; there were *so* many souls.

"Rest, be at peace. Return to Sanctum to be born again."

As I spun and moved in time with the beat of the spell, I stepped through the field. I had danced half across the clearing, leaving Diego behind me. My feet moved on their own as I swooped and glided. The magic flowed freely from me, and the souls glittered in the air like suspended raindrops. I held them there like I had stopped time itself and felt a little drunk with the Priestess' magic.

My hands were together at my chest, as if in prayer. Was I praying? I wasn't sure—the souls knew my request as my staff hovered in front of me. It shone emerald green, as they all tumbled one by one into the sphere.

When I opened my hands, I saw that a small orb had formed between them. It was different from the others. Silvery like it was made of platinum instead of actual silver. There were hints of gold, and I watched as it sparkled. There was a shift in the magic; the Resting spell seeped into the ground, trying desperately to soothe the burnt soil as the souls continued their path into the crystal. The vision came back, playing itself out in the silvery orb.

I saw golden eyes and blue feathers. I saw curled horns and black hair. I saw the determined set of shoulders and the danger that hovered just above his skin, like a coiled threat.

Desmond.

I knew his name.

Chapter Two

DIEGO

I stood in the center of the clearing, what was a battlefield just hours ago, and numbness seeped through me. Muted and drowning, I'd seen this scene play out a hundred times or more in the past but I was helpless to look away. Jack danced through the Resting spell. She moved with easy grace, like she had been training all her life to do exactly this. I watched her as she twirled and spun, her staff dancing with her like an elegant partner. The souls of the fallen came to her willingly, and she pulled each one into her staff.

It was a little sickening—each life decimated to nothing but the light of their souls.

Her staff took them all greedily; the magic glowing brighter inside with every addition.

She's not Snapdragon, I reminded myself as I glanced at Jack to make sure she wasn't listening. I let the words cut deeper than I should. She wasn't Snapdragon. Of course she wasn't. Jack saw her life in danger with her visions and she ran straight into the fray instead of hiding. She gently laid

Snapdragon's soul to rest in her staff when she could have–and probably *should* have–destroyed the fragments.

Her visions of another man with blue feathers gnawed at me too. Where was that coming from? How could it be true?

Had the Seer's magic already started twisting her too?

My hands reached instinctively for the heart link. I fingered each little charm knitted into the metal of the chain around my wrist. Love. Eternity. Blossoms. The promises from the Goddesses and the blessings for a happy life. Jack's heart rate picked up as she moved, beating faster from exertion, and I felt every thump radiate through my arm. We were connected.

This *is* different.

She's different.

The past wasn't doomed to repeat itself.

I wouldn't make the same mistakes again.

Jack's spell finished and she was unsteady on her feet. I rushed to her side–she was all the way across the field, closer to the treeline now than the openness she left me in–and I extended a hand to her.

"Thanks," she said, out of breath.

"Steady," I said more to myself than her. Jack's smile was radiant; everything about her was radiant, really, but when she smiled and her eyes crinkled, the light of her soul shone through. She caught something flickering across my face but the smile faded as quick as it came, and I felt the walls of my mind going up.

"Diego?"

"Yes?" I shifted under the weight of her gaze and she folded her arms across her chest. She was still wearing one of Snapdragon's dresses.

"Look at me," she said and I realized I was suddenly studying my feet quite intently. She was wearing Snapdragon's shoes. Sherwin found them in a market so many seasons ago. He remembered her mentioning that she wanted something more fashionable than just sandals. But this wasn't

Snapdragon standing in front of me, with the lingering smoke from Wild-fire clinging to her skin and her hazel eyes staring back at me. It was Jack. She cocked her head and her bun wobbled. My heart lurched. She was different.

"You're gaining such confidence in your magic as a Priestess," I said evenly. The years on the throne, sitting in courts and feigning polite-ness through my discomfort served me well now. My voice was even and smooth, although my heart wasn't. It would never be smooth again.

"You're a terrible liar," she said, the wicked smile back.

"Actually, I'm an excellent liar. Comes with the kingly duties." I tapped her nose, keeping my face neutral and calm, pretending I was a still lake instead of a rushing river.

She arched an eyebrow and I realized my mistake instantly, "So you *are* lying."

"No, ah, I just–"

"Diego Ortiz, even without my magic I'd know if you were lying. So, let's try again. What's going on?" The sound of my name–my human, chosen name–on her lips made me shiver.

"You just... remind me of Snapdragon," I said cautiously. It was a clear statement. Of course they were similar. They had the same magic. They knew the same spells. They had visions. They both loved me.

At least, I thought they did. I hoped.

"I'm nothing like her," Jack snapped, more viciously than I think she meant. Her spine was too straight and she stood with balled fists. The sharp tone surprised us both, and I took a step back.

"I know," I said, and I did know that. I did. Bowing my head to submit, to show that she was right, I kissed the back of her hand. Slowly, she relaxed with my touch. "I know, my Blossom."

Jack's hand was limp in mine and the heart link tightened against my wrist. Our connection had just taken a hit, and I think she realized it then too. She breathed in and out slowly, releasing her breath fully before looking at me.

"I'm not her and I need you to believe that. I need you to trust me," she said. I nodded; my throat was dry and my tongue too heavy to form words. The tightness of the heart link lessened a little.

"Wh-what are you going to do with the souls?"

"I'm not going to *do* anything to them. Not until I can figure out how to get them to Sanctum, anyway."

"Can your crystal hold them all?" I wondered how many souls were in there now. The bright green dot of Snapdragon's spirit floated around and I squirmed. I prayed that Snapdragon couldn't see me, that she was truly gone, and I hated that I wished for that.

"Think so. Let's cross that awful bridge *if* we have to. Now, which way to the castle?"

I pointed through the treeline, toward the tattered banners flying in the distance. Arturo would likely be there; walking in wouldn't be the easiest option or the smartest. Jack had magic practically falling out of her, but I wasn't ready to toss her into another fight. I didn't want to fight through my old home either; there had been too much destruction already.

"Tell me more about your vision," I said.

"The guy that isn't you but could be your twin?"

"Yes. Him."

"I saw blue lakes and blue skies, with little bridges and huts. It looked like he was floating on the water."

"Chilijan."

"Chilijan? That's where Puddin is from. Is it all Catfolk?" Jack's staff settled at her side, and she tapped the crystal. I wondered if Snapdragon was whispering to her again, but didn't press it. It wouldn't help either of our moods.

"Not all, but most of the Catfolk live there. There's a lot of Fae that live in the waters of Chilijan too. Including their Empress. She isn't very social though. I've only met her a handful of times. I'm not even sure if she's still the Empress."

Jack bumped my shoulder, and the warmth of her affection bloomed in my chest. This was different. Things would be different.

"How far away is Chilijan?"

"A week's travel? Less if we can get a mage-hound to ride."

Jack grimaced at the mention of the mage-hound. They *were* quite smelly, but they weren't violent beasts. Not unless they were commanded to be, anyway. Flame was gone, and I didn't see or smell any sign of the others. Smokey, Blaze, Fira. I didn't know if they were even still alive.

That seemed to be the theme of my sum knowledge of Trellis now: what-ifs and guesses. My chest tightened at the thought and then the heart link followed suit. It sparked Jack's attention and any smile I forced on my face was as flat as the burnt land in front of us.

"Are we pretending that I'm not supposed to notice or know why you look like that?" Jack asked.

"Yes, please." The heart links held powerful magic and combined with Jack's natural psychic abilities, privacy was an illusion. At first, I welcomed it; the knowing, the being seen. It was a heady thing to be noticed after centuries clinging to the edges of life, but now the spotlight of Jack's attention never seemed to dim.

I didn't remember feeling like this with Snapdragon, but then again, were her eyes ever truly set on me?

I shook the thoughts away and watched as Jack relaxed. The tension of the heart links faded and the comforting weight they brought settled my nerves.

"There has to be something we can do about the land," Jack mumbled. She spoke more to the staff than to me. The crystal glowed bright and she nodded.

"Seeing anything promising in its depths?"

"Harold. I named the crystal Harold when I bought it online. Seems silly now, right?"

"Seems like you," I said, the surety of my words startling me. I was sure; of course Jack would name her crystal. She named the plants in her gardens and knew the spirit of every living thing around her.

"Snapdragon was ranting about soul revivals. Do you know anything about that?"

Scrubbing my hands over my face, I groaned. Soul revivals. Of course she would know about that magic; it *was* part of the Seer's Blessing. A soul revival is much like what it sounds; bringing the soul back to a body. It could work on a grander scale, like say, an entire forest ravaged by cruel flames, but the sheer amount of magic it would require–

"That groan went bone deep," she laughed.

"I know what a soul revival is. It's rare magic. I didn't even know that Snapdragon knew about the spells, but I'm not surprised. It's ancient magic, even by Obius's standards. As far as I know, there hasn't been a Priestess to cast one since the alchemy was created. Priestesses are *taught* about soul revivals, but no one *performs* them."

"Why not?"

"Because they'd probably die casting it," I finished weakly. Jack chewed on her bottom lip, taking in my words. Her eyes darted to the crystal, and she waved it away.

"Maybe we need to start smaller then," she said.

"Smaller."

"Yes."

"Such as?"

"Opening the link to Sanctum? Finding more of your heart? Finding your unlikely-twin-but-definite-blood-relative-and/or-clone?"

"Only one of those things sounds appealing to me." I pinched the bridge of my nose. Falcon told me a thousand times that it made me look like a grandfather when I did that. Thinking about how badly he was injured made it hard to breathe. Another piece in the wreckage that I caused. He was back on Earth and I prayed that Peony's magic was helping. I prayed that Peony would *keep* helping him.

I glanced back to the long, flat stone where the portal was. It was a stage years ago; this was where Fae children would dance for the start of the Bloom Festival. Was that even still celebrated? I remembered the streamers and the banners; the colors of the forest, the crest of Trellis proudly hung and everyone smiling. My throat closed up and I rubbed the knot that formed in my chest. Walking through Trellis was like walking through an echo, like reaching and only touching shadows, and I hated it. I hated what Trellis had become. I hated what I'd done to it.

"Any ideas on where we should start looking for your heart then?" Jack's words were coy and soft, trying to draw me out of my thunderous mood. I bowed deeply, at the waist, just to make her laugh.

She did.

"Ah, but my Blossom, my heart stands before me. Perhaps I'm in better shape than I originally thought."

"You're *such* a cheeseball." Jack tapped the tip of my nose and I caught her hand, pressing kisses to each finger.

"You love cheese."

"Lucky for you."

"Perhaps we can find some Trellian food. Cheese, even." I didn't know how likely that would be, considering the majority of the forest was gone, but the outer villages should still be fine. Brimming even, with all of the Fae that fled from Wildfire. The idea sparked alive in me; the outer villages.

That's where we had to go. The land would have to wait to be healed. The links to Sanctum weren't going to miraculously open again.

But I could show Jack what Trellis *was* like. I could show her the home I loved, the people I loved, and I could damn well prepare a meal for her.

Her stomach growled, and I grinned, wide and wolfish. Her cheeks tinged pink, and I drank in the sight of her. Things were going to be okay. *Eyes forward, eyes on her*, I repeated to myself over and over, like my new mantra.

"I think my body just realized how hungry I actually am. Is there really cheese here?" she asked. She covered her belly with her arms, trying to muffle the sound. It didn't work.

"Is there cheese–*honestly*, what kind of hovel do you take Trellis for? Of course we have cheese!" I gave her my best smile, the brightest parts of me because she deserved them.

Eyes forward, eyes on her.

"Lead the way, Diego." This time she bowed, mimicking me and I laughed, loud and full of life. She bowed to the waist, rolling her wrists and swinging her arms wide, fluffing the gesture even further. Bowing was typically only something the royals did in court. We bowed to our people to honor them. I never wanted to reign *above* anyone, I was there to serve, and I took that seriously. Jack rose and reached for my hand and I held it gingerly. I remembered how the imbalance of power between Snapdragon and I made things hard for her. I was her King first, partner second. It wasn't like that this time around, and I tried to stay aware of how easily it could change. I tugged her and she followed.

There were a few sets of smaller villages a few hours' walk from here. The suns in the sky were my guide, and I remembered the trails that my feet had traveled so many centuries ago.

Eyes forward, eyes on her.

CHAPTER THREE

FALCON

Everything hurt and I had to be dying. I sort of remembered returning to Earth. I remembered the feeling of being torn apart only to be miraculously put back together in the same atomic arrangement. Pretty sure I blacked out shortly after that.

It would explain why I was in Marigold Groves' bed. Flat on my back and under her covers. Smelling the scent of almonds and honey that I knew was the scent of her skin. Maybe her hair–it was the smell of Mari, of what a home could be, and I was keenly aware of how dangerous that thought pattern could be.

What I couldn't explain was why Mari was laying next to me, her eyes fluttered closed in sleep and her breathing deep and even. She was on her side, her back to me, and it only accentuated the curve of her hips. She was close enough that I could pretend to stretch and have her in my arms.

I was pretty sure I still had pants on, but peeked under the blankets just to confirm. Pants, check. That was good. Mari had a little tank top on with some sleep shorts. That was... some information. She had a birthmark on the back of her knee. Maybe it was just the light. Maybe she'd flinch if I licked it.

Maybe I needed to calm down.

She stretched, her hand jamming straight into my throat and it startled her awake. I made a strangled noise. The light punch didn't hurt but it did remind the remaining parts of my body that didn't ache to get on that.

"Hey," she said in the sweet, soft tone of a woman waking up and feeling safe. Her voice was thick from sleep, but when she opened her eyes I saw the flames of Wildfire in them with the ruins of Trellis reflecting back. Those trees would haunt my memories forever.

"Hey, yourself," I said. The flames grew brighter before flickering back to be contained in her blown pupils.

"How're you feeling?"

"Confused, mostly? Also like I should be on painkillers. Loads of them."

"You're going to the doctor today for sure. You passed out once we got back to Earth. Sherwin carried you in here. There wasn't really much space to lay you down."

"You could have just put me on the floor," I said, suddenly feeling too close to her, too close to something that could ignite. The air was heated between us, probably from her, but I was burning up under the sheets. I tossed them off and immediately regretted moving.

"We were not putting the most injured of the lot on the floor, you doofus."

"Forgive me for asking, but why are *you* here then?" I flashed a smile, hoping she saw the question as innocent as I meant it. Being in bed with Mari seemed like a dream, but this wasn't how it would have played out for me. Her laugh was husky as she ran a hand through her hair, shifting the braids so she could somehow snuggle closer to the silky pillow.

"Because it's my damn bed and it's comfortable," she said, stretching.

"Got it, makes sense. And where is the rest of Team Hawthorne?"

"We are not calling ourselves Team Hawthorne, and Peony is at Sherwin's place I assume. I didn't ask. She looked like she needed to have a good cry and that's not really my strong suit." Mari shuddered involuntarily, thinking about how to comfort a sobbing Peony, and I followed suit. A woman who could literally move the oceans was probably not the easiest person to console.

"Can you move? Stand?" she asked.

"I can feel my legs, but I wish I couldn't, so that's a good sign. Not really excited to try my luck at my legs supporting me though." I stretched my legs, trying to get the knots in them to loosen and release. No luck. The pain was sharp and shooting like someone had poured lava through my veins. Every breath reminded me of the Lightning.

"Well, we can get you up together. Peony and her mama were casting as many healing spells as they could. Puddin used some alchemy to create a healing crystal. She had me put it in the pocket of your shirt. Hopefully, it's helping."

I fished the crystal out of my pocket and it thrummed with magic. The healing spell made the small agate pulse with power, and I felt the effects easing the ache in my knuckles. I was getting too old to be punching folks left and right. Mari's gaze turned the air between us too warm and I squirmed. It made my ass hurt.

"Thank you," I said. I cleared my throat to let the words flow better. They owed me nothing; they could have left me to die, but they didn't.

It's what I would have done.

"Once we get you up, it's on you to shower. I'll make some coffee," she said. Mari was already up, stretching her arms over her head and I caught a glimpse of the smooth skin of her stomach. It wasn't the Wildfire that made her hot, that's for damn sure. Mari's movements weren't intrinsically graceful. She moved with purpose, alerting the ground that it was supposed to be there for her next steps.

"Not going to wash my back for me?"

"Baby, you haven't even bought me dinner and you're already trying to get me into the shower? Shameful Falcon, shameful."

"Ever the optimist I suppose."

"Opportunist, you mean. Go on. If you can make a pass at me, you're strong enough to carry your own self into the bathroom." Mari winked at me and I swear she added more swagger to her walk as she headed for the kitchen.

Groaning, I hauled myself upright. It was easier than I expected, which was good–but weird. My ribs ached but I could breathe without wincing. My arms were still a mess of webbed Lightning scars. I didn't see that going away anytime soon, if ever. I always liked my hands; I thought they were one of my more attractive features. I had hands that had seen days in the sun and spent time fighting and working. They were rough, but they were the only part of me that seemed like I wore the truth of my life for the world to see.

They were gnarly now. Not quite *mangled*, but not the sun-worn palms I was used to. The braided and leaf-like scarring made my skin lighter than it usually was. It was burned, but not red; the healing spells from Jack's staff and her family had pushed me through some of the healing process but now my hands were withered and veiny.

My tattoo was gone too, like the Lighting had purposefully obliterated it.

Maybe it had.

The smell of coffee and bacon forced me to my feet and I slowly made the short journey to Mari's bathroom. Her apartment was just as I remembered it from the last time she took care of me. I never knew why she was willing to help me then, but I was thankful.

I needed to stop showing up at her place half-dead; it wasn't a great look.

Without my clothes as a barrier, I saw the full extent of how badly I looked. The Lightning spread across my chest too, across my pecs but stopped right before the scars touched. I was probably lucky for that; it likely meant the Lightning missed my heart. They were leafy and vine-like, spreading out in a shocking disaster. I touched the raised skin and forced myself to swallow. They were just scars. I had plenty of others. In time I'd take my shirt off and not even see them.

But today, I did see the scars. Mari's huge bathroom mirror reflected every ugly mark. My left side was black and blue. My right hip bone had a nasty gash that was already scabbed over. I had bruises everywhere, including my nose and right eye where Diego punched me. I scrunched up a washcloth and dabbed at the bruises on my face. Someone—probably Mari—had done a decent job at getting the dried blood off of me, but I needed to scrub to get the rest of it off.

The heat of her shower cleansed my skin and relaxed some of the tighter muscles. I soaped up with Mari's almond and honey soap, washed my hair with her almond shampoo, and felt the flame that was Mari thaw my heart as her scent filled the small shower. I pretended that I didn't notice her there, like staying silent would buy me a couple extra seconds in her orbit.

"Just checking to make sure you didn't die in the shower," Mari called through the door.

"Haven't I proven that I'm a bit more indestructible than that?"

"Still don't want you dying in my bathroom. Food's ready," she said, but I heard the smile in her voice.

Don't catch feels, Falcon. She's gonna light you on fire. Probably literally.

"Be right there. Any chance my bag is here? I'd really love some fresh undies."

"Because I am an actual angel, yes, you do have clothes. Sherwin guessed you were his size, and dropped off a couple things. I left them on my bed."

"You are a goddess among men," I said.

She laughed, wild and bright. This girl was a Wildfire all on her own. "I'll be in the kitchen."

"Be right there."

JACK

Diego's thoughts were a mess and occasionally switched from English to Fae. I knew that it was Fae from the way it tickled in my mind like a whisper instead of a word. It was the language of magic, but I didn't understand the words and I tried not to pry. He was working something out in his mind, and I wanted to give him the space he needed to do so. Even though I was *dying* to know what was causing the lines around his eyes to be pronounced and why his heartbeat picked up steadily. It was beating as one solid piece, even though there was still over half of it missing.

At least he was still holding my hand.

We had been walking for hours and my feet ached; I knew they were covered in blisters. I wasn't used to wearing such stiff shoes, and shoving my feet into them after they were already a mess of cuts and bruises from roaming Trellis barefoot only made it worse. I did my best to keep my pace with Diego, but I was slowing down.

"We're almost there, my Blossom. We're going to a village called the River Glades. It's close to the Treis River."

"Close sounds good. I think I'm gonna need to stop and put my feet up for a bit."

"I'm sure we can find something to heal your pains in the village. River Glades is known for having strong healers. The river water is very restorative."

"Any chance they sell shoes?"

Diego scooped me up, his arms under the crooks of my knees and my back. He pressed his cheek to my forehead, our skin sticking together under a slight sheen of sweat. He moved like he wasn't carrying a grown woman who was mostly dead weight at this point. Diego's steps were sure and confident, but his silence was still too heavy, filling the air.

"Tell me about River Glades," I said.

"The folk that live there are water folk. They live in harmony with the river and make sure the waters flow. Most of the people are connected with the river, and their magic is a lot like Peony's. Minus the truth magic."

"They sound lovely," I said.

"They are. Were. Assuming River Glades is still there," Diego said as his voice faded. We didn't know how far Wildfire had spread, or how long it raged. I felt life stirring around us, so that gave me hope that River Glades was spared from the flames. Maybe the river helped them.

He walked for at least another hour with me in his arms. My back ached from being carried, along with my hips and shoulders. My knees and arms were stiff from Diego's steady grip. I shifted a few times, trying to make it easier for both of us, before I finally insisted that he put me down.

My feet protested immediately. The blisters had time to realize how swollen and painful they were, and each step was agony. Diego tried to pick me back up, but I playfully swatted him away. There was something off with his mood, so I tried to keep things light. The storm of his emotions churned in those golden eyes, and I felt the depths of them through the heart links.

I kissed the bracelet on my wrist and watched Diego's smile brighten.

"Look," he said, turning me to face the path before us. The path was well-trodden and mostly packed dirt. The edges were lined with flowers and pebbles. We'd been trekking through so much forest that my feet practically cried in relief at the very flat road ahead.

"Are we here?"

"River Glades is at the end of the path, about nearly a furlong. Think you can make it?"

"Yes," I said and started down the way. I had to pry into his mind to figure out what a furlong was, but it didn't seem *too* far. The shoes had to go; I pulled them off and let my messed up feet breathe and feel the soil. Magic tingled in the bottoms of my feet–I connected with the land differently here.

Back in Trellis proper, where the forest was in ruins and the ground was covered in debris and rocks and decaying trees, the land was weak and lifeless. Here, magic was alive. I felt the stirring of the planet and the people of River Glades before I saw them. Curling my toes in the dirt, I reached deeper, grasping for the soul of the land that was missing around the castle.

My staff hovered in front of me, a horizon bar to stabilize myself.

Magic arced through me, racing up my spine and down through my fingers, spreading through my chest and curling itself around my heart. It pulled me deeper into its energy until I lost myself. It was like a vision; my body unfolded in front of me, growing larger and longer with every root and vine. I opened my hands and felt the flowers blooming in my palms, leaves sprouting from my fingers. Green, green magic poured from me and I was a bystander to how it flowed. I connected deep into the core of Obius, the core of the world, and I smiled. I saw the history etched into the layers of the land and wanted to pause in this moment.

This was *right*.

River Glades welcomed me with open blooms and open branches. The spirit of the river rose up in my mind and welcomed me too. I saw the spirit as the shape of a woman, her hair flowing like the river itself and her features clear and blue.

"A Priestess! We are honored," the river spirit spoke. Her words were whispered and soft; people in Trellis didn't seem to raise their voices unless there was a party. Everything was soft, gentle. Words were spoken with care because they understood how intent could shape them.

"I'm honored. This place... it's so beautiful," I said. We were connected in spirit, like Diego and I had done so many times through the heart links. But this time, I didn't need the link to connect us. With the magic flowing like the river's tides, I waded into it easily.

"This is what Obius is meant to be."

"How did you preserve the magic?"

"Sacrifices must be made, my lady." I watched her memories, as she poured more and more of herself into the land, into the people around her. Her body was clearer and softer now than it was before. Before she seemed to be made of ice and now she was water.

My heart clenched.

"Peace, my lady. We survived and we are happy. But you are injured. Come deeper into my waters.. Come to me."

"I'm not alone, is that alright?"

"Bring your friend," she whispered.

"You don't recognize him?"

"No, my lady, should I?" I chewed on my lips, hoping it wasn't showing wherever my physical body was. The warmth of Diego's hands pierced through the connection, and I felt them settle on my hips. Gentle. Assertive. Holding me steady so I could lose myself in the magic and find my way back again.

"I'm here, Jack. You're safe. Enjoy the magic. This is how I remember my home," Diego's words filtered through my mind, so I drifted again.

Souls were strange things. They sparkled and glittered like they were made from diamonds and stars, but some looked like ink blots and some like watercolor paintings and some like faces etched in stone. Everyone here was made of ink blots and watercolors.

I saw my star lights knitting together, just like when I connected with Diego. I turned my hands over, looking at the details, and the lights filled in the shape of my soul.

My soul was shaped just like me.

And then there was Diego.

He shimmered. The star lights worked to build him in front of me, the heart links singing with magic, happy at last to be surrounded by this much alchemy. Diego was carved from diamonds. His horns and feathers were exquisitely detailed, like each curve and line was dipped in diamond dust. Molten, turbulent golden eyes stared at me and I couldn't breathe. He was a masterpiece of emotion and love. The star lights were working overtime to build Diego's soul for me and hot tears welled up in my eyes.

"My Blossom, please don't cry," he said, and I felt his arms around me, all of me. I had expanded and grown to stretch across River Glades and Diego reached and reached until he had his arms around me fully.

"I see you," I said, hoping he understood, hoping he knew what I was seeing, and how I'd do anything to keep seeing this version of him. Open and glittering, shining for me like I was the only flower in this sun's universe.

His hands soothed the edges of my hair, sending shockwaves through me. I couldn't tell if it was his hands or just another part of his soul, but I couldn't get enough. I was floating from his magic, from the well of magic that ran so deeply, and I clung to him.

"Jack, my Blossom, my Priestess, my treasure, I see you too. You're blooming."

I glanced down and saw myself again; the star lights had built my frame, but he was right. Flowers of every color–no, they were the colors of the Rainbow Forest–sprouted down my arms and legs and over every part of me. A huge, perfect Jack-in-the-pulpit flower had bloomed in the center of my chest. I saw peonies and marigolds, too, and my eyes welled up. The flowers and herbs I grew in my garden back home sprouted on my legs and feet. I felt them again grounding me in my magic, rooting to my feet to remind me of my home. With the stars and souls in my eyes, I watched the path to River Glades grow brighter and brighter. Each flower's spirit twinkled until it stretched out like a star-lined street.

"I'm blooming," I said.

"You're blooming," he echoed. Diego's voice was back to that reverent tone I'd heard from him a few times before. He spoke like he was praying, like everything about me was special enough to inspire awe. I felt more than saw his hands reaching for me, reaching for the flowers that popped up everywhere. I wondered if my petals were soft to him or if I still seemed too human to have flowers. Was I still just human? It was hard to remember that when my body was just a memory from my magic.

But then it started to fade and I grew smaller, more contained within the confines of my human body. I was small and cramped, but as my eyes came back into focus, Diego was standing there grinning at me.

"What was–"

"That's Obius. That's how magic was before–" Diego's words fumbled, and the heart link spoke for him, the truth humming through us without him needing to say it. ***Before I ruined it.*** His eyes flashed brown, flashed *human*, but when I blinked they were gold again.

"So we're here? This is River Glades?"

"The entrance, yes. Let's go."

River Glades reminded me of the watery village I saw in the vision with Desmond. I was sure that was his name; it rang true in my mind and I was certain if I called it, he would respond. But that was where the similarities ended. The village in my vision was blues and browns, but River Glades had the same colors as the Rainbow Forest. The reeds that swayed in the breeze were yellow and orange, with the river cycling through every shade of blue imaginable. I tried to see if the river spirit was there, but I didn't notice her. Light wind chimes caught my attention, and I turned to see the rest of the village. The houses were up on stilts, bright and cheerful like the houses that lined my street back home. The closest one was pink and my heart leaped into my throat. It was small, the roof was thatched and sort of yellowish, just like the door.

It looked like someone had formed my house here in Obius. There were small flower pots and bushes near the waterline, where the house hovered above. Wind chimes and decorations hung from every possible purchase; there were dangling charms and shiny crystals along the window sills and along the roofline too.

It was everything I wanted my house to be.

The next house was green with red accents. Blue and green. Blue and purple. Purple and yellow and orange mixed together. The houses lined up next to one another, the buildings not quite touching but the roofs were close enough to kiss.

The colors flowed into one another like crayons melting to create a mosaic.

"Are those... mermaids?" I asked, pointing at the very-mermaid-like person breaching through the river, and Diego nodded.

"Yes, but here we don't call them mermaids. They are just water sprites."

"Is mermaid a bad term here?"

"As far as I know, I don't think it *is* a word here. That's a very human-sounding word," Diego scratched at his chin, thinking. It was one of those gestures that he learned from watching humans, imitating other humans. It was also too exaggerated to be serious, but I knew that he was. Diego was thinking hard, plunging the depths of his brain trying to answer my questions.

I ruffled his hair, my hand bumping his horns as warmth flooded through me. This ridiculous man was *mine*.

"Always, in any universe, in any realm."

Diego tucked my hair behind my ears, smoothing his thumbs against my cheeks as he kissed my forehead. The heart link buzzed with energy again, and I tucked his hands tight against my chest.

Rustling made Diego stand straighter with his arm wrapped protectively around my shoulders. I felt the energy of several souls, but I sensed no malice, no ill will. Just loads of curiosity.

"Who goes there?" he shouted, kingly and full of force.

A few Fae poked their heads out of the houses, from around some smaller trees and bushes, until it felt like the town had answered his call.

The Fae folk were... a lot to look at. People with gills and scales and fins swam up to the edge of the water. Their eyes were wide and glassy, too fish-like to get a read on. There were Fae, like actual fairies from children's story books; small and fluttering with shiny, gossamer wings and frilly, leafy clothes. They had the same playful energy as little kids about to get into trouble, and I instantly liked them.

There were folks with scales and tails, more reptile than human-like. They stood about three feet tall, head to foot with their tails curled around their feet as they watched me cautiously. Lizard-like and cautious, each one regarded us and whispered.

Everyone's thoughts came streaming through my mind like the current of the river.

Who is that? Look at his horns! The feathers! They're blue, how could that be? Who is he? Is that a human? Did the humans finally arrive? The Priestess was right! Wait, is the human a priestess? How is that possible? Her magic is so green.

"Hello," I said, louder than I meant and the Fae folk startled. The fairies hugged each other in the air and the water sprites hid their faces so only their fishy eyes peeked out. The lizard people–I needed to know what to call them, *lizard people* felt awful to say–hissed but stayed still.

"Peace, please. My name is–"

"Are you Trellian?" a small fairy asked. She was green and yellow, and reminded me of a dandelion flower as she buzzed around Diego's head.

"I am–"

"Why do you have blue feathers?" another fairy asked. Purple, like an iris.

"Well–"

"He's very dodgy, why won't he just answer us?" a third, pink fairy said.

"He's trying," I said, and they all turned to me. I held my hands up in surrender and the fairies ducked behind a tree.

"Please, she's human, she means no harm. I'm Deign, I'm from Trellis," Diego said. He used his old name; it sounded like an Obius-thing. Diego sounded too human in this world, and the more I said his name, the worse it sounded here. Diego was not meant to be in Obius, but Deign would walk on Trellian ground with his head up.

"Deign!" they all shouted. The fairies buzzed, the water sprites splashed and thrashed, and the lizard people slapped their tails on the ground.

"How?" one of the lizard people said. He was old; his scales were the grayish tone that could only come with age, and his skin was wrinkled and worn. His tail tapped gently next to his clawed feet, the tip crooked and bent.

"I was able to repair the link, and I came back–"

"Why would you think that anyone would welcome *you* here, Shatterer?" a water sprite said. She hauled herself out of the river, and I was shocked to realize that she had legs and a finned tail. Her skin was iridescent and purplish, with small fins on her arms and legs; a larger sail went down the length of her spine.

"I..." Diego's words fell away, but he rose to his full height and the water spite flinched. It was quick–but I saw the fear trickle across her face and vanish again.

"We don't have to stay," I whispered to Diego. The heart link's pulse raced against my wrist, the thrumming bordering on painful.

"I never expected to be welcomed. I didn't come here for your approval. I came to aid the Priestess in her work. Once it's done, I'll leave." Diego's words were made of stone and I shivered. I'd heard the ice of his tone before only in a vision, but experiencing it first hand was something else. Each word was a bite at the crowd, a dare to challenge him. I heard the click of his teeth as he spoke, the threat plain on his face.

"What Priestess? Snapdragon has no need for you. She's the reason Trellis is in ashes!" the water sprite spat. Literally. She finished speaking and then spat on the ground in front of us.

"Snapdragon is no longer the Priestess of Trellis," I said, stepping around Diego to stand in front of him. He growled, low and soft, more frustrated than anything else. I reached for him, and Diego held my hand like he was following orders. He didn't wrap his fingers around mine; his hand acted like a hand rest and that was all.

"Who are you?" the fairies chittered. Their voices were shrill and high, making my ears hurt.

"I'm Jack Hawthorne, the new Priestess of Trellis."

"But you're just a human!" the water sprite yelled. My staff glowed emerald green, crossing itself in front of me. The Seer's magic welled up in my chest, tightening and expanding like a balloon ready to pop.

"Look at her eyes," the fairies said. I knew they were bright green; I felt the magic surging and I didn't try to slow it down or control it. The Fae here needed proof of who I was, and they needed a reason not to attack Diego on the spot.

"How is this possible?" the old lizard asked.

"I've been on Earth since the Shattering. I found Jack, and she has the Seer's Blessing. She reconnected the link between Earth and Obius," Diego said. He gave me more credit than I deserved, but the Fae nodded, slowly warming to me.

"We won't stay long, but we'd like to rest and get some supplies," I said. Diego finally curled his fingers around mine, actually holding my hand.

"A Priestess and her... guardian are always welcome in River Glades. We'll find a place for you," the old lizard said. His beady, black eyes stayed on Diego. Diego met his gaze and held it until the lizard looked away first.

"Stay near me, Jack. I was expecting this," Diego whispered through the heart link.

"Can you take me to the river?" I asked the water sprite.

"Why?" she hissed.

"Because the river spirit came to me in a vision and asked me to. I wanted to meet her," I said. This caused another small outrage among the Fae folk until the water sprite slapped her tail on the water.

"We haven't seen the river sprite in a long time," she said. The heat in her words had vanished; she was full of sorrow, the kind that reminded me of Diego, and my heart sank as her energy washed over me.

"She's still there," I said.

"Of course she is!" the fairies yelled.

I walked over to the edge of the river and watched as the water churned through varying shades of blue. It was like mixing paint and washing it away; I knelt and touched the surface of the water, expecting my hand to come back tinged with blue.

It didn't, but I felt the river spirit.

"I am a little weak today, my lady," the river spirit's voice rippled through the waves. I pushed a healing spell into the babbling water. The spell brightened the river, and then the river spirit rose from the currents, like she did in the vision.

"You look pretty good to me!" I said, smiling. The Fae folk all erupted in happy, joyful cheers as they came to the riverbanks. Diego stayed put, watching from afar with a gleam in his eyes.

"Nod to her, eyes cast down." His voice tumbled around my mind. I winked at him and nodded to the river spirit. This earned me more cheers. The Fae folk warmed up to me and came to poke and prod at me. I tried to stand very still; some of the fairies were really tiny, and I didn't want to accidentally hurt anyone.

"My lady, you are so gentle," the river spirit said.

"Just cautious, I haven't been in Obius very long. I don't want to hurt anyone."

"Wade deeper into my waters, let the alchemy of my currents wash over you. Your body is very tired." I cast a glance back to Diego and he gave me the smallest of nods. Sucking in a breath to calm my nerves, I walked fully into the water. My feet ached from the cold, but soon the pain faded. I was suspended in the water, and felt lighter than I had since before the fire at my house. The magic from the river spirit wrapped around me like the ribbons of Peony's healing spells, but these went deeper. They soothed the aches in my muscles but they also wrapped around all of the bruised parts of my feelings. The ache of losing my home and store. The disconnect from Mari and Peony. Mama. The destruction of the forest. Snapdragon.

Diego.

I dove deeper into the river; it looked bottomless. I swam until my muscles burned from exertion. I wasn't a great swimmer, but I could move through the water without flailing too much.

"Swim all you like, my lady. I won't let you drown." Air filled my lungs and I grinned; I pushed deeper down, until the light started to fade and the colors stopped churning their blue rainbow. The water here was navy blue, only illuminated by the plants and little creatures that lived here. Soft

greens, yellows, and whites glowed in the deep, and I swam up to a small, white flower.

It looked just like a jasmine flower as its petals swayed gently in the currents. I touched the petals and saw the little flower sprouting from a seed until the bloom fully opened.

There was so much beauty in Obius; I had to remember that. The forest was burned, but we were going to make it right. Flowers were going to bloom here once again.

"My lady, your guardian is starting to get worried. He is very fussy, isn't he?"

"Very fussy," I laughed.

The little jasmine flower's petals hugged my fingers before I started swimming back to the surface. The magic had seeped into every part of me, and I felt good. My body didn't hurt. My mind was refreshed.

"Thank you," I whispered as I swam closer to the surface.

"Thank you for coming to Obius, my lady. We need you," the river spirit's watery voice was so soft.

"I think I need to find a way to heal the land, like you did for me. How can I do that?"

"Healing spells work best with love-filled intention. You will be just fine."

When my head popped above the water, my eyes immediately found Diego. His shoulders relaxed and some of the edges around his eyes eased. His mouth was still a hard line, but I felt him relax in the heart link. I pressed a kiss to the bracelet and Diego smiled.

"Priestess, your guardian said that you needed clothes and shoes. Will these work for you?" the lizard asked. He handed me a parcel tied with a very fine twine. Diego draped a blanket around my shoulders and I wiped my hands before taking it from him.

I opened the package slowly, not wanting to drop anything and upset someone else. There were a pair of shoes on top that looked sort of like loafers. They were emerald green with a slightly pointed toe and ribbons to lace them around my ankle to keep them in place. The soles were thick but bendable.

Diego held them for me as I looked at the rest of the clothing. It was a deep, forest-green jumpsuit with lots of fine embroidery on it; flowers and sigils and the crest of Trellis on the arms; the material was soft and breathable.

"If you're going to be out trying to save the realm, you need to be able to move without your bloomers on display," the lizard said. I cackled and he smiled a reptilian grin.

"Can I ask your name?"

"Luther," he said.

"Thank you, Luther. I also don't want my ass hanging out while I'm trying to get my magic on," I said, sensing the edges of his humor. He chuckled, slapping me on the back *just* barely above my butt. It was all he could reach.

"I think we're going to be fine friends, Jack Hawthorne, Priestess of Trellis."

"Just Jack is fine," I said. Luther held a hand out to me and I shook his scaly claw.

"Jack it is. You go rest. You need to pray," he said.

"But–"

"We will care for the fallen King," Luther said, and Diego's eyebrows nearly shot through the top of his head. *Fallen King* scratched at every healing scab he had. He grimaced, trying and failing to smile and be gracious, until Luther laughed again. "I remember you having more of a sense of humor."

"I grew up, I suppose," Diego replied. Everything about him screamed defeat–the set of his shoulders and the clenched fists, trying to hide behind his back, the smile that didn't reach his eyes, the splay of his feathers.

"No, Your Highness, you had your heart broken with the rest of us."

The fairies ushered me away while Diego was grilled by the other Fae folk. There were four fairies now; the dandelion, iris, pink flower, and another that reminded me of a daisy. They flew around me, sitting on my shoulders and trying to sit in my hands.

"Will he be okay?" I asked as they guided me through the village.

"Sure," Dandelion said.

"Probably," Iris said.

"That's really up to him, isn't it?" the pink one said. I couldn't place what kind of flower she was; maybe a rose?

"I don't think he's ever been okay. The Priestess before you used some kind of magic to bewitch him. No one is that doe-eyed," Daisy said.

"You'd be surprised," I said and the four of them laughed.

They lead me to the heart of River Glades. There was a small waterfall with stones arranged in a semi-circle around it. The cliffs that the water fell from were covered in greenery and flowers. My breath hitched and I got goosebumps.

This has to be what heaven looks like.

"Priestess! Come! This is the house that we use for important people," Dandelion said.

"Am I considered important now?" I smiled as the fairies laughed. They liked someone who would banter with them, and it reminded me of Peony and Mari going at it. They would love them. I paused at the threshold of the house; the magic stirred in my chest and I wanted to feel it.

"I guess, but it's also the only open space. After the old Priestess went crazy, we started taking more people in here. The elders wouldn't let us put anyone in that house though," Rose said.

The energy shifted between them, memories and unease floating in the air just as freely as they did. I forced myself not to look at all of their frayed memories and took a centering breath. The sound startled them from their thoughts and they buzzed around me some more.

"I'll just be a minute to get changed," I said, giving them an excuse to flee. I took a moment to examine the jumpsuit again. It was probably the prettiest thing I'd ever had the chance to wear. The fine gold details and the soft fabric moved so easily. I slid off my dirty clothes and shoes and felt the energy shift in me as I smoothed the jumpsuit into place. It was a perfect fit. Another moment of rightness, of belonging washed over me as I caught glimpses of the tiny hands that made this.

I rejoined the group feeling I had found another piece of myself.

CHAPTER FOUR

DIEGO

The fairies ushered Jack away before I could follow, and Luther patted my hand and gestured for me to come along with him. He led me in the opposite direction from Jack and warning bells sounded in my mind. *Don't leave her. Stay close. This is not your world anymore.* Luther ambled down a thin dirt road lined with Fae circles and rings, his tail creating another trail in the dust.

"Come along now, don't keep an old man waiting." I trotted to catch up to him as I studied the circles made of pebbles and rocks.

My heart caught in my throat at the memories of when I was just a boy, long before I even knew Snapdragon, and my friends and I would spend hours and hours building Fae rings. We would build circles and rings as big as we could, moving massive hunks of rocks and filling in the gaps with pebbles and sand, enchanting every grain. Sherwin loved making the smallest, most delicate rings that he could, building intricate designs within them, subtly adding sigils with pebble patterns and layers and layers of magic. It had been a game–something to pass the time until lessons and training would take over. We would run through the forests for as long as our legs and wings would take us and then the trees would give us shelter to rest.

Seeing River Glades was just as hard as seeing the ruins of my forest; remembering Obius as it was hurt as much as seeing it destroyed.

Every ounce of Obius would break my heart again and again.

"You were a lot livelier as a child," Luther said, as if reading my mind. His voice croaked out the words; more from age than anything else. If he had been around pre-Shattering, he would be close to three thousand years old, or more. The days in Obius seemed to pass just as slowly as the days on Earth, but while everything on Earth died, Obius grew wiser. The lines of Luther's face were older than all of the humans currently alive. His bones creaked, but Obius softened around him, making the ground easier for his old frame to bear.

"I remember," I said much more bitterly than I meant to let out.

Luther stopped, turning to cock an eyelid, and stared at me. He reminded me of a tutor that I hated. Exacting, nothing ever measuring up, disappointment etched into his face like it was the only expression he could muster.

"How did you manage to fall so far from grace, Your Highness?" Luther stopped to sit on some logs fashioned into a table and chair set.

A tea kettle and some earthen cups were waiting. This was a scene from days past too—tea time in Obius was sacred. The preparation of the tea, the presentation of the cups and saucers, everything was meant to convey love and welcomeness. His setting was one of the more simple ones, showing an earnestness that was never found in the castle walls. The delicate shapes carved into the cups were the sigils of tranquility and the Seer. Her magic was everywhere in Obius.

Luther waved for me to join him, pointing up at the sign that swung by a small door frame carved out of a tree trunk. I winced at the tree, hoping that it was happy with being a small shop, but Luther just smiled.

"This is my shop, Your Highness. The world can fall apart, but at least we still have a decent cuppa tea." Luther poured some honey and milk into his tea and breathed in the scent. Trellian berry tea: my favorite.

"I haven't had Trellian tea in a very long time," I whispered.

"I thought as much. You need something to restore your soul, boy. King or not, you're as much of a mess as I've ever seen."

"You have a way with words," I laughed, pouring milk into the piping-hot cup of tea. The milk combined with the tea, mixing like the magic I'd see in coffee shops back on Earth. The aroma of the coffee brewing filled my memory and I missed the Earth's mellow mornings.

"Heh, more like I'm old enough that I don't mind offending or telling the truths no one else wants to speak. Tell me your story, Deign. Entertain an old man who has seen the world on both sides of your reign."

So I told him. I told him how Snapdragon saw her own death, how the humans would come, how the forest would be destroyed. I told him how I'd been so terrified to lose her, that I did something unspeakable.

I told him how my heart had been shattered.

Luther nodded, not once interrupting. He sipped and sipped at his tea, poured us both another cup, and took in my story. He patted my hand and his scales lightly scratched my skin.

Confessing made me lighter, but it didn't *fix* anything, and I was the last one who deserved to lessen the burden that I carried. Punishment wasn't meant to be easy.

"To me, it sounds like you were isolated and manipulated. It sounds like perhaps the Goddesses knew that falling in love with a Priestess was a bad idea."

"It's hard to control who you fall in love with," I mumbled out. Snapdragon, before things changed and before the magic warped her mind, was gentle and caring. She was delicate like the flowers of the forest she sprang from with mischief in her eyes. Snapdragon loved performers and watching live music and dancing the nights away. She would sit with her vines hugging her together and watch the moons rise and the stars come out, greeting each one by the names she gave them.

"Indeed, and here you've gone and done it again," he laughed, choking on his tea. I clapped him on the back a couple times before he regained his composure.

"Not very bright, am I?"

"Well, Your Highness, you certainly have a *type*. Perhaps, this time, listen to *your* heart instead of hers. Perhaps it's time you start trusting yourself to stand on your own two feet."

"I–"

"You are more than capable, but while we wait for your lovely human Priestess, maybe you should take a dip in the river too. The river spirit likes the Priestess; that's the first time we've seen her in centuries. She was conserving her magic, but it's not every day you meet a new Priestess. And a human one at that! What was the Seer thinking?"

I wondered that myself; blessing a human with Her holy magic was beyond unheard of, it was practically *unholy*. Jack was special, even without the Seer's magic, but there had to be a reason for her to be chosen.

"Aye, well, don't try to puzzle out the logic of a Goddess. You should really consider taking that swim though. I'm no healer, but I sense the wounds in your heart."

I smiled over the cup. "Well, it was shattered."

"There's the wise-cracking princeling I remember. You know, I was there at your coronation. Your mother, may she rest in grace, knew how to throw a party."

"Want to know a secret?" I asked as I sat the cup down. Luther was already at work to fill it again. My heart fluttered and my hands got sweaty. I still remembered Snapdragon's face clearly before... before everything.

"Hmm?"

"Snapdragon planned most of it. She loved parties, and my mother was so excited to have a cohort, that they spent three seasons sorting it out."

"Three seasons! Hah!"

"I don't remember a lot of it now. I feel like my memories from before are fading, getting muddy. It feels like I'm forgetting what it means to be Trellian." The harder I tried to scan my memories, the foggier they got. I remembered the feeling of Snapdragon's newly blossomed petals more than the day they happened or what I did that had made her smile.

Luther patted my hands, holding them in his claws. There was a kindness in his eyes that wasn't there before.

"Now you listen here, Deign, Wise King of Trellis, son of Orainia and Lionus, you *are* Trellian. You are the blood of our people, the color of royalty, with the magic of the ancients in your veins. You *are* Trellis. Memories are finicky things, and you've been shattered. There will be missing pieces, but none of that changes your birthright."

I swallowed hard. *Deign, Wise King of Trellis, son of Orainia and Lionus.* No one had dared say my title since the Shattering. Luther held my eyes steady, not blinking, not looking away.

"I'm not a king anymore," I breathed out the words like they were the last bits of air in my lungs.

"Doesn't mean that you never *were*."

"I'm not going to try to take back the throne."

"As you shouldn't. That whole part about you being wise was a little exaggerated, don't you think?" Luther slapped the table as he laughed, and now it was my turn to choke on the tea. I laughed until my eyes teared up.

"Maybe *you* should be the king. You certainly know more than me," I said.

"Aye, but I'm not covered in blue feathers, am I Your Highness?"

"I don't think there's anyone still bearing my feathers."

"No one, save maybe, your brother." The age seemed to vanish from his features, and I could imagine the wily youth that he had to have been. Luther's eyes twinkled with mischief the same way that Snapdragon's did, and I scooted to the edge of my chair.

"My brother?"

"Mmm, perhaps you should go take that swim now. The Priestess will be returning soon, and I'm old. I shouldn't have to be telling the same story over and over again. Go, I'll make more tea. Has she ever had Trellian tea?"

I shook my head and Luther sighed like I had admitted something worse than breaking the ties between the worlds. He tsked and moved away from the table, heading back to the shop.

"Absolutely tragic. I'll make a spread. You both need to eat. Your face is too shallow for my liking. Now go on, no arguments Your Highness."

Luther picked up a stick next to the table and poked me in the ribs. I stood and he pointed to the river, just behind his small tea shop. I took a deep breath before I removed my shoes and headed for the river.

"I'm going to fetch you some more clothes too. Can't be having a former king roaming around looking like that."

"Like what?"

"Like a human," Luther said as he retreated into the shop.

JACK

I examined myself in the full-length mirror; it was still a little small for me to see my head to my feet, but the mirror took up the entire door. The woman in the reflection seemed so foreign. I blinked a few times, expecting to see Snapdragon appear to hiss at me again.

It was my face, clearly, but my eyes had changed. More than just the magic, there was something deeper in them, some part of myself that I had yet to understand on Earth. The river water made my messy mop of hair more tidy, curling more than my pin-straight strands were used to. My skin was glowing, the freckles across my nose now more pronounced from the intense suns.

It was me, just, the version of myself that I never thought would exist. The woman staring back at me was stronger and looked wiser. She looked like someone who gazed into the future with ease and found only clarity. Emerald green lit up my staff, and Harold came floating over. The magic enhanced the colors of the jumpsuit and the elaborate, delicate stitching.

"You... look like a Priestess, now," Snapdragon's voice echoed through the crystal.

"I do?"

"Yes, probably more than I ever did."

"Don't go all emo on me now, Snapdragon."

"I don't think I ever looked that settled. The Seer's Blessing is wrapped around you like a silken cloak, and it dragged me down like a soaked wool blanket."

I wanted to object, but I knew in my heart that she was right. The Seer's magic flooded Snapdragon's senses in a way that it didn't for me, and it made her hide in the corners of her mind. Every shadow of the future clung to her like a dread-filled promise until the weight broke her branches.

Whereas I felt like the doors I'd locked myself behind were thrown open. Magic unfolded in me like a secret. The more I cast, the more I learned about myself. I glanced back at my reflection again, and this time I was smiling.

"You will be a good Priestess if you stay."

"If I stay?"

"Jack, we both know that you don't belong on Earth. It's why I found you so easily. You don't belong there any more than I do, or Deign. Obius is your home. You don't need me of all people to tell you that."

Home. The heart link heated up again and I rolled it around my wrist. Home went up in flames. But then again, so did Trellis.

"Priestess, are you ready? I think Luther has made some food for you and the grumpy one. You need to eat," Dandelion said as she fluttered around me, trying not to outright stare.

"Thanks, I'm coming." The four fairies trilled around me, examining the clothes and double-checking that I had laced my shoes correctly. Iris tapped my crystal, watching the glittering specks float around.

"What are those?" she asked.

"Souls." The fairies hovered in midair, huddling together to stare at me. "The souls of those that died in Wildfire. I could hear them, but I couldn't send them anywhere to rest so I just–"

"Thank you," Dandelion said softly. The other nodded, flying in a circle around me. A thin ribbon of magic tied itself around my waist, resting against my hips before settling into my skin.

"What was that?"

"Another blessing, Priestess. You wouldn't know this as a human, but when the Priestess visits, we're supposed to bless her for the work she does," Rose said.

"This time, we laid a blessing of bravery on you. Saying goodbye to all those souls when the links to Sanctum are restored will not be easy."

The hair on my arms stood up, and I fiddled with my staff, "Why won't it be easy?"

"Goodbyes are never easy," Daisy said, patting the crystal like she was trying to comfort the souls too. They bounded around in the crystal, following the traces of Daisy's fingertips.

"Come on, before Luther notices that we're late," Dandelion said. She fluttered in front of me and brushed her nose to mine. Her features were so small and dainty, she reminded me of a miniature doll. "We really are happy that you're here." And with that, the four of them flew out of the house, leaving me to trail after them.

DIEGO

I dove deep into the river, not bothering to strip off my clothes. I wanted to wash away the scent of the battle, and to just *be* in the water as quickly as possible.

A brother.

Luther said I had a brother.

How could I have forgotten that? Was he born after the Shattering? When did my mother die?

Did she die because of him? Because of me?

Anger churned through me again, hot and tugging like it always did, and I swam deeper. My lungs burned, but I didn't relent. Little spots danced at the corners of my eyes, and I pushed further.

"Please, don't punish yourself. Breathe deeply, you are safe in my waters," the river spirit spoke. Air filled my lungs and it only made the anger flash through me even brighter, stinging every nerve in my body, until I wanted to thrash in the water until the air was gone again.

"Do you know who I am? Who I was?" The words were muddled in the water, but I knew she could understand me. A soft current brushed against my face, trying to comfort the storm in me.

"I think it's time for you to start forgiving yourself, Your Highness. The world has changed, but we are still here, and Trellis will thrive once again."

"But not because of me," I said bitterly and told myself to check my emotions. The river spirit was here, working her beautiful magic, to heal all of the tender places in my body and I was making her work harder.

"I think taking credit for healing Trellis will do little good to heal the wounds in your heart. I can feel how deeply it was shattered. Only three small pieces working to support the heart of a King. It's not an easy task."

"Do people really still see me as a king here?" I floated, suspended, as I watched other Fae swim on by, frolicking and playing like they didn't have a care in the world. Like the world wasn't a heaping pile of garbage that I created.

"Those who remember do."

"Are there still a lot of those?" The river spirit paused, pushing more magic through the currents, wrapping around me tightly.

"No, Your Highness," she whispered through the waves.

The tightness in my chest eased; one day I would be forgotten entirely, just a fable to warn the children not to be too cocky or too reckless. One day, I could walk through my homeland and people would ask my name, and I would say, *"Hello, my name is Diego,"* and they would believe it as truth. The whole truth.

Because it was.

"The folk are gathering. It's time to get cleaned up, Your Highness."

"Can I stay here for another minute?" I trod water, pumping my legs just to know that I could, feeling the resistance of the water.

"Of course, and you're always welcome to come back."

The water washed away any tears that threatened to fall, and I swam for the surface. Jack was there, sitting on the log that I had been earlier, eating some fruit, smiling wide at the Fae around her. The clothes suited her perfectly, complimenting her hazel eyes and fair skin, making her beauty shine even brighter.

My heart, small and broken, pounded hard in my chest.

Jack looked like she was home.

And I felt like an outsider, staring through the window of a warm, candle-filled home, fogging up the glass while wanting to be invited back in.

I wondered what comment made her laugh, how she would take her Trellian tea, and if she would love the bread made by the sprites more than the fairies. There was a world of things for Jack to know about Obius, and I couldn't remember even having a brother.

She felt my presence and winked, as she raised a cup to her lips. I toweled off and made my way over to her.

"You look lighter," her voice threaded through me.

I kneeled next to her, the laugh already forming in her throat, and kissed her hand. She pushed my face away, gentle and playful, her fingers a reminder that she was still here and hadn't run off yet. Her kissable hands were already too far away for me to pull her close. Jack's touch felt like home, and being just inches away felt like I had been cast adrift.

"Your Highness, stop wooing the Priestess. You think he would have learned," Luther said to the fairies and everyone laughed. Even me. Jack patted the log chair next to her, and I sat. I offered my hand, palm up, for her to take, and she teased her fingertips across mine until she squeezed my hand tighter.

"You mentioned a story, Luther," Jack said.

"Yes, yes, but please be sure you eat," Luther handed her a bowl of salad greens and then another with bread and cheese.

Meat wasn't a common dish in Obius. Of course, there were some with a preference for it, but overwhelmingly my people were vegetarian. Obius-folk preferred to eat the things that the world gave freely, made with their own hands in collaboration with the land, instead of reaping what they could from it. I wondered if the Earth had ever been like that, trading and living happily in tune with nature underfoot. It never seemed to last there.

"Your Highness, you need to eat too," one of the fairies said. She was white and yellow, with flecks of dark brown on her wings, a daisy sprite.

"Thank you," I said, accepting the plate of cheese quickly so she didn't need to strain to hold it for me.

"I would start with the beginnings of Obius, but I think we need to skip ahead a few thousand years in our history," Luther said smiling.

"You're an oracle," I said, grinning.

"I am," he confirmed.

"Oracles are living storytellers. Our stories are passed on through the years and they tell them to the people they pass. Most oracles are shop-keepers or own small cafes. Places for people to gather."

"Aye, but we're going to start with a story that neither of you know. Unless of course, our fair Priestess has already started digging through the past."

"I know nothing," Jack laughed, chewing through a piece of hard cheese.

"Well, get settled, this is a longer tale."

CHAPTER FIVE

A TALE FROM THE ORACLE, LUTHER

The world had crumbled. No one knew what was going on. The King, always full of sunlight and energy, had become smaller, timid. He looked over his shoulder constantly, some unknown threat or terror waiting around every curve.

And then there was the Emerald Priestess, Snapdragon.

Ahh, how lovely she was. Never had a priestess been so doubly blessed as she: the Seer's benevolent blessing, future sight, and then to be blessed with a beauty that would defy time, defy the ages. She moved with soft, graceful steps, her eyes shining with magic and always so prayerful.

Her frail hands were constantly clenched, confirming the fear that the King felt. She stayed by his side, and the people were happy to see it. They loved them both so, and everyone knew how much they loved each other. It was as plain as the suns in the sky, constantly chasing each other but never being allowed to catch up.

Then word spread: Snapdragon, sweet, beloved Snapdragon was going to die.

She would be struck down by humans, looking for more magic than their bodies could hold. She would be an easy, obvious target to cripple Trellis. The King would be too, of course, but he was a lion of a king, fierce and loud, and wouldn't go down as quickly as the frail Priestess.

Her visions became more bloody, more violent.

Trellis would burn.

She would die.

King Deign, brave and unyielding, would fight through leagues of men but nothing could possibly save her. He turned away from his advisors, from the Dowager Queen Orainia, from Snapdragon herself.

He had a plan, and he would execute it because there wasn't a soul in Obius strong enough–or stupid enough, truly–to oppose him. This was the side of the King that no one really knew, that no one wanted to talk about. At the height of his rule, there had never been a Fae with magic that could rival his.

But how far would he go? To save the Priestess, whom he loved so dearly, so clearly, so openly for the realm to wish for their marriage, even though all knew it was forbidden? To save Trellis from an unthinkable fire? To stop this madness from unfolding?

Aye, we all know how far he would go. How far he did *go.*

And so, King Deign shattered our world to keep everyone safe, to keep the realms separate and free.

And alas, we know how that turned out.

But then he was gone, cast out of Obius as punishment for his brazen hubris, never to return since the links that bound our realms together were shattered beyond repair.

Snapdragon cried out from Trellis Castle; her cries were heard throughout the kingdom and there was no comforting her.

The Dowager Queen, now older and gray, was pregnant. Who is the father, you ask? None can be certain. Some say that the father was her late husband, Prince Lionus, who came back from the dead to make sure that another child was there to keep the Trellian bloodline alive. Some say it was one of her guards. Some say that the father was just a Fae she met during a lovely night on the town, away from the prying eyes of the castle.

Who he was matters little.

Who came to be from that union matters greatly.

A child.

Born to the Dowager Queen during a trip to Chilijan; she hid the pregnancy from the Trellian court. Snapdragon had begun her descent into madness, forcing the Queen out of the castle, out of Trellis. Snapdragon forced everyone out, save a handful of guards who refused day in and day out until she finally relented and let them stay. The castle became a fortress; no one was allowed in, and Snapdragon never left.

The people thought—prayed—that Snapdragon had died just to find some peace.

But the Dowager Queen was alive and well in Chilijan. She gave birth to a son, a lovely child with the same dark hair, curled horns, and cerulean blue feathers that his older brother was known for.

The boys could have been twins, if not for the age differences.

Raising a little horn was a lot, and Queen Orainia was not used to the weather in Chilijan. Rumors say that she stayed with the Empress there, but no one really knows what happened to her.

Eventually, the townsfolk all started whispering about her death, the passing of the Great Queen, the last link to King Deign, and the world before the Shattering. Of course, some people claimed that there was an heir! The child! But where was he? Who was he?

Did he survive?

So many questions and so few answers.

Chilijan struggled without magic flowing freely, but they were better off than Trellis. People left in droves, and soon the whisperings of the child were gone. The people in Trellis stopped asking, stopped looking too.

A hush settled over the lands as magic seemed further and further away. Who cares about a king when there isn't enough magic to grow food? To keep the Fae casting and understanding the magic that is a part of their souls?

No one in Trellis, I'll tell you that much.

But then the hush was gone, and Trellis Castle was alive and bustling again. Soldiers pouring out through the gates. Emerald green magic glittering from the rafters. Snapdragon's horrid laughter filling the air.

We all knew something was coming. We all could sense the shift. We felt the links trying to revive themselves.

And then we all saw the fire and fled.

Now, you ask, "Luther, what about this child? Deign's brother? Did Deign ever even know he had a brother?"

All fine questions, but what we should be asking is not if Deign knew him, but whether he wants to know him now. Because the boy is not a boy anymore. He's grown, his magic immense in this droughted world, and the ground will rumble beneath his feet.

No, what we should be asking is if we truly want to find him.

Chapter Six

JACK

Luther's story unfolded in my mind so clearly. His words were the paint that my magic needed to bring the memories to life. Diego as a boy, growing up too fast, and falling in love. I saw how shyly he looked at Snapdragon and how she would look away before he could catch her. His mother, Queen Orainia, smiling with the same grin that I'd seen on Diego's face time and time again.

I watched again as Snapdragon grew smaller and smaller, shrinking in on herself, her mind becoming nothing but paranoia and darkness. She pulled away from everyone, and the more that Diego tried to chase her, the farther she ran.

I'd seen the first part of the story before–the before clicked in my mind, and I saw so clearly how Diego was gently nudged and nudged until he was standing on the edge of a cliff that he had to jump off of.

But then I saw his mother, grieving the loss of her son, and taking in all of the details of Snapdragon's madness. She watched as Snapdragon became more violent, ready to strike at anything that opposed her, and she saw her way out.

There was a guard with very kind eyes and a sweet aura that clung to him; he looked similar to the way that I imagined Diego's father, with wings and fine bones, but deadly magic. She announced a trip to Chilijan, her dear friend the Empress, falling on hard times.

And then she was gone.

I saw her raising Diego's brother; she smiled again, and I knew that it had been too long since that had happened. She only smiled like that at her son, and now another child stood before her, so young but already so much like Diego.

The Queen grew weaker and weaker, until the boy was a man, with horns that had fully curled against his head, and bright blue plumage that lined his arms.

He cried for weeks when she died. The Queen passed in her sleep, the guard with the fine bones at her side, kissing each of her knuckles in the lush bedroom that she lay in. The room was full of blues and greens, like the ocean had crafted a palace, and Queen Orainia lay there with her son on one side, the guard on the other.

He loved her, the guard. I couldn't get a read on his name, but I felt the love through the words of Luther's story. Her son stayed very still, very close. He clung to her hands, knowing this was the end, his last chance to say goodbye.

"He will come back one day, Desmond. Welcome him, love him. Please. You are the warrior, the heart of the storm that your brother cannot ever be again. You will be the one to set the banner of Trellis right again. And one day, Deign will be there with you."

"I don't care about some brother that I'll never meet. I care about you, Mum. How do I let go of you?"

"Oh my darling, you don't. I will be in your heart forever. I want my soul poured into that sapphire you love so I am with you. You know the spell. Once my body passes, you know what to do."

"I can't–"

"You will, because Desmond, my sweet child, one day you will return to Trellis, and one day, you will lead our people back to a place of grace. And one day, you will lay my spirit to rest on a lovely hook in my old rooms so I can watch my gardens bloom again."

He did as she asked–he pulled her soul up and out of her body, a platinum orb of light that was too bright to look at directly, and coaxed it into the sapphire around his neck. It shimmered until the soul relaxed into the crystal, refracting light.

Luther's story had ended, but the vision had morphed into its own, coming more alive and real than my body seated at the small log table. The attachment to my body felt far away. I unfolded into the land, spreading out everywhere until I was connected to each blade of grass that still stood. This was part of the Blessing–the connection and the knowing of every spirit. Obius taught me what magic truly meant, and how deeply it ran in my veins. My small, human body was never designed for this magic, and I felt that now more than ever.

I was soulwalking again, like I used to do on Earth before I could control the magic. But now, I moved with intention and everything, everything, everything around me responded. My body hummed to life, energy and light weaving through my chest; each sunbeam tying itself to me, each molecule of air blending with how I expanded and moved.

I stopped for a moment and let myself exist in this in-between existence that was becoming more of my home than anywhere else. I felt like I could reach across the universes and just keep going, greeting each star and moon that I met along the way until I connected with the sunbeams of another land.

"*Eternal*," something whispered and adrenaline pulsed through me, through all of me.

Obius unraveled itself for me like I was unrolling a map, and I let my fingers travel the lines of the rivers, looking for a way to Chilijan. I needed to get to Chilijan—that was the key, that was where we would find our answers.

That's where Desmond would be waiting for us.

"Deign can show you the way, Priestess," he said. Desmond. Horns. Feathers. Hardened mouth and dark clothes.

"You can hear me?"

"Yes. It feels like you are reaching across the world to rattle my mind."

"I'm sorry, I didn't mean—"

"You never need to apologize to me, Priestess. Come to Chilijan. I will be waiting."

"Diego—Deign—is here, and I'm sure—"

"I know. I watched him fall from the sky like he was a wishing star. Maybe he finally heard me. I've been calling him for a very long time."

"We're coming," I said.

Desmond's voice was already farther away now, and I was drifting back to my body, back to Diego, to the small log table with Luther's tea and his plates of food, the fairies, and the river spirit.

Blinking my eyes several times, I waited for the magic to finally clear. My head was lying on my hands, on the table in front of me. Harold bobbed behind me, the magic in my staff brightening again as I sat up.

"Who were you talking to?" Diego asked. He stroked the back of my hands with his thumb, moving in small circles, over and over. His other hand tapped the table—*one, two, three, one, two, three*—as he studied me.

He knew already; if he didn't from the look on my face, then he did from the heart links. Maybe one day, he could experience soul walking with me and he could see how far the world really extended. Maybe then he would forgive himself for thinking that he destroyed it.

"Your brother, Desmond."

"He heard you?"

"He's in Chilijan, and he's waiting for you."

"My lady Priestess, please let us prepare some things for you before you leave. Chilijan is not very far, but you will need to be prepared. Obius is not the sunflower it used to be, I'm afraid," Luther said, biting into a goddess fruit.

Diego's thoughts popped into my head, telling me its name along with a memory of him biting into one as a child. I saw the juice dribbling down his chin, and how he wiped it on his feathers.

"Has Chilijan changed as much as Trellis?" Diego asked, fingers still tapping again and again.

"Dear boy, everything has changed." His words felt like a prophecy, and I swallowed hard.

Chilijan will have the answers. Chilijan is the next step.

"Safe travels, Priestess," Dandelion said, rubbing her nose to mine. The fairies had prepared two packs for us, full of food, medicines, and an extra set of clothes.

"Thank you," I said.

Diego stood, hefting both packs on his back, and bowed to them. The fairies giggled and Luther tugged on his hair.

"You're both welcome in River Glades anytime you find your feet on our path."

I took one last long look at this little village with its brightly painted houses at the river banks and the magic here that was more alive than anything else we'd seen in Obius. The river rushed on behind us, ever flowing and the colors cycling through an endless blue color wheel.

We said our goodbyes, and Diego led us onward to Chilijan.

FALCON

The hours ticked on, Mari sitting perilously close to me on the couch, but not *too* close. Her almond scent filled the air around us, intoxicating and comforting. We binged K-dramas and watched endless crime documentaries and police procedurals with two BFF chicks that were a lot like her and Jack. Lots of snacks. Pizza. Thai delivery.

Lots of things to keep us in this apartment, locked away from everything happening beyond the walls of her home.

Mari was hot–literally, heat poured off of her like she was an inferno and the close contact was making me sweat. She was also gorgeous, but I kept my hands and thoughts to myself.

"Are we going to talk about why we're not leaving your place?" I had to ask her; I was climbing the walls and I knew she was too.

She shifted on the couch, laying on her back with her feet resting on the top of it. Her fuzzy blue socks had long been discarded, and her bare feet felt like an invitation to tickle them. She jingled as she moved; the little charms in her hair rustled to make their own kind of music. Everything about her jingled, from the bracelets around her wrists, to the charms in her hair, to the golden bands around her ankles.

"Nope."

"It's been three days, Mari."

"We're *resting*, Falcon. This is what you do when you rest. You should try it more often."

"I'm not great at resting."

She laughed. Oh man, what a laugh. Brisk and sharp edged. This girl.

"Or following directions."

"That too."

I grinned and got another laugh from her. A bigger laugh, more from the belly instead of her amused huff. Her eyes had fires burning in them. I was ready to douse myself in gasoline and let her light a match.

"And what is it exactly you want to do?"

Kiss you. That sounds like a good idea.

"Not resting would be great."

"You have about a million bruises and at least a couple cracked ribs. Also the whole lightning thing. And you want to go off galivanting?"

The fire in her blazed up, sparking to life and overtaking the entirety of her eyes. I leaned back, the heat coming from her making the air in the room too stuffy to tolerate. My gut told me to cast, to put my shields up because another blast was coming, but then it didn't. Mari tried to shrink into herself and I touched her arm like she was going to burn me. She didn't.

"Mari, what's going on with the fire?" I pulled back, giving her space—giving us both space—and waited. She blinked back tears, little sparks falling from her eyes. The flames went out and only her lovely brown eyes stared back at me. She looked away first. *Please don't keep burning, Mari. Please.*

"I don't know," she said.

My fingers still had phantom pain from the Lightning that seared them, but I held my hand out anyway. She could burn me if she wanted to, but I didn't think she would. Not intentionally. Mari was so like the Wildfire that she consumed; beautiful, burning, free. She would burn out before she tried to hurt anyone, but my fingers trembled nonetheless.

When she squeezed my hand and it didn't catch fire, I exhaled again.

"We'll figure it out," I said. Declared. I hoped it sounded more confident than my shaking hands felt. The energy had shifted so fast that I wanted the awkward binge-watching vibe to come back.

She stayed quiet for a minute. Then another. Her giant, blue and yellow clock ticked loudly in the silence of her home, and I realized how unnatural silence was for her. Mari crackled and jingled and was surrounded by sound everywhere she went.

"I think I'm feeling something other than pizza today. Nachos?" She picked at her nails and then switched to picking at some scum on the tv remote. She bit her lip, but then schooled her face again, so I smiled and held a hand to my heart. Mari seemed to read my mind, seeing that nachos were the deepest desire of my life.

"It's like you can read minds too!"

"Everybody loves nachos, Falcon."

She uncrossed her feet and flipped upright to go to the kitchen. Mari leaned on the breakfast bar too heavily, flipping through some paper menu like it had offended her. A few swipes on her phone later, she proclaimed that dinner was ordered. I watched in silence because she was the one made for music, and I was here just to listen.

I'd stay here with her in the safety of these walls–likely laced with so much alchemy that a Goddess couldn't break through–until she felt like she could leave them. I said a prayer to the Judge out of habit, asking for a clear mind and a solution to the fire that was eating Mari alive.

Chapter Seven

DIEGO

River Glades was closer to the Chilijan border than I remembered, or we had just been walking longer than I realized. I couldn't shake the feeling of being watched, of eyes everywhere in the forest and along the paths that we walked. Jack didn't seem to notice, so the logical part of my mind told me that sneaking up on a Priestess, or surprising her in any way, would be difficult. My magic was weaker but I could still tell when someone was watching me. Even my horns seemed to react, tingling against my scalp. Something was coming.

Jack and I laughed as we walked, our hands fitting together and falling apart easily. She tilted her head back to let the sunlight wash over her, a smile bright on her lips. I tried to keep the conversation light and flowing so she didn't detect the itching I felt on the back of my neck, the watchful stares that I knew I wasn't just imagining. I didn't want this moment to end.

The suns were getting low in the sky, neither setting but getting closer. She stopped to breathe it all in—the magic and the light. She shimmered and now I was the one breathless

"The light feels different from each of the suns," she said.

"Hmm? It does?"

"Yeah, I can feel the difference. One is warmer, and the other is brighter." She scrunched up her face, thinking about the differences, touching her cheeks as if to confirm her theories.

"I don't think anyone has ever noticed a difference," I said.

"Well, I like paying attention to the details. It's important."

"Agreed, don't the humans say the devil is in the details?"

"Yep. And I'm really good at details." The playful lilt of her voice made me want to pull her into my arms, against my chest. She walked backward in front of me, narrowing her eyes at me, staring at my face. Then my neck. Then a little lower until my cheeks tinged pink.

"Really. Such as?"

"You blush when I stare at you. You have a freckle next to your nose. There's a mole between your index and middle finger on your left hand. You tug at your sleeves when you're anxious, like you're doing now," Jack said as she tugged on the sleeves of her jumper. I forced my hands down, not even realizing she was mimicking me.

"None of those things sound particularly appealing," I said, hoping my voice came across as fun instead of embarrassed. I rolled my shoulders and looked away, something catching my eye.

"I love all your details, Diego."

She stopped walking so suddenly that I nearly crashed into her. Jack laced her fingers with mine, redirecting my focus back to her, as the heart links brushed against each other to send jolts through us both. I felt her heart beating with her standing this close, the scent of the river water—clean, fresh—on her skin, and the warmth of her breath brushing my collarbone like a kiss. I leaned down, inclining my head just to be closer to her eye level when her hands pressed against my cheeks.

"Hey," she said.

"Hey." I think I flinched—my body spasmed but it happened so fast that I wasn't even sure it *did* happen.

"Where are you retreating to?"

"I'm sorry?"

"Diego." Her magic wound its way through me, starting at the heart link before it settled around my chipped heart. "I'm asking because I don't want to pry, but I definitely could."

"I–" My throat went dry, closing in on itself to keep the words in. *"I don't want to break this too. I don't want to make the same mistakes. I don't want to lose you too."*

"I'm not going anywhere."

Jack's eyes were closed now, and her arms wrapped around my neck so she was pressed against my chest. I held her lightly, not wanting to ruin this moment by squeezing her too tight, not wanting something else to crack around me.

The heart links worked their magic again, and even in my mind, I saw Jack standing with outstretched arms. She was made of her starlights, and watching her glitter made my breath hitch.

"I'm here, I'm standing in front of you, in your arms. I'm here."

When I opened my eyes, she was there, just like she said and just like I knew she would be.

Only there was something else here too—some*one* else–and dread flooded through me just as quickly as her fierce love had just seconds before.

Jack's staff raced through the air, circling us with emerald light until it crossed behind her back. My focus snapped up, scanning for whatever the staff saw that I had missed. We were still in Trellis, but just barely. There was a long, thin, wooden bridge over a river as the entrance into Chilijan.

A man stood at the wooden gate. It blocked the entrance further into the realm of Chilijan, and the sigils covering it warned of deep waters and strong currents.

He had dark brown hair, not quite black. Curled horns. Strong nose. Deep-set eyebrows and a scowl to match.

Blue feathers. Cerulean blue.

He pulled on the edges of his sleeves, but they didn't quite cover all of the feathers. My eyes were glued to his forearms. The more he tried to hide the feathers, the more I stared. They were cerulean blue.

"Diego? What is it?" Jack slowly let go of me, but I held her against me.

He truly did look just like me; maybe more stern, more intense. He pulled on his sleeves again, but it was still like looking in the mirror.

Jack took a few steps away, out of the safety of the circle her staff had erected. She turned back to me, grinning. Every step she took now was bolder, more confident. Obius made her shine brighter. I balled my fists, forcing them to stay by my side because I refused to force her hand. I wasn't going to reign over her. I wasn't going to make the same mistakes again.

"Desmond?"

"My lady," he said, bowing deep. There was nothing playful about his manner. No laughter in his eyes. No joy in the corners of his mouth. No ease in the way his hands flexed and released at his sides.

"Desmond," I repeated and his face jerked to me. The bridge swayed in the breeze behind him; the old cables of the suspension looked worn, but the bridge was solid. The bridge moved more than Desmond did.

"Deign."

"You're my brother." The words were small.

He nodded once, and the silence stretched out around us, suffocating and heavy. Where to even begin with him? A handshake? A hug? This man in front of me was my last living relative; the only link to the family I left in Obius.

"We have a lot to discuss," he said.

"Indeed we do," Jack said. She glanced between us, like she was looking at reflections, looking for the differences.

I wondered what she saw, if there was anything at all. Desmond–*my brother*–didn't stand like me. His shoulders bunched up around his ears, discomfort in every muscle. *Wound up tighter than Dick's hatband.* I remembered Falcon saying a hundred times before. Was that how he saw me? I forced my shoulders to unclench, pushing them down to appear relaxed.

Jack's raised eyebrow told me she was eavesdropping on my thoughts again. I didn't mind–it was just, sometimes it was easy to forget that my mind wasn't fully my own anymore.

"Do you know of a place we can talk or is out here on the bridge good?" Jack asked, lightness rolling off her in waves. She didn't feel light right now; she felt as nervous as I was, but she could hide her emotions in her smiles, and I couldn't.

"Follow me," he said, his eyes staying locked on me, moving like I was a threat.

In his eyes, I probably was.

JACK

Diego and Desmond could pass for twins. Assuming Desmond's face could remember how to make literally *any* expression except a scowl. Diego was like a warm cookie: soft and gooey, very sweet, making your day better just by existing. But he was also in those moments right after savoring that cookie: forlorn, sad, cookie-less. Heart-less instead of heartless.

Desmond looked like he had swallowed a rock and couldn't decide if he would have another.

He pointed across the bridge to Chilijan, the land of water. He cast some spell to open the gates and I found myself holding my breath to see what would happen next. I'd heard Puddin and Diego both mention that Chilijan had an empress, not a king or a queen, and I wondered how that changed things. Did an empress have something that the kings of Trellis lacked? Vice versa? Every question made me realize there was still so much about Obius that I didn't know.

"There's a border village just beyond the bridge. We can stop there, if that pleases you, my lady." Desmond wouldn't raise his eyes to meet mine, but he couldn't keep them off of Diego. It must be like seeing a ghost.

Desmond's mouth grew more grim and I hoped I didn't grimace myself. He was *salty*. Definitely not like Diego.

"Please, just call me Jack. All this 'my lady' stuff is getting kinda weird," I said, trying to ease the tension.

It didn't work.

"I'm Di–"

Desmond turned and walked away before Diego could even say hello. He was halfway across the bridge before Diego and I started moving.

"What's his deal?" I said to Diego.

"Maybe he's just... cautious?" Diego looked as convinced as his words sounded, but he followed him nonetheless.

Desmond was already waiting for us under a tree that reminded me of a weeping willow. It was purple though, and its branches and soft petal-like leaves blew in the breeze.

The bridge was sturdy beneath my feet, but I crossed it quickly. The rushing water of the river below sent water droplets up, splashing on my shoes and ankles. The currents were churning with magic and I wanted to jump in. There was an energy in the water that was missing from my current companions. Diego and Desmond both kept waiting for something to happen, some attack to dodge, some words to cut through them. Desmond's energy was similar to Diego's but it lacked depth. Desmond's feelings all hovered near the surface, but Diego was buried underwater.

The currents were hypnotizing. I could scry in the rivers here, the urge to let myself get lost was nearly overwhelming. My hands tingled and the pull to let go of my human body rushed through me as swiftly as the currents.

"Jack?" Diego startled me from my thoughts and I snapped back so roughly, fully into myself that I flinched. "Jack?" he asked again, this time much softer, coming back to the bridge to help me across.

"Sorry, yes. The river is just distracting."

"They say that memories can be seen in the waters of Chilijan. People from all over Obius come to stare into our waters," Desmond said. He crossed back to us incredibly fast; the willow tree was several feet away, more than a few gliding steps.

Diego took another step away from the river bank. If I didn't know him so well, I'd miss how high his head was tilted away from the water. I'd miss how his back was too stiff and how tried not to chew the inside of his lip. There was no missing how his eyes would dart away as soon as they caught a glimpse of the tides.

"I wonder what I'd see," I said out loud. Diego had drawn me across the bridge and I knelt at the water, running my fingers across the top.

"Everything, would be my guess," Desmond said.

My staff dipped the crystal into the water and green magic flooded through the sphere. I felt the rush and grabbed the staff, riding the high of the magic and smiling. *Yes.* This was who I was meant to be.

"The town is just beyond the valley," Desmond said. He didn't make eye contact. He didn't turn back to see if we would follow. He moved like it was his purpose to just keep going. When his shadow mingled with Diego, I paused to really examine them.

He was the same height as Diego; they stood almost next to each other now, and both looked like they would spontaneously combust.

"Okay, I know it's weird being here, but you two are so awkward. Maybe you should just hug it out or something."

"No," Desmond said.

"I don't *hug it out*, what in the world–" They spoke at the same time, and glared at each other. Diego was flustered, his cheeks turning pink as he stepped away, closer to me. Desmond stayed very still, like if he just didn't move, he could disappear.

"You two are ridiculous. Does this town have a place for us to stay? Food?"

He blinked at me, curious but confused.

"Y-yes, of course, come with me." So the stutter and the awkwardness were genetic then. Desmond had the same rigidity I'd seen in Diego, long before he let down the walls of his mind for me.

They walked like two similar magnets, pushing each other away the closer the other moved. This was going to be a long chat, even if it only took minutes. I took in the scenery so I could try to quiet my mind of their thoughts. Listening was getting too easy, too natural; the assumed privacy that people sought in their own minds was not a comfort they could have with me any longer. The realization was heady, my staff glowing brighter as it was so in tune with me.

"Be careful with that line of thinking, Priestess," Snapdragon whispered.

"Why is that?"

"Because that's when you start seeing the shadows in everyone's words."

The short walk was silent. I walked between them, and took a few extra steps so I could be out in front. Space helped; I didn't immediately scan someone's thoughts if they weren't close to me. My feet ached again from the walking, but it was a good distraction. The energy bouncing between them was too much for me to deal with.

The little village that Desmond alluded to was huge and sprawling. We crossed through the valley, and I focused on all of the flowers and trees. I took in the colors of them, tried to memorize every detail so I could visit this place again in my dreams one day, and touched every piece of greenery I could reasonably reach. They all had names, and I wanted to learn them all.

Huge, luminous Jack-in-the-pulpit flowers grew by another river bank. The blooms had that signature swooping petal over the top, but here they grew in more colors than just the green and maroon-black I was used to on Earth. They were yellow and gold, red and white, pink and green. The combinations were strange and complicated; the thin stripes were sometimes a different shade than the rest of the flower, sometimes another hue altogether.

They were perfect.

Their berries were huge too, ripe and red, shiny in the sunlight. The flowers tilted a bit in my direction, and a berry dropped. A small, curly vine nudged it in my direction.

"Is that for me?"

The vine nudged it again.

"Pulpit berries. They're very good this time of year," Diego said, looking up at the sky. Clouds passed overhead, bright and fluffy. He brought my hand to his lips to press kisses on each knuckle.

"Is she your lover?" Desmond asked, voice slicing through the moment and making me feel like a scolded teenager.

"I fail to see how that is *any* of your business, brother," Diego spat the words out, one by one. He covered my hand with his.

Desmond's humorless, angry huff of a laugh rang alarm bells in my head. A bitter smile formed on his lips. Cold. Angry. Spiteful.

Their faces were similar, but that was all.

"Well, *brother*, I think it's everyone's concern if you fall in love or lust or whatever this is with *another* Priestess and destroy what little we have left here. There isn't much left, but it's ours. You've no right to show up here and–"

"I would never hurt a blade of grass in Obius. Never." Did Diego even say that out loud? His words reverberated through my chest.

"History tells us a different tale."

Privacy be damned, I let the floodgates of my magic open and delved deep into his mind. Desmond's memories spread out before me like I was shuffling a deck of cards. I slid all of the happy, smiling cards away to see the parts that broke this man. I wanted to see where this anger came from, to see if there was ever a chance for him not to be broken.

Stones being thrown at him. Covering his feathers. Covering his head. Hiding. So much hiding but from who?

Everyone, everyone, everyone, his shaking voice whispers to me.

His mother, the beautiful Queen Orainia, crippled and dying. I felt the pressure of their clasped hands until the joints in my fingers ached. I remembered the words from Luther's story, how they had to say goodbye, and then more words from her. The Queen whispering to him, the last words, the last things she will ever say to him.

"I love you more than the suns in the sky, more than any Goddess, more than the heart in my own chest. Forgive him. Find him. I know you will."

He didn't need the links between the worlds to be shattered for his heart to break. It broke when she passed.

The pendant that hung around his neck called to me as I shuffled his memories more, digging deeper and deeper. Years of research, years of reading. Lonely nights spent in cramped rooms, hovering over a candle. The loneliness ate at me; where Diego was full of sorrow and regret, Desmond held a black ocean inside his heart. Massive and roaring, the waves of his isolation were only buffeted by the presence of one other person. I hoped this person was a friend.

What were you looking for, Desmond?

I focused harder on the books he read, looking at the words on the pages written in a script I couldn't read. But I didn't need to know how to read, because the Seer's magic did, and I knew the spells now.

Bindings.

Gravity.

Lightning.

Holy Revival.

"Desmond, how long has it been since your mother passed?" I asked. I wanted him to trust me. I wanted Desmond to see that I understood the roaring in his ears and that I could quiet the storm.

"Years," he said flatly.

"Where are you taking us?" Diego asked. He used his kingly voice again; commanding and loud, letting it carry.

Desmond stopped, squeezing his fists tight before releasing them. He worked so hard to maintain a civil face, and I wondered for a second if that was for my benefit, or for some promise he made to his mother.

"To your doom. I'm going to stab you in your sleep and throw you in the river."

Not one muscle moved on his face as he spoke, and I laughed. Horrible, embarrassing belly laughs. The joke sailed right past Diego and he was ready to fight, until he noticed the laughing.

Desmond's thoughts played in my head, *What a chump*, and I laughed again. Harder. I snorted.

Finally, Desmond smiled.

"What kind of response is that? There's a *Priestess* here and–"

"Diego," I said through my giggles, resting my hand on his arm, and he yanked it away.

"Joking about harming a Priestess is *never* funny."

He sulked past us and the anger that radiated from him made my stomach clench. I knew he didn't want me to reach for him; the heart link felt like a vice and it tightened and tightened. I tried to pry my fingers under the heart link, but I couldn't.

"What foul magic is this?" Desmond asked, seizing my arm and yanking it up. He flipped out a knife from somewhere and had it against the heart link in one sweeping motion.

"Hey, stop, don't! That's–"

"Our heart links." Diego was back, and he ripped Desmond away from me, tossing him like he was weightless. Diego was in front of me, arms out with his feathers fanned out. He lowered his head just a smidge, just showing his horns.

It was a battle request.

Desmond dropped his head, the sleeves of his shirt bulging, but he didn't pull them up to let his feathers fan out. Cerulean, striking blue, peeked through the straining black fabric.

"Heart links? You *bound* a Priestess again. What kind of monster are–"

"Bound? What are you on about?"

"Heart links are dark magic, you fucking beast. I don't know why Mum thought you were worth saving." Desmond's tone had lost any and all warmth. He practically spat at Diego, the rage coating his words like he had chewed on something rotten.

Diego lunged. He launched his entire body at Desmond and Desmond didn't stand a chance. He hit the ground hard enough that I felt the thud rattle beneath my feet.

My staff was back in my hands, ready to cast. Lightning was building in the crystal. Falcon's face and burnt-up arms flashed in my mind and I tried to force the magic back down.

Diego swung at him, his fist connecting with Desmond's face. The sound of the *thwack* that came when he landed the punch spurred me into action, and I raced over to Diego. Grabbing his arm and pulling him back, pulling him to me, I shushed him gently. My hands were tangled in his black hair, Diego's face buried against my stomach.

"Okay, let's try this conversation again, but this time like adults instead of a couple of idiots itching for a fight," I scolded them both.

Diego breathed hard against me, his breath hot through the fabric of my jumpsuit. He was shaking.

"Priestess, please, you need to–"

I held up a hand to Desmond and he quieted too.

"Nope. You *both* need to be quiet. One step at a time. Desmond, you need to work on your joke delivery. Maybe don't sorta threaten me in the process. Clearly a hot button for this one." I stroked Diego's hair more, scratching at his scalp. His breathing still hadn't gone back to normal.

"Diego, he *was* joking. It was a bad joke," I lied. It wasn't–Desmond delivered without an ounce of emotion to give it away, and I loved dry humor–but he didn't need to hear that. He needed to see me supporting him.

"It was funny," Desmond said, kicking at the dirt. He smoothed his sleeves down, getting the feathers to relax, so the sleeves would sit flat again. Diego's feathers were still fanned out, and his breathing *still* wasn't normal.

"Heart links are not evil magic, or dark magic, or whatever else. They're... gifts between people who love each other," I said carefully. Diego and I hadn't had the "what are we" chat, and throwing out a label when he was nearly hyperventilating didn't feel like the right time.

"The only heart links I've seen were not for lovers. They bound people to Mum's service and they died with her."

"What?" Diego squeaked out. His voice was practically gone. The lion's roar had vanished completely and it was a slap in the face reminder of how weak Diego still was. His heart was functional but incomplete. How could I have forgotten that?

"Believe me, Jack, I would never bind you to me. I wouldn't. I would never–"

"Shh," I said, hugging him tighter to me.

"They were a gift to us, so we could stay connected. Diego didn't make them," I said.

The truth slowly formed in my mind. Bound together. Communication. Soul linked. I pictured Abuela's face, remembering how she promised me that we would stay connected. How she created them. How she created the amber stones that messed with Mari's magic what felt like ages ago.

"They're... cursed?" I asked.

"They're dangerous in the wrong hands. For your sake Priestess, I hope my brother is not the man I've been taught that he was. I hope he's the man my mother told me about, not the demon that wrecked this world, because if that's the truth, then you're bound for life to a monster. And I won't be able to save you. No one will."

CHAPTER EIGHT

PEONY

I couldn't bear to go back to the beige and gray hotel room from hell after the vibrancy of Obius. My senses felt duller here, and there was an ache in my chest that I wasn't expecting, like every time I've left Cape Margaret. I *missed* Obius. Magic took root in my body there in a way I'd never experienced on Earth, and the strength of it lingered. It bubbled up through me, wanting me to cast and cast. I'd never enjoyed my magic, not on Earth, but in the land of magic? Now that was something.

So Sherwin collected their things from the hotel rooms, and brought everything to his apartment. Jack, Diego, and Falcon's things were mixed together in a pile in his foyer. Seeing the pile of stuff sitting there haphazardly felt a lot like the emotions churning in my heart.

I could see the ocean from his window, and the turbulent waves called to me. The dark blue crashed in a lovely aqua with white breaks against the shoreline. The beach in the winter was my favorite; the summer was great for people to soak up the sun, but the ocean's true nature came with the winter.

Part of me wanted to launch myself into the sea. The very insane, not logical part. But the call to the water was overwhelming, so I closed the curtains and headed into the kitchen. Jack's burnt and battered purse was splayed out on the counter. Small citrines, ambers, a pearl, and some other base stones like quartz and moonstone littered the bottom of the bag, were tucked into the pockets and crevices. Jack's soft magic was laced through the crystalline structures of each one of them.

Soft magic, I thought again. Her magic wasn't soft any longer; it was grand and ancient. Obius opened her magic up in a way it couldn't bloom on Earth, and seeing the strength that settled in her eyes made my big sister heart swell with pride.

Sherwin hummed as he buzzed around his kitchen, happily working and quiet. His features were calm, but I saw the thoughts flipping through his mind as he chopped up some vegetables.

"You're hovering, Pea."

"Oh, sorry." I'd wandered over to him, standing closer than I realized.

His body had shifted back to his human form. The beard was gone. The horns were gone. The purple feathers along his forearms were gone. But he still smelled of pine and the earthiness that only can be found in forests. He smelled like Trellis, I realized then. I hugged him from behind, squeezing tight and breathing him in.

"It was beautiful, wasn't it?" he asked. The chopping rocked me a little, and I laid my head against his back. It probably made his work harder, but Sherwin didn't complain so I didn't move.

"Yes," the word came out hushed but Sherwin heard me.

"It was more so, if you can believe it. Before the fire, it was so much more."

"Was it hard to see it like that?"

Sherwin cleared his throat and set the knife down. He turned around so he could look at me. "It was the worst thing I've ever seen."

"But you still thought it was beautiful?"

"Scars don't make something less beautiful, Pea. The beauty wasn't just the liveliness, it's the world itself."

I nodded. Obius was enchanting, that's for sure. Thinking of it made the pull to the ocean stronger.

"You ready to go check on Mari and Falcon?" he asked, pushing my glasses back up on my nose and tucking my hair behind my ears. He found every opportunity to touch me, and I hoped he never stopped.

"No," I said.

Mari swallowed holy magic like she was taking an aspirin. She was unstable and Falcon had been badly injured. Letting her focus on taking care of someone without me hovering around her would be best for everyone. Plus I still wanted to punch Falcon for starting this avalanche to begin with.

"Then let's have some dinner, and we can figure out our next move."

I blew out a sigh. The ocean practically roared in my ears. I wanted to swim until my arms and legs burned with exhaustion.

Mama and Puddin had disappeared from Mari's place when we arrived back on Earth. The portal plopped us right into her living room, but they were gone. I wasn't surprised that Mama was gone, but Puddin too stung. She was Jack's shadow, and ever since the fire, Puddin has been distinctly missing.

I knew what the next move would be; I needed to find them.

And I needed someone that could help me.

"I don't like that face," Sherwin said. He had pulled out a large pan and drizzled some oil. Sherwin loved stir-fried vegetables, I was learning. Everything he ate was very veggie-heavy, and fragrant. His home smelled like a home; the kitchen came to life in his hands. I hated cooking and only did enough to get by, or to make Jack feel better.

"What're you making?" I asked, eyeing the stove.

"You're changing the subject," he said.

"Yes, I am."

"Peony, we can't go back to Obius to get Jack–"

"She's not the one we need to find."

Sherwin stopped. He'd need to stir his onions and peppers before they burned. I tried to inch around him to help but he blocked me. "She's not?"

"Nope, we need to find Mari's shitty grandma."

Sherwin laughed. It wasn't a pleasant sound.

"The crazy woman that tried to kill us at Jack's place?"

"I wouldn't say she tried to *kill* you, so much as she… chose not to assist in any life-saving measures."

Sherwin held my hips and pulled me back to his chest. He was solid and warm. He felt like sure footing, and it made me want to head for the hills. It made me want to never leave this little cocoon of safety.

"I forgot that you're a lawyer," he said as he placed a kiss on the top of my head. Being this close smooshed my glasses against my nose.

"And do you have any idea where to find her?"

"I have a few."

"Dinner first. Bed. We can start tomorrow." Sherwin trailed his hands from my shoulders to my back, and my face heated. Bed. We hadn't shared a bed before. *Would* we be sharing a bed? *That's a bit presumptuous, Peony.*

"You look like you just saw a ghost," Sherwin's voice was adorably deadpan. His low man-bun was falling out, and I reached to pull the hair tie out. His dirty blonde hair fell around his ears and chin, not quite to his shoulders and I wanted to touch it.

So I did. I was allowed to touch his hair. He made a soft *hmm* and stirred our dinner before everything really did burn.

"Do you want me to–"

"Get a solid night's rest next to me while I'm on my best behavior? Yes, that was my plan."

"Let's talk about this best behavior," I said, letting my voice drip with honey. Another perk of my magic. Sherwin added something to the pan, his eyes never leaving mine. They darted down to my lips and then back to my eyes.

"You're a menace," he growled, pressing another kiss to my forehead.

The logic part of my brain told me this perfect moment wouldn't last, so I tried to soak in every little moment. The look in his eyes. The smell of his skin. The strength in his hands and the feel of the calloused parts on my face and neck and in my hair. The way that he looked at me like I was special, like I was the stars in his sky. A lump sat heavy in my throat and I swallowed it down, forcing the thoughts away to stay present in this moment.

"I'm starving, actually. Can I help?"

A smirk played at the edges of his lips and I smiled back at him.

"Set the table? Not sure I trust you with a spatula yet." Sherwin waggled his eyebrows and I laughed. It might not last forever, but I sure as hell was going to ride this train until it crashed.

JACK

Desmond guided us to a building that was formed from large stone boulders, cobbled together to form an inn. His pace was steady even though his breathing wasn't. Desmond didn't like glancing back, but he kept looking in Diego's direction. The boulders were the entrance to the inn, but the rest of it stretched out into a very large, very blue lake. I knew that Chilijan was the land of waters, but I guess I didn't expect that to be quite so literal. The guys seemed so small next to the doorway, and it threw me a little off balance. Obius knocked the wind out of me again and again.

The lake was huge. It could have easily been an ocean, and I wouldn't have known the difference. The entire inn swayed with the currents, and instead of being freaked out, I found it soothing.

Okay, I was a *little* freaked out that the inn would collapse and dump us into the lake with the huge stone pillars and the roof tumbling on top of us, trapping us beneath the water's surface—

"I've booked us a couple of rooms here. This village is called Ubbin Lake. We can stay here for a few days and then head further inland to Aquarine, the capital city in Chilijan," Desmond said. He spoke quickly to a mermaid—water sprite—and handed us a small key also forged from stone. It was carved with delicate swirling patterns, like waves, and I traced them with my fingers.

"What do we need in Aquarine? That's quite a ways—" Diego started.

"I just thought you'd like to see your mother's grave," he spat back, already ready for the next fight to break out.

I saw the retort die on Diego's lips as he stopped himself, his shoulders already dropping.

"She was buried in Chilijan?"

"She didn't want to return to Trellis. Too many ghosts, she used to say." Desmond also found the key interesting. His thoughts were so loud and filled with so much anger that I was back to putting the walls up in my mind like I did on Earth.

"Enough, both of you. You're going to have to learn to get along," I said.

The guys stopped. They glared daggers at each other, and the sibling rivalry reminded me of Peony and I as kids. Diego stepped away, instinctively closer to me.

Desmond led us through the winding bridge-like hallways until we got to our rooms. They were small huts that fed off from the main hall.

"Priestess, do you require your own space? I thought since you were traveling with him, you would want to stay close, but perhaps I misjudged," Desmond said, not quite meeting my eyes, not quite looking away.

"Nope, we're good, and you're going to start calling me Jack. I feel like an aunty or something with all that Priestess-this, Priestess-that talk."

A small smile formed on Desmond's face and I felt like that was a victory. He would be a hard one to crack, but there was more to him than the grumpy face. He tugged at his sleeves again, bowed, and went into his room.

"My Blossom, you should rest," Diego said. His thoughts broke through my barriers; the heart links kept us closer than any magic could repel, and all of his fear clawed through my mind.

"You should too," I said.

When Diego closed the door behind us, I threw myself into his arms and he held me like his heart was going to break all over again. His fingers dug into me, one hand on my shoulder and the other on my hip. The feathers all down his forearms brushed against the exposed skin at my waist and I shivered, causing Diego to subtly, barely push away. His body tensed as a flash of fear played across his face.

"Your feathers. They tickle, that's all. Diego, where are you going? In your mind? The only thing I can read from you is panic. Talk to me," I said, closing the gap he made between us. I intertwined our palms, the heart links and our pulse points gently touching, and it brought him back to me.

"Talk to me," I pleaded, and then I waited. The words were so jumbled in his mind that he didn't know where to start.

"I feel like I need to beg your forgiveness, and I'm not sure how," Diego said, and I caught the edge in his voice. It hitched and cracked, and then I saw the redness ringing his eyes.

"Diego, love..."

His eyes shot up to me, the word *love* resting so easy on my lips.

"What do you have to apologize for?" I put my hands on his face so I could get his gaze firmly on me.

His bottom lip trembled, and I thought I was going to cry if he didn't.

"The heart links," he finally choked out.

"The heart links? What about them?"

Desmond's words replayed in my head and tried to remember the look on Diego's face. Was he mad? Scared?

"He's right. Desmond. They *are* a form of binding magic. I didn't think about that when we put them on. It was just supposed to be a link, but now you're *bound* to me, and I–"

"You're bound to me, too."

His lips were so red, and shiny. He had been chewing on them, willing the tears back, and smoothed my thumb across them.

"But Jack, you don't understand, these can't be broken. Not unless I–" His voice really broke then, the sob he held back threatening to come out.

"Diego, what makes you think I'd *want* to break them?"

"Because–"

"Because?"

His thoughts came through loud and clear. ***She's going to realize this was all a mistake. Why would a Priestess want to bind herself to the man who wrecked her world and her home? What if I screw this up again. What if–***

"I don't want to ruin you," he said softly, hanging his head.

I hugged him, crushing him to me with all my might and Diego squeezed me back. I guided us to the bed and pressed him down to the mattress with my weight. Diego stayed perfectly still, his eyes darting around, the panic clear on his face.

"I'm not so easily broken," I said as I drew his hands to my lips, kissing them like he had done so many times before.

Diego's chest rose and fell rapidly, so I laid my hand on his shattered heart and waited for it to slow, really letting myself take in his details. Everything had been moving so swiftly since he arrived in Obius, that I hadn't had time to just *look* at him.

His eyes were golden here, not the mellow, lovely brown they were on Earth. I saw a few more freckles that dotted his face, one stubborn one hiding in his right eyebrow. Diego's horns almost seemed to hide in his increasingly messy mop of curls, and my hands itched to tug on the ringlets. I rubbed his feathers, massaging his arms. Diego was a ball of knots and tension, and I kneaded at the tender spots.

He sat up, leaning on one elbow, and pressed forward to place a kiss to my lips. Soft. Gentle.

Shy?

"My B-blossom–" His cheeks blushed a cherry red, highlighting the array of tiny freckles and flecks of different golds in his eyes. "I, uh, it's been a very long time since–" His heart pounded until the bed seemed to shake. Its beat thundered in my wrist.

"All I need from you tonight is to be in your arms. Is that too much?"

Diego's skin heated under my palm, and I waited for an answer. I didn't know where the night would lead, but wherever it went, I wanted Diego fully on board and smiling at me. I wanted to see the mischief in his eyes, not the panic that was there now.

"N-no, that's, that's perfect." He ran his fingers through my hair like touching me too much would make me shatter too, so I leaned into him.

I took off my shoes and helped him out of his–such a small gesture, but the moment changed and deepened until he glanced down at the heart link, feeling how mine had picked up the pace too. Diego opened an arm and I cuddled up against him, until he turned, pressing us together chest to chest, heart to heart.

Sandalwood filled the air between us; the scent of his skin was warm and musky, making the weight of his arms surrounding me even more comforting. His linen shirt was going to be a mess of wrinkles, but I snaked my hands under the hem and heard his sharp intake of breath. His chest and stomach were hardened muscle, but there was nothing hard about him. Well, maybe *one* thing.

"*I love you.*" The words echoed in my mind, and I nuzzled my face against him. The words didn't make it to his lips, but I heard them nonetheless.

"I agree, this is pretty perfect."

PEONY

Waking up in Sherwin's bed, with his arm lazily around my waist and his hushed breathing tickling the back of my neck felt like a rare treat. Such closeness and quietness when the world was so chaotic and loud was a sanctuary that I didn't quite feel like I deserved. I stayed as still as I could not wanting to wake him.

This was too perfect, it couldn't last.

He stretched and when he pulled his arms back in, he pulled me with him, dragging me across the bed and against his chest. Sherwin kissed my shoulder and the top of my arm.

"Mornin'," he said, his voice still heavy with sleep. Sherwin wasn't a morning person. Cute. Everything about him was cute. Infuriatingly cute.

"Hi," I said, rolling over to face him.

His breath was warm on my cheeks and I didn't even mind the morning breath.

"Sleep okay?"

"Yeah," I said.

It was the best night's sleep I'd had in ages. I actually slept instead of pretending to sleep, letting anxiety claw through me until I had to reach for the antacids for some relief. I just slept, deep and dreamless, and woke up with the sun shining through the windows. It had to be nearly 9 o'clock.

I grabbed my phone and saw the missed calls from work, my inbox had seventy-four emails, and the bubble on my message app read fifty-eight.

Work was blowing up, and I didn't care. I needed to care; I was going to get fired.

"Would that be so bad," the awful, wishful part of my heart whispered, *"when you could wake up every day next to him?"*

I put my phone back on the nightstand.

"I need to take a shower, and then we can get going. Do you mind making coffee? Can I trust you with my coffee pot?" Sherwin said between kisses—my face, my hair, my nose, a few on the lips. He was already getting up, and the lack of heat from where his body was made me shiver.

"I know how to work a coffee pot, Sherwin."

"Just checking. Fancy lawyer and all that," he said, the smile that made my knees weak on full display.

"I'm not that fancy. And I need a shower too."

Sherwin kissed me again, light and sweet, and stripped off his shirt to head for the bathroom. I pulled the covers up to my nose and watched him.

"Pea. Coffee. Please." He laughed and closed the door behind him. I loved his different nicknames for me—Pea versus P. Pea when his voice was warm and welcoming, P for the world to hear him to announce our closeness.

After we were showered, caffeinated—with my very drinkable coffee—and a quick stop for some breakfast, we were on the road and heading to hit up all of the local crystal markets. Abuela would be there. She was always trolling through the markets, and it was just a matter of time before we found her. I wanted to be excited, to make the next step, but nerves clouded my thoughts.

My phone rang and I jumped—it was my boss. I declined the call.

"Are we going to talk about how you've stayed in Cape Margaret way longer than your day job expected or no?"

"Nope," I said.

Being a lawyer was functional. I liked going to school. I liked learning. I liked the law. I liked how all of those things equated to something that I was good at, but mostly because of how my magic could influence the tides of an interview or an examination. I didn't like admitting how *often* that was, or that I probably would be a terrible lawyer without my magic.

"Pea, you're going to have to face your–"

"I know. But I'm not ready to leave the Cape. Jack still isn't home, and she doesn't even *have* a home–

"We'll figure it out." He so casually threw out a "we" pronoun that I nearly choked on my bagel.

"Which market should we start with?"

"Let's stay at the oceanfront. There's a smaller one there, and she might want to lay low."

Sherwin drove, which I was also thankful for because my focus wasn't great right now. Part of the reason for that was that Sherwin was so damn cute, but mostly that clawing feeling was coming back. He rubbed my thigh as he drove, and I soaked in all of the comfort he gave me. The closer we got to the crystal market, the more I felt the puzzle pieces forming in my mind; this truth that I was certain we were nearly onto. It was like when I was about to break a case wide open.

It took four markets before we found her. She was at a larger one that operated in an open field behind an abandoned church, much to Sherwin's surprise. He didn't frequent the markets often, and it was odd to find one at a church. I wasn't really a fan of crystal markets, but they served their purpose. Pop-up and whimsical, they were fun and called to alchemists and normies alike. This market was set up in tents with a large sign that read *Local Market Today Only!* There were streamers hung from the tent tops. Each one in its own color, bright but worn.

This was what the marketplace in Treis probably looked like.

"Peony, there," Sherwin said, his hand on the small of my back as he guided us through all of the stalls.

It was run by mostly women. Older, embracing nomadic roots they likely didn't have but I still supported the vibe. It worked for the markets. Artists, artisans, and hustlers all had their stuff up and ready to talk anyone into a sale. There was magic in the air, and my gut told me to follow it.

Sherwin was pointing to an old woman with a small tent. She had wind chimes set up and tacky prints leaning against the front of her table. She laughed loudly and I cringed. It sounded so fake to me, too over the top and too jovial, but that was Abuela. We'd only interacted a handful of times since she was more interested in Mari and Jack than me. She fixated on Mari, showering her with affection over the years.

I knew Mari needed something from her that Jack, Mama, and I couldn't provide, but I didn't trust Abuela. Something about her always raised warning flags, but this time I needed to put it aside for the greater good. Reopening the portal. Finding Mama and Puddin. Bringing Jack and Diego home.

"Yep, that's her," I said but he was already guiding me over to the table. Magic buzzed through me, tightening in my chest. The truth was a powerful thing, and Obius just amplified my connection to it.

"Peony Hawthorne! Is that you, child? And... Sherwin, isn't it?" Abuela said.

He nodded, the sunny, surfer personality had all but evaporated from him. Sherwin stood just behind me, quiet and waiting. Just like a shadow.

"Yep, it's me. I was hoping we could talk?" I tried to keep the lightness in my tone, but seeing Sherwin seize up made the red flag that was Abuela wave even more. He sensed something.

"Of course, come back here and out of the crowd," she said, waving us over as she opened the back corner of the tent to let us in. The small tent wouldn't hold the three of us comfortably, so Sherwin stayed outside, back against the tent flap.

"You seem well," I said. The light, breezy mood I went for fell flat, and Abuela's smile dropped as soon as the flap closed.

"What're you doing here?"

"I was curious if you had seen my mother, and my sister's cat." I forced eye contact. I was good at this; being a trial lawyer had some perks, and I could intimidate nearly anyone with enough eye contact.

"I haven't. You can leave now."

"I have more questions–"

"I have no answers for you. Go." Abuela tried to push me out but I planted my feet and stood my ground. This deposition wasn't over yet. Sherwin's face flashed in my mind and it was gone once I blinked. Did I imagine that? How did–

"I see you've met Sherwin before?"

"Hmm? Oh, yes, must be. I meet so many people. Now, you need to leave–"

"Aren't you the least bit curious about Mari? How's she doing? And then, of course, Falcon. Isn't he like your son? Or did I misread that? I don't think I did." I let the ice of my magic settle into my voice and strengthen my stance. *Lie to me, I dare you*, I thought, my lips curling up.

"Mari is as good as someone can be for swallowing holy magic. Falcon will survive, it's just some bumps and bruises–"

"So you *have* talked to them. Interesting. Mari hadn't mentioned it."

I pushed down the urge to smile; Abuela couldn't see the victory yet. She couldn't see how I had laid out the puzzle pieces in front of me, arranging them until the full picture came into view.

She moved her hand so fast and gripped my arm until I squeaked. It was sure to leave a bruise.

"I see you, child. I see what you're doing, what's calculating in that tricky little mind of yours. You need to watch yourself. You don't know the game you're playing." The sweet, grandmotherly voice melted away. She was cold and distant, icier than I ever hoped to be, and the emerald green magic that flashed in her eyes was *so* familiar.

I'd seen it my whole life. In my sister's eyes.

Focus, Peony.

"Where's my mother?"

"Recharging. Jazzy should know better—use a locating spell if you're so worried. Which you aren't, are you? You came here, instead of using a simple spell. I do wonder why, Peony Hawthorne, truth speaker."

Something electric shot through me when she said, *truth speaker*. I held eye contact even though I was the one that wanted to look away. I wouldn't give her the satisfaction. I shrugged out of her grip and she let me. I was certain it was truly a *let me go* instead of me breaking free; Abuela could have kept holding on if she wanted to.

"Sometimes it's easier to ask the source," I said carefully. The pieces were arranged in front of me and I was taking a leap here. Just like in the courtroom, sometimes a feeling would come to me and I would go with it.

I knew I was right though.

The green magic practically pouring out of her ears was all of the confirmation that I needed.

"Everything okay here?" a redheaded woman asked. Her long, fiery hair hung to the middle of her back when up in a high ponytail. She had thin braids mixed in with the ponytail, and little dangling charms in them that instantly reminded me of Mari. She was curvy and showed off every curve she had with her tight shirt and hip-hugging jeans. Another vendor—had to be.

"Peachy, and you are?"

"I'm—"

"My niece–"

"Sister."

They both glared at the other, and I saw the truth on their lips. It was as bright as the young woman's hair. And she was young–closer to my age.

"Do you want to try that one more time? Consolidate the lie, make it a little more believable," I said. Victory was sweet, but the magic that swelled in my chest, and feeling the heat of Sherwin's body through the tent made me brazen.

"I'm Candela," the redhead said. Her eyes were too green.

"And you're? The niece?"

"Sister," Candela said, Abuela glaring daggers at us both.

"Interesting," I said, eyeing the two women. Young, ginger, and fair. Old as sin, suntanned, gray hair that was likely black at one time.

"It is," Candela said. Abuela grabbed her arm with the ferocity that she did to me, but Candela didn't budge an inch. She held my gaze and winked at me. "I'll be over here, *sis*. I'm sure Peony needs to be going."

"Indeed," Abuela said, eyes green with magic.

Candela knew my name. I didn't say my name. Abuela didn't either.

"What's your name?" I asked, "Your actual name?"

Abuela smiled with all four of her teeth. "Oh child, names are powerful things but they are vastly overrated. Call me whatever you like." The warmth and love that she used on Mari practically dripped from her words, and I wanted another shower to wash them away.

"I'll be going then. Do call if you hear from Mama or Puddin."

"I won't be doing that." Her voice changed back to ice, and she let a bit of her magic loose to run wild around the small tent, "And Peony?"

I turned, already opening the flap to retreat back to Sherwin. "Yes?"

"You already know my name."

Lightning sparked in her eyes and a wicked grin spread on her face. My stomach dropped, and I glanced up to see Candela looking back.

She had fires in her eyes.

Oh shit.

CHAPTER NINE

DIEGO

"You have to be joking," Desmond said. He stopped mid-sip of his tea.

This wasn't my favorite plan either, but it was the best one we had. I stayed awake long after Jack had fallen asleep in my arms. She was a warm reminder of everything that I needed to fix; Trellis, the kingdom, my heart. I needed to be whole to take care of her.

"I'm not," I said matter of fact. Jack was fascinated by the breakfast foods instead of paying attention to the conversation. She'd never seen these fruits before, or tasted Chilijan jam, or had porridge made from the corn stalks in the fields of Trellis. She sipped our morning tea, made from the flowers of water daisies, and sighed happily.

She was falling in love with Obius.

"We cannot just *waltz* into Trellis Castle–" Desmond's ears turned red, like he was trying not to explode from within.

"Wait what?" Jack said around a mouthful of toast.

"Of course we can. It's our birthright. It's not like they can deny–"

"You're clueless, aren't you?" Desmond said, cutting me off and rising from the table.

Jam colored Jack's lips a brighter shade of pink and I smiled at her; all of Desmond's huffing couldn't deter me from the one that would ever truly hold my attention again.

He leaned out a window and raked a hand through his hair, staring at the vast Ubbin Lake. The motion was unnerving. I'd done that so many times, but Desmond's hand didn't messily bump into his horns. His feathers stuck out of his long-sleeved shirt; the blue caught my attention every time I saw it. It was a perfect match to the feathers on my own arms. Today's shirt was a dark red that made his skin look warmer than his personality ever could be.

"A lot has changed, that much I know," I said.

"More than you realize," he huffed.

"Desmond, can I ask? Why do you hide your feathers?" I sensed that I was on thin ice, but Desmond needed to see that I wasn't rotten to the core. I wanted him to see that maybe one day we could stand eye to eye as family.

"Blue isn't a popular color here. It gets people talking." Desmond yanked hard on his sleeve, but one feather still showed.

"Talking doesn't sound so bad–"

"You didn't really leave a great taste in the mouths of the Fae folk, Deign. You were born a king. I was born a reminder of everything that you destroyed." He was up, storming back toward the table–a bull ready for the kill–when Jack stood and put herself between us.

"No more fighting. It doesn't help anyone."

"I'm sorry," I said to Desmond.

Shock flickered across his face, his eyes going wide before he regained composure.

"I appreciate that, but words won't fix the links between the world."

"What's your idea, Diego?" Jack asked, sitting back down. She gestured for me to sit with her, and I reached for her hand without thinking. Touching Jack kept my feet grounded and my head clear.

Fix Trellis. Right the kingdom. Heal my heart.

"We need to go back to Trellis Castle. Desmond is alive, and he's the rightful heir," I said before I could stop the words.

Rightful heir.

My time was done, I knew that; but passing the crown and everything that I loved to Desmond, who seemingly loved nothing, made me uneasy, to say the least. My chest ached, the dull, familiar pain and I swallowed hard to try to push it down. Jack slid a cup of tea over to me.

"Deign, you have to be joking. There's no way I could–"

"Lead? Be a king? Why not?"

"Because I'm not–"

"You are. Whatever you were going to say, you are. This is who you are, Desmond. I'm sorry if anyone has told you differently. I came back to Obius to find Jack, but now that I'm here... I won't leave until things are *right*. And this is *right*."

Jack's magic swirled in my mind and I tried to push it away; she was worried that I wasn't okay with this–I wasn't–but it wasn't up to me anymore. I didn't wear the crown, I didn't protect Trellis, and I damn well wouldn't mess it up a second time.

She studied my face, and it reminded me of Snapdragon. The soft eyes, assessing and blank all at once, the slight smile. I shook the thought away. I wasn't going to destroy whatever I was building with her, either.

Desmond's eyes focused on his hands. I wanted him to take that ridiculous shirt off and let the world see his plumage. Something dark and angry nipped at me when I thought too hard about him hiding them.

This was the play, this was our only option. How in the Goddesses' great names would we be able to fix this hellscape without someone to *lead* Trellis?

"Then... we need to go to Aquarine," Desmond said. His voice was quiet and he tugged again on his sleeves. I was going to get him a proper-fitting shirt.

"What for?" Jack asked.

"I need to say goodbye," Desmond said.

He was far away now, looking out the window of the small gathering space in the hotel. Desmond hadn't touched his food. He didn't even drink any tea or water. He sat there motionless and processing.

"Goodbye?" I asked.

"Believe it or not, Deign, I have a life here without you. If I have to leave everyone I know, I get to at least say goodbye. Get your things, we're leaving." Desmond stood again, turning to leave the table before he stopped and spun back to Jack, bowing.

Once Desmond had retreated to his room, Jack asked, "Are you sure this is the best thing, Diego? He doesn't seem thrilled."

"I'm not sure joy or excitement is something that he's capable of," I muttered and Jack playfully punched my arm.

"Some people probably thought the same thing about you, you know."

"Not here, not in Trellis. I was happy here," I said, remembering how easily I used to smile and how I felt like *maybe* that would come back. My heart rate sped up making my chest ache but I smiled anyway. I *wanted* to be the man who smiled because there was more joy in his life than sorrow.

"Then we're going to Trellis. After Aquarine."

"We really should just press on–"

"Diego, you didn't get to say goodbye. Don't do that to him," she said, playing with the tip of one of my feathers. Her eyes came alive with magic, green and shining, "And besides, I think you will need to lay some things to rest there too."

She blinked and the magic faded. Everything in Obius was another ghost to face; I didn't want to charge into yet another one.

JACK

After three or four failed attempts to apologize, I stepped in to help walk them through saying, *I'm sorry I'm an asshole because you're too much like me and it's freaking me out.* Once Desmond stopped seeing red, they chatted off and on through the path to Aquarine. It was nice to watch Diego talk to someone else. He was so oddly private when he wasn't talking to me. Or Falcon, I suppose. I saw how his energy shifted, tensing and releasing like answering a question could somehow snap him open again.

"I hardly even recognize him," Snapdragon whispered. Her voice was velvety, sweet and seductive, like a true damsel in distress from a kids' movie. Maybe that's who she was before the magic changed her.

"What do you mean?" I thought back to her. She didn't need me to say the words aloud. I was so in tune with Harold that my thoughts and feelings would reflect back at me even before the Seer's magic really came to me.

"This man is a closed-off fortress. Deign was regal. He was loud, laughing more than anyone around him. He was the first to smile, the first to speak. Deign greeted everyone he met, kindness etched on his lips like he didn't know how to spread thorns."

"He's still like that, but I think he can be thorny now, when he wants to be."

"My heart aches for him. He should never be made of thorns."

"Do you remember your life? After the Shattering? And the—"

"Wildfire?"

"Yes," I answered.

"Some. I remember the fire..." Her words trailed off, and I wanted to ask her if she regretted it but she continued before I could ask. *"I remember Deign mostly. I remember him at court, and walking through the forests, and dancing. He loved to dance. Does he still dance?"*

"He hasn't really, not with me anyway."

"Make him dance again. I remember the Shattering. That's when I truly died, no matter the date of my death, I died when he left. I died in stages, I think. I don't remember most of the years between then and the fire. I remember you waking up and hearing your magic echo through Obius."

The green sparkle in my crystal floated to the opposite side, like she was looking for Diego. I couldn't bring myself to call him Deign. It felt wrong. It felt like I was speaking to the dead.

"I wish I hadn't disturbed you," I said, surprising myself with sincerity.

Snapdragon heard me casting when I was scrying under the moon. I don't know what she heard, but it didn't matter.

"Don't say that. It happened because it is written, it is our fate. It happened because Deign needed you."

"We're not becoming friends now, are we?"

"Hardly. But I can see you clearly now. You're not a False Priestess. And the king needs you. Do your duty." With that, Snapdragon stopped speaking, and the link between us fizzled out. She floated in the crystal, and I wondered what she saw. I hoped that the magic in there was healing her bruised soul.

"My Blossom, are you alright? We were just talking about stopping to eat," Diego said. He was next to me, my staff hovering on the other side, and I stopped to catch my breath. We walked all day, and I was feeling it now. My feet, ankles, and legs throbbed like hell.

"Tired, but I'm good. My feet are killing me though."

"Priestess, there's another village just up ahead, can you walk?" Desmond asked. He kept bowing his head anytime he addressed me, and I hated it.

"Yeah, but I'm going barefoot."

Diego offered to carry my shoes and I let him. He was smiling again, and I wanted those smiles to stay on his face. Snapdragon was right; he wasn't made for thorns.

I took a couple of steps and winced. The stopping broke any forward momentum that I had. Desmond was several feet ahead already, looking for the next stony path to another village.

"I can carry you," Diego said, his hand trailing down to the small of my back. Just the slight pressure eased some of the muscles.

"Aren't you tired too?"

"I'm not, actually. It's been years since I've walked this easily. Before you repaired my heart, I could only walk for short periods. Especially in the last few months before we met. I could barely stand some days, other days I couldn't sit up. Falcon would move me from place to place with him, never straying too far. But here, I can walk for days. Run. Cast. I could carry you from here to whatever inn we find and straight to your bed," his voice dropped and his cheeks pinkened. There was a sparkle in his eye and a twist on his lips that had nothing to do with magic. The timbre of his voice changed, lowering until I felt it low in my belly; the heart links heated up and he noticed too, mischief running wild through him finally.

"Straight to bed sounds great." Diego lifted me with ease. Face to face, nose to nose, my legs were draped over his arm and he kissed my nose.

"Jack," he exhaled and the warmth of his breath was nearly too hot on my skin.

I hugged him, pressing my face into his neck to give our lips some space. As much as I would love to kiss him, doing so in front of his little brother didn't sit right.

"Maybe let's have some dinner first," I said, and he nodded.

"I'm not putting you down. You have blisters."

I raised a foot to confirm, and yep, red, angry blisters had formed on my toes. I loved the closeness but I wanted to be on my feet, barefoot, and soaking up the feel of Obius.

"Priestess, you're hurt?" Desmond was back, and already casting something on my feet. The blisters were healing, slowly closing and the swelling was going down.

"You can heal?" I asked.

"Yes, my father was very gifted. I learned from him," he said, performing the spell again until the pain in my feet had practically vanished.

"I can do some healing, but I'm not that good at it. I feel like I can heal the land more than myself. Not that I actually practice it–"

"My Blossom, most people can't cast healing spells. You've just been blessed with healers in your life." Diego still held me like the ground was lava instead of the greenest grass I'd ever seen. It was soft underfoot, and I was probably fine to walk now. Probably. I leaned my head against Diego's shoulder, feeling his heart rate tick up and up. Thoughts were coming in fragments instead of full sentences and images and raw emotion.

My guard immediately went up. I reached through the heart links, reaching for the realness that kept us–me–grounded.

"Diego? Are you alright?"

"Yes, my Blossom, why?"

"You feel... far away."

My thoughts were chaotic, trying to tune into him without tipping Desmond off that we were in our own world. Diego gently adjusted his grip. I'd been in his arms like this a few times before and each time I felt like I was as close to him as he would let anyone be, after what happened with Snapdragon. He held me like it was the last time he'd have his arms around me, and I squeezed his neck.

The distance from his mind seemed galactic even though my forehead was against his neck.

"I'm not, I'm here," he said, but the words were flat. He was here but not *here*.

"I can't hear your thoughts, or see your emotions in your star lights."

"My Blossom, you don't have to see every thought that filters through me to know that I am here. I'm not going anywhere. I am forever linked to you." He shifted me in his arms again, angling the heart link enough for me to feel it press against my back.

Bound. Yes, he was bound to me.

I patted his shoulder, asking to be let down. Diego eased me back to the ground like my feet would suddenly break and I took a couple of steps to prove I wouldn't collapse. My feet still ached with fatigue, but they weren't a mess of blisters, so that was a victory.

"Where are we stopping?" I asked Desmond.

"Jack—"

"Should be about ten more minutes of walking. Are you alright to walk? You look a little faint," Desmond said, raising a palm to touch my face but stopping just short.

"Jack, listen—"

"That sounds great. I could use some more of that tea. The one you made for us, yesterday," I said, keeping the distance between Diego and me.

I shouldn't have been *angry*. He was allowed to have his own thoughts. Of course he was. Realizing that I wasn't happy about him *wanting* that privacy was something else altogether. I felt the fragments of his thoughts jabbing at me, memories of Snapdragon, memories of Obius and his mother, the seasons changing just like his moods, him huddled in the corners of his mind covering his eyes.

I didn't like these thoughts—feeling him recoil and hide while still some part of his mind pleading for me to see him. It made me dizzy, searching for some part of him that didn't feel miles away. I wanted to dig deeper, but I knew that I shouldn't. The magic in me was desperate to find the answers and my conscience was telling me to stop.

"Oh, of course. I brought some, but it's easily found here. It's made from the roots of Chilijan mint. It's not hard to make–"

"Don't turn away from me. Don't look too close," Diego's voice had dropped in my mind, darker and deeper than I was used to, a tone he'd never used toward me and I shuddered. His push and pull made my head spin.

"Priestess, you're shivering. Let's hurry, you need to rest–"

"I'm fine!" I snapped out loud, a little too loud, at both of them and marched onward. I was fine. I *will* be fine. I needed a hot bath and a full night's sleep. And I needed Diego to sort his thoughts out before I did it for him.

DIEGO

Jack's thoughts were constantly in my head, so much so that sometimes I couldn't tell the difference between hers and mine. That's how it should be–a closeness that no one else can feel, no one else can see, and yet–

I slowly built the walls back up in my mind, shutting out her magic, shutting mine in. My memories were getting stronger the longer I stayed in Obius. I remembered my mother's face more clearly. And my father's, even though he passed long before the Shattering. I remembered the fun and joy of childhood, how Sherwin, Arturo, and Bitterroot would romp through the forest playing until the suns had long set. Images of Snapdragon too, of course. The curves of her body and her curly vines. The braids of her hair and the leaves that would sprout on her fingers when something startled her.

Looking back, I can see how she started to change, how the magic took her mind and made her someone I no longer recognized.

Looking back, *I* was someone I no longer recognize.

Just like the trails in these plains, and the paths through the rocks to the rivers. I didn't spend a lot of time in Chilijan, but I was there enough to know the lay of the land, and now I didn't.

I just didn't *know* anything about Obius, even though I should know *everything.* A weight settled against my chest. Jack's probing, the looks, and the nagging thoughts in the back of my mind that felt like an itch, made me tense up until I snapped at her through the heart links. They squeezed until the skin underneath pinched and felt raw. The absence of her in my arms made my chest cleave but she wasn't gone; this was just the heart link reacting to her emotions. Ones that I couldn't see like she could.

Jack chatted with Desmond, smiling but I saw the tension in her eyes every time our eyes caught each other. She would look away, her magic flashing like a beacon in my mind, and leaving before she could press me.

"Jack, my Blossom, I'm sorry-"

"Don't shut me out," she whispered back, her back still turned while she continued listening to his lecture on the incredible tea blends found in Obius. I'd give anything for Desmond not to be here, so I could just let her see whatever it was that she needed to see.

A shadow of doubt flickered across her face and I nearly tripped. I remembered seeing those shadows before.

Right before I lost Snapdragon, too.

MARI

Peony and Sherwin were back in my house. Peony buzzed to and fro. Something had her hackles up, but pushing the issue wouldn't do a damn thing. I made chai for everyone just to have something to do with my hands, something that didn't involve magic. Falcon arched an eyebrow and glanced at her, and I shrugged. This quiet sort of communication that we were building was comfortable. Easy.

Confusing.

He was up and moving and alive, and the best way to *stay* that way was to stay out of Peony Hawthorne's way when she was in a *mood*.

And my girl was moody.

She plucked at pillows and then paced. Sherwin tried to soothe her, and it would work for about five seconds before she was hovering again. My fingers were hot and ready to start a fire. I grabbed some candles and quickly got to work. Falcon's eyes were on me but I couldn't look at him because then Peony would know. She would see what was building here, give it life and a name, and then I wouldn't be able to contain it any longer

"Peony," I finally said. I had to speak. The silence was too much. Too many everyday noises that didn't belong in my house because there were too many people here.

"I'm not crazy, Mari. I know what I saw."

"It's not possible, how does that even make *sense–*"

"Actually," Falcon chimed in, and I shot him a look that could kill. Maybe literally; the Wildfire burned through me and sometimes I did set things on fire. Sorta. Sometimes it was more of a *kaboom*, but that's semantics. Falcon was oddly hard to kill, that much we all learned, and I greatly appreciated it.

Peony's dagger eyes were ruthless. Sherwin handed her a couple antacids and a glass of water. Sherwin was a warm blanket of a man, soft and cozy but likely suffocating. He seemed perfect for Peony.

"Actually?" I asked, wanting him to focus on me and not how Peony might stab him. She had a hard time letting go of grudges.

"It... kinda makes sense. I mean, she hasn't aged since I've known her. And that's almost forty years."

"Damn Falcon, how old are you?" I teased and he groaned out a laugh. The ribs weren't healing as fast as I wanted them to.

"Mid to late thirties."

"What kind of non-answer is that?" Peony said, her magic thundering around my house, and I grabbed at my cookie jar near the edge of the counter. I'd cleaned up enough glass and porcelain for a lifetime in the last couple of weeks.

Falcon's lips twitched as he tried to hide a smile, and the fire that wouldn't stop sparked alive in my belly. Falcon was going to cause me to set this whole damn building on fire, and I hated that I didn't care.

There wasn't much I did care about these days, to be honest. Jack. Peony. Puddin. Jazzy. Falcon. I had an inkling that my heart would one day include Diego and Sherwin, but they felt like side characters in my story.

Abuela used to be a large part of my heart, but now she felt like my villain.

"Mari, did you hear what I said?" Peony said, still snappy, crunching through another antacid. She's had at least three in less than ten minutes. That was intense, even for her.

"Sorry, I think I zoned out."

Falcon stared at me, stared through me, seeing something that he would surely tease me about later.

The fire leaped up to my lungs.

Peony sucked in a deep breath and I did my best not to mimic her. The flames would ignite with more oxygen, and my magic was just dying for a reason to let loose. "Mari, I think Abuela is a goddess."

I heard the words, I knew Peony was speaking, but they passed right through me.

I tried to remember when I met her, when my mother was still alive. I saw her when I was a child, at the markets. I wondered if Falcon had ever been there, at the edges of the markets, watching for a chance to join the energy of the crowd. His worn clothes and weird bandanas and long hair practically screamed alchemist to the regs; he was *different* and it was plain to see, easy to identify the otherness about him. The bandanas were gone now, and it felt like Falcon was constantly trying to hide the Lightning marked skin of his arms.

I thought about the summer I spent several weeks in an old cabin in the mountains of Virginia with Abuela. It was after my father ditched out and my mother didn't want to be alone. We spent the days walking through the woods and casting until we were lightheaded with magic. My mother smiled so much. She loved being among the trees, touching the bark to feel the life under her fingers, and she would cast her earthy spells.

That was the first time I ever made a *spark*. It was so small and flickered out so quickly, I thought I had imagined it. Abuela told me that it was beautiful, that the spark of magic in my soul ran through the realms, wild and free.

She looked at me with such love in her eyes that I believed it implicitly.

I remembered the walls being etched in sigils—the old language, the old magic. I remember her smacking my hand, telling me to stop messing with them because who knows what I could call down on us. I remember the sigil for fire, the first one I could ever identify, glowing gold and orange when I touched it.

Her eyes were so green, bright, emerald green—

"Holy shit, Abuela is the Seer!"

Was I shouting? Maybe. My voice was hoarse and *so* dry. Falcon had a hand on my shoulder, the other tilting my face to look at him, to focus on him.

"Hey, hey, hey, Mari, look at me. Look at my eyes. I'm here, stay with me, girl. Stop burning up. Stop casting–" He flinched but didn't let go.

My hands were on fire. My arms were on fire. The sweater I was wearing was melting, dripping bits of fabric on my counters and Peony worked to stop it from spreading. Falcon guided me to the bathroom, stumbling over things he didn't know the place of. His body was still large in my home, and he hadn't adjusted to it yet. Would he ever? Adjust to my place? Would he ever see this as a home he was welcome in?

My arms were really hot.

My neck was pricked with sweat too, now that I thought about it.

Why were we standing in the shower? Falcon's brown eyes were laser-focused on me, and I realized that I wanted to kiss him. The shower curtain was melting. Would Falcon melt if I touched my lips to his?

He was shouting something, I could tell. The words formed on his lips and I saw them moving, but all I heard was the crackling of the fire all around me.

Cool water rained down on me and I blinked through it. Falcon stayed right there, saying something, but the words were lost in all the noise still.

My sweater was ruined.

Peony's healing magic wrapped around my hands and they itched. I flexed my fingers and Falcon jumped.

"Mari! Breathe! Release it! Please, can you hear me? Mari–" Falcon's voice jarred me back, and I backed into the shower wall. The tile cracked, but it was cold and wet, and it cut through the fire enough for me to realize that I was burning *my* house down now.

"What's going on?" I whispered. I remembered the events. I recalled walking here and seeing the fire, but how did I start it?

"You went supernova on me," Falcon said, breathing hard and soaking wet in the shower.

His ponytail was a mess, clinging to his face and neck, streaming into his eyes. I raised a hand to tuck it behind his ear, but my fingers were still on fire. They looked charred, flaky. Like every time Jack tried to make biscuits. I clapped my charred hands over my mouth just in case I accidentally spit fire all over Falcon.

"I'm good," I said.

Falcon shook his head. "You're trembling."

Damn if I wasn't. The charred skin was peeling off, leaving my normal hands underneath. The skin should not be normal. It should be red, bleeding, and raw. I should be in an ICU.

"I feel fine," I said. Was I lying? My body did feel off. Stiff. I felt like I needed to cast for a few hours, like an athlete in need of a run.

"Let's get you cleaned up," Peony said. She was just outside the shower, and Sherwin was there, holding a fire extinguisher. I had no idea where he even found one, but I didn't ask. He held it up, at the ready, in case I were to combust again.

"Peony–"

A flame popped out of my mouth and she ducked before it hit her. Sherwin sprayed the little flame and Falcon laughed. Someone had to, I'm glad it wasn't just me.

"I've got her, Peony," Falcon said, winking at me.

The flames died down so nothing on me was actively burning and I took his hand. He helped me step over the side of the tub and wrapped a towel around me. Steam rose from my skin.

"I'm not going to just combust," I said dryly, while everyone side-eyed each other. Fair response; my wall tile was cracked and the curtain was melted and singed.

"I'm gonna grab you some more clothes," Peony said and left the bathroom with Sherwin in tow.

"Do you think it's true?" Falcon asked. He rubbed my arms, drying and soothing me all at the same time.

"Is what true?" I said, the last half hour or more was a blur in my mind.

"Nana. Abuela. Whatever you call her–"

The memories hit me like a ton of bricks falling on me, threatening to make me collapse. Falcon watched the complicated dance play out on my face and he strengthened his grip on my arm. My knees felt weak. "Yeah, I think it is. And I know where we need to go to find her."

"Cabin? Shenandoah?"

"Yep."

"You good to be in a car that long? Not gonna blow us up?" Falcon took the towel off of me and dropped it over my head.

"Can you even sit up that long with those busted ribs?" I poked his chest softly. He still flinched.

"Guess we're gonna find out. Otherwise, I'm gonna be lying down in the backseat."

"Guess you're lucky that I make a good pillow."

PUDDIN

The portal was unstable enough that Obius called me as Jazzy and I held it open. I felt the brush of magic against my whiskers and a wave of homesickness hit harder than I could ever remember. Jazzy held strong with the portal magic, securing it so the four of them could pass through. I wanted to jump through so badly; I wanted to help my girl, but I wanted to be *home*. I wanted to swim in the waters of Chilijan. I wanted to see if my house still stood. I wanted to climb trees and breathe so my lungs were filled with magic.

I wanted to go *home*.

After they got through the portal, we collapsed. It wasn't graceful; Jazzy and I were beyond spent, just trying to get the damn thing open, and there was no way we could hold it. No matter how badly we wanted to.

The sun had long since set when we woke up. Jazzy woke up before me, and she sat on Mari's couch, dabbing tears from her eyes. She knew I wasn't her biggest fan, but if I could have cried then, I would have too. With the portal closed, it felt like the only chance to get the girls home evaporated with our spent magic.

It'd been a week since they left, and about a day since we felt the shifting of the realms again.

We'd been in a small cabin in the Shenandoah Valley the entire time; after we finally straightened Mari's home, Jazzy said we needed a backup plan.

The backup plan was a grumpy old woman with very few teeth, lots of attitude, and an ever-changing name.

"She should be back by now," Jazzy said, constantly pacing the well-worn floor of Abuela's cabin. There were sigils engraved on the walls, around the door frames and window sills. She had them painted into the flooring, on every flat or textile surface had some kind of sigil. There were scrying bowls and crystals on a small altar that I felt like I'd seen before. Somewhere in Obius; so long ago that the memory was more of an impression instead of a real thing.

"She said it would take a few days. And you still need to replenish your magic. You look... feral," I said, letting my words have more growl in them than they needed.

Jazzy had a well of magic in her that seemed to never end, until the portal, anyway. She was ragged and seemed much older than she was. Her healing magic should have helped her, but she had so little left in her that she couldn't manage a basic spell.

"It's been a few days. Where are the girls?" she snapped at me, but I didn't take it personally. Her daughters were gone.

I curled my tail around myself and laid down in a patch of sun. Nature held magic on Earth, and as the sun slowly warmed my body, it recharged my waning magic.

"You need to heal yourself."

"I can't. I'm too—"

"Are you from Obius, Jazzy?" I asked her. She cut her eyes and pulled her shawl around her shoulders tighter.

"No. But I've been lucky enough to be blessed with extraordinary magic, and a great sense of where to find magic."

"And what did you find?"

Her eyes were silver-ringed and shining. Jazzy pulled out a small medallion that was hidden under her shirt. The chain was long and silver, and I knew the markings of the coin instantly. A caladrius. Chilijan healers. The power it gave her made her feel almost like an Obius being, but she wasn't. Jazzy was human, despite not wanting to be.

"I've always had an affinity for healing, but then I found this, and the affinity... strengthened."

"Be careful of the darker side of that coin, Jazzy. Death magic always comes with a price," I purred.

The front door opened, and we both startled. Peony stepped through the door and dropped her keys. Her eyes went from Jazzy to me and back again. Sherwin was right behind her, a gentle hand on her hip as he guided her into the cabin. Mari and Falcon came through next, and I held my breath.

Jack should be next.

Jack should be here–

"She's not here," Peony said. She tried to keep her voice sweet, gentle, but there was an edge to it that neither of us missed. Before she could finish her thoughts, Jazzy was hugging her, combing her fingers through her hair, trying not to cry.

They actually made it back. But where–

"Jack and Diego stayed in Trellis. Oh Mama, the forest, it was awful. She stayed because she said she had to, she couldn't leave it like that and–"

"I know, darling, I know. She wasn't done. I know, shh, shh, my darling, you're safe."

Peony had started crying, and the weight of realizing that Jack was still trapped in Obius settled through me.

Magic sparked through Mari, fires burning bright in her eyes, and I floated over to her, inspecting the stink of magic that came from her. She smelled like chaos, like the Goddess was still crafting her but tossed her away before She put the fire out.

"Mari?" I purred. I was going to perch on her shoulder, wrap my tail around her face to make her laugh and shoo me away, but the heat that came from her was suffocating.

Falcon leaned heavily against the doorframe, holding his side. Not one ounce of sympathy was in me for him.

He made eye contact with me and I hissed.

"You!" Jazzy shouted, pushing Peony behind her to fully take stock of Falcon.

"Me. Yep. Hi, I'm Falcon, the fuck up catalyst for these shenanigans. Mind the ribs, please, I nearly died a few times," he said, wincing as he tried to smile. Jazzy wasn't impressed, neither was I.

"Enough," Mari spat, her hands catching on fire.

She shook them, trying to get the fire to stop, to slow down, to release whatever magic she was casting. Falcon leaned over, groaning, and blew on her hands like they were candles.

"Mari, what have you done?" Jazzy asked, stepping closer to her until she felt the heat coming off of her.

"She swallowed Wildfire, like a fool. Child, you *know* better than that," Abuela said. She came in through the back of the cabin, and everyone jumped when she spoke. Sherwin pulled Peony close as she dried her eyes.

Falcon and Mari went rigid, and my instinct to attack raised my hackles. Abuela. Nana. Whatever name she wanted to be called. Why were they all so afraid?

"Moira, how can you be so callous to them?" Jazzy spat. Moira? Another name. Another face. Which one was real?

"It's probably easy for a Goddess. Humans come and go so quickly in their eternal lives, what's a few decades to her?" Falcon said, all teeth and pointed looks.

Maybe I would like him. One day, far in the future, assuming he lives long enough for me to stop hating him.

Now it was Abuela's–*Moira's*–turn to be rigid and fixed in place. Her hard eyes studied Falcon, likely noticing his heavy leaning, the dark circles under his eyes, and how he tenderly held his side. I had enough magic in me to heal him, but I needed to know where the battle lines were drawn and where he intended to stand. Right now, it was next to Mari. Her eyes were ablaze, and her hands were sparking.

"Falcon, don't take that tone with me. I've been nothing but love to you," Moira said. Nothing softened about her when she spoke, and Falcon's laugh was so humorless, so dry, it could be used for kindling.

"And her? Have you been nothing but love to *her*?" Falcon jutted a finger at Mari, and her eyes were shining with tears through the flames.

"I've been watchful because I knew one day, Mari would need a firm hand to guide. She would need someone to keep her from burning the world down. She would need you, Falcon," Moira said. She dropped her purse on a wobbly table, straightening her back. The bones creaked and popped, but it was more like a predator working out the kinks before attacking instead of an old woman hobbling around.

"So I was just something to be handled?" Mari said, not bothering to hide the tears anymore. Her eyes were full of fire. The flames were coming out of her eyes, and I worried that she was going to burn herself, but her hands were already on fire.

She was already burning up.

"Mari," I purred, trying to get close, but Falcon *scooped me up* like I was nothing more than a common housecat.

"Don't get too close," he whispered "She can't really hear you right now. Gotta get her back on stable footing." Falcon swiftly sat me on a counter next to Mari, but not touching her.

"No child, you weren't just a thing to be handled. You're magnificent, look at how you're glowing," Moira said, the tenderness in her voice almost believable.

"I am?" Mari's arms were on fire now. Peony was casting something, soothing healing spells that mixed with water. That was new; when did she learn that?

"She's *burning,* not glowing. This is what all your scheming was for? So Mari could burn?" Falcon's words dripped with ice and venom, and my respect for him increased.

Abuela–*Moira,* I kept forgetting–laughed, cruel and low. The temperature in the house dropped, a chill forcing my back to twitch and my claws to extend.

"She's fulfilling her prophecy. She's being who she was *meant* to be. Mari isn't just burning, she's being reborn. Now the others just need to learn to play their part. Their fates are written, and Jack keeps trying to rewrite–"

"What are you talking about?" I growled, feigning a bravery I didn't feel.

Moira turned to me, eyes alight with the greenest magic I'd ever seen. Her smile was wicked, the curve of it suddenly changed to something sinister, and my whole body tensed in preparation to flee or fight. "Jack Hawthorne, the human priestess, unique and full of love. Who else could be crafted from my sister's hands to heal a fallen and forgotten king? Who else would even bat an eye at the husk of a man that crossed their path?"

Jazzy stiffened. She was still drained, still struggling to be standing, but she put herself in Moira's face. "What are you talking about? What do you know about my daughter? Where is she!" Jazzy shrieked, the leftovers of her magic bouncing around the house–bolts of magic shooting themselves at Moira with no effect.

"She's the Seer," Peony said. The truth was a powerful thing, just as strong as any alchemy I'd seen. The words lit something in Peony, igniting a deeper well of magic that no one knew she possessed.

The house was silent save for the sounds of the fire burning through Mari.

"Did... did you ever love me?" Mari asked. The fire burned brighter, and she sank to her knees. The tears that rolled down her cheeks were all sparks, igniting as they fell.

"Of course I did, my Marigold. I love all of you. I always will. But you needed to be guided, your mother saw that too. You needed to be pushed so you would step out into the sun. 'Mari, you're a shield, be a shield.' No child, you are no shield. You were made for war, and I made sure that you would ignite. Look at you now!" Moira was smiling, truly smiling.

Mari hung her head, and I jumped down and ran over to her. Fire be damned, Mari was one of mine. I batted her cheek with my paw, getting her to look at me. My fur was burning.

I'd never forget the fire in her eyes.

Jazzy raised a hand and slapped Moira so hard the sound echoed through the house. Her rage was a living thing, backed into a corner and wild. She swung and swung at Moira, until Sherwin grabbed Jazzy's hands and tucked them to her side, his arms wrapped around her as she kicked fiercely to break free.

"How could you do this to my girls? You manipulative fucking bitch! These are my girls! How could you do this to Daisy? How could you do this to Daisy!" Jazzy struggled against Sherwin's arms, but he didn't let go. He had himself between Moira and Peony too; a physical body to bear the brunt of whatever came.

"*Because* I am the Seer, Holy Goddess of Vision and Time, and I will *do* as I damn well please, you insignificant speck. You are nothing but dust, crafted from the mud of my sister's heel. You will *not* defy me."

"They're not your daughters, you wretched bitch!"

"They're all mine. Just as you are."

The house shook. Mari's arms gave out, and Falcon scooped her up. She was still burning and he was weak, but he stayed upright. His shirt was on fire. Peony was casting healing spells at the speed of light, keeping them both alive, putting out as much of the fire as she could. He held her tight and kicked the door open before the cabin went up in flames with her.

Jazzy screamed and screamed, her words lost to the roar of the magic around us. Sherwin had Peony tucked into his arms too, and he was pulling them out of the house as the roof started to crumble.

Moira locked eyes with me and I didn't move.

She opened a portal.

The smell of Obius–the grasslands of Aggria, the forests in Trellis, and the seawater of Chilijan–it all hit me at once, everything like I had forgotten what senses *were*, until I saw her stepping through the portal.

I jumped through after her.

CHAPTER TEN

JACK

Aquarine personified the essence of beauty more than I could have imagined. The palace was majestic in a way that Trellis wasn't; it also had spires and turrets, but there was a *grandness* to Aquarine that didn't exist in Trellis. The castle in Trellis was bricked and covered in vines and flowers–purposefully, not from neglect–and the vibe was warm and welcoming. The gates were open for the people to come through. At least, that's how I saw Trellis in my visions. Now, it was run down and closed away. I thought back to the halls that Arturo had dragged me through, to the decaying dungeon, and how the castle walls crumbled so easily.

But Aquarine shined and glimmered. The palace gleamed in blues and greens I'd never seen before, with shining tiles in spiraling designs across its walls. Pearlescent, rounded tiles that reminded me of fish scales lined the roof. A long, thin bridge from the main entrance to the courtyard of the palace swung back and forth softly in the breeze. The posts that held the bridge had the same, shiny, pearly feel like the rest of the palace.

I felt my breath hitch when the suns' light made the palace gleam. Every surface of Aquarine glinted like a jewel. The water surrounding the towering palace was crystal clear, and I could see that more of it extended into the depths below. The castle seemed to go to the bottom of the lake, with gems glittering all the way down. I caught flashes of years past as the castle was built and decorated, how it slowly transformed into a true palace. The walls were covered in pearls and the iridescent glow of seashells. There was a large, open gate under the water where Fae folk swam back and forth. They moved too fast for me to see their details, but I felt this place teeming with life in a way that the rest of Obius had lacked. Aquarine was a city above and below the waves.

"Jack, before we go back to Trellis, I need to see the Empress," Desmond said.

I heard the tail end of his thoughts, all jumbled and filled with emotion. He needed to pray and there was someone he wanted to see. We'd walked for about fourteen hours straight; Diego and Desmond kept insisting that we stop to rest, but I was restless. I wanted to keep moving. I wanted distance between their thoughts, and Diego's gentle prying and apologies.

I felt the shift in him, the clanging of his voice heavy in my mind. The darkness that I knew from the earliest visions hadn't fully cleared, and it was a surprise to both of us. Anger permeated through Diego's mind but his face was a cool, emotionless mask.

I reached with magic to calm the little fires popping up through him, and he immediately gave me a timid smile. It gave me butterflies, that smile. So confident, so full of pride, but so, so shy. ***"Thank you,"*** he said to me, the corners of his lips turning up.

"The Empress is well? She's not in hiding?" Diego asked.

Desmond noticed the smirk forming on Diego's face, and he snarled. "Hiding? Hardly. She just decided that once the drama in Trellis started she would stay out of it. With Snapdragon at the helm though, I'm sure everything seemed like a threat. Empress Sereia closed the borders. The people of Aquarine have struggled with their magic too, but overall we have fared better than those in Trellis."

"We?" Diego asked, and I found the edge in the tone again.

"Breathe," I urged him.

"Yes?" Desmond said.

"Do you not consider yourself a Trellian?"

"No, I don't. I have no home. I've been graciously allowed to stay in Aquarine, and I won't spit on the acceptance I've found here."

"Oookay, both of you need to step back. Your thoughts are giving me a headache," I said, pinching the bridge of my nose.

Diego rubbed circles on my back, and the touch soothed me some, but I didn't lean into him. This distance between us still felt too raw. Diego stopped a minute later, sensing that he wasn't helping. ***"Forgive me, my Blossom, just tell me what I need to do—"***

"Who do you need to see, Desmond? The Empress?"

"Well, I'm sure she would like to meet you, Priestess, but um, there was someone else I needed to say goodbye to." Desmond's voice trailed off and he reminded me of Diego just then: the sweetness in his voice, the shyness in asking instead of declaring.

I saw flashes of Desmond standing in Trellian colors, a crown sitting on his head, with a courtyard full of people cheering, and his voice boomed through me. Loud and victorious, I saw flashes of the man Desmond was going to become. His hair was longer but pulled back to show his horns more fully. Flowers twined around them. Blue, five-petaled blooms covered his horns. His arms were out, the skin fairer than his face from all the years that he had his feathers hidden.

"Jack?" Diego pressed his hand to my back again and the images faded.

"Yes, sorry. Let's go."

"What did you see?" he asked.

"A king."

Desmond already crossed the bridge, gently tapping on the larger posts as we passed by. A different number of taps each time, some longer, some shorter.

"What are you doing?" Diego asked.

"Announcing ourselves. That way we can see the Empress."

I swallowed harder than I meant to and my chest ached. I wasn't *nervous* about meeting the Empress, but I wasn't excited either. I didn't want to be some dancing monkey to prove myself to yet another person. It made me think about all of my customers back at my shop, *Visions and Trinkets*. That felt so far away; a lifetime ago, in a world that was truly a universe away. I thought about the rows of crystals and my trays of teas and bracelets. I thought about the skeptical look on my customers' faces, thrilled to be so close to *real magic* but not believing in the magic that they were breathing in.

But here, they would be expecting real magic. Grand displays and a show of power that I didn't have. Harold glowed and I gripped the staff's shaft tighter. Small lightning bolts popped up in the crystal, the emerald green sparkle of Snapdragon's tattered soul floating near the surface.

"The Empress of Chilijan is kind but vain. She likes her beauty to be praised. Don't be her pet or entertainment. You are a holy Priestess, remind her of her place should she forget," Snapdragon whispered.

"I can't just tell an Empress to stuff it," I whisper-thought back to her.

Desmond kept tapping along the way across the bridge. It was just like the one to cross into Chilijan, but this one was longer and had more sparkle to it.

"Of course you can. What is she going to do? Hold a Priestess hostage? Hardly. With not one, but two Trellians of the royal family? Her people respect her level-headedness."

Diego's energy was behind me, solid and warm. He didn't need to touch me for me to feel him there; the heart link pulsed with his affection.

"How long has she been the Empress?"

"Two thousand years or so? Something like that. She gets bored easily."

I imagined I would get very bored if I was alive for that long. Longevity seems appealing until you think about how the body needs rest and how the mind looks for ways to wander. Living for thousands of years seemed more lonely than even Diego could fathom.

"Jack? Priestess?" Snapdragon's voice barely carried itself to me, her words getting more and more strained to reach me. *"Don't make the same mistakes that I made, please. Deign is not your enemy. He's the sun in your sky; let his light bring you out of the darkness, Priestess."*

"What about his darkness?"

"It's time that his wounds be healed." I only heard the impressions of her words instead of her voice. The spark in my crystal had faded and mixed with the other souls still in there. A tiny, tiny speck of green was still visible but it was lost in the center.

The hair on my arms raised and my skin chilled. I said a prayer, maybe even a spell, to whoever listened that whatever was left of Snapdragon would be healed too.

"I want to make a stop before we see the Empress. Deign, you should come with me," Desmond said. The wind picked up as we crossed the bridge, making it sway. Diego seemed hesitant, but Desmond's steps were sure as he strode across. I had stopped moving, and Diego stopped with me.

"Oh?" he said.

Panic pulsed through Diego's chest, which made it race through me too. The heart links were powerful magic, and his emotions ran so deep that it was impossible to shut them out, even if that's what we both wanted. I tried to show him quickly how to calm his breathing down, how to count the breaths and feel the details of things around you, but his mind was a wall.

"I want to show you our mother's grave. You... deserve to see her too. She's at rest," Desmond said and his hand went to his heart. To the pendant hanging around his neck, I knew.

"Another goodbye," he mumbled. Panic surged through him again. "That's very kind," he finally said, smiling softly with a slight deferential bow.

The glittering water seemed surreal. It reminded me of peering into my crystal, like when I'd search the depths while scrying. I saw flecks of white and silver and streaks of gold. The water teemed with magic, just like the river back in River Glades.

Diego held his hand out for me to hold. I saw the offering in his eyes—peace, a truce, an apology. The heart link tugged my wrist closer to him until our fingers touched. Tip to tip. Diego held his hand face up, letting me trail my fingers and nails across his palm. Diego's hands were soft but worn. They were calloused but he had long, fine bones. He shivered as my nails grazed him, and I pressed a little harder before taking his hand.

Diego brushed his lips across the back of my hand before he took the lead, guiding me across. His heart link thrummed with magic, so much so that I could see the aura coming from it. By the time we got to the gates of the palace, Diego's panic had started to calm. His heart beat slower, more regularly. His heartbeat still got out of sync; the fragments forgot that they were back together and thumped painfully against his ribcage.

"This is the entrance to the palace. Just inside is a grand foyer that leads back to the throne room, the ballrooms to the sides, and then up the stairs to some of the bedrooms. The Empress' quarters are in the underwater part of the palace. Only the water sprites and naiads can access it. I've swam down a few times, but I couldn't stay for any length of time, obviously." Desmond plucked at some thread on his shirt or yanked on his sleeve as he rambled off more castle facts. The underwater section of the palace was twice as large as the above portion. The Catfolk lived mostly in the huts on the surface with some of the water sprites. He talked about the construction of the palace and how the Empress had been modifying it and adding more every couple of decades.

He finally led us to a small but well-tended bedroom after saying hello to a dozen different people that we passed. The bed was wooden with large knotted posts, and fluffy dark blue bedding. There was a small desk and a bookshelf, both piled high with books and papers. Desmond had a few different brushes out that he wrote with, and a painting of a man smiling back at him. It was small too, sitting on the edge of his desk in a frame with worn edges.

The man in the painting appeared to be about his age, had a loving smile and a shirt that exposed a large portion of light blue skin. He had short, blue hair with several thin, blue braids that touched his ears. There were jewels in his hair and a small crown on his head. Desmond instinctually picked it up and rubbed the back of the frame, touching each of the corners, and tucking it into his small bag. I saw a flash of Desmond with pink cheeks, holding that picture to his chest, and knew he had spent more time with it in his hands than on his desk.

"Who is that?" I asked, touching his elbow.

He jumped. Of course he did.

"This? Oh, um, this is High Prince Atam. He's the Empress's son. Atam is my friend," Desmond said.

I caught the implications of the word *friend* immediately, and more flashes came to me. Desmond and Atam with tangled hands and tangled arms. Desmond braiding his hair. Atam smiling and laughing, getting some strangled noise that should have been a laugh coming from Desmond. I saw them crying together when the Queen died, and Atam making water droplets dance and sparkle to soothe Desmond.

The love there flowed as deep as the seas in Chilijan, and I squeezed his arm.

"Will we get to meet Atam?" Diego asked. He watched and I saw the understanding in his eyes, and smiled at him. Diego beamed back at me, and I felt the ice in me thawing. A little.

"If... you want to. But first, we need to go see Mum," he said.

"Where is she?" Diego asked.

"I had her buried in a garden. It's not far. Her remains are there, but she had her soul tethered to a crystal." Desmond's hand went back to his chest, and Diego understood his meaning there too.

"So she's always with you," he said. Sorrow crept up through him, edging around his heart, and I hugged him from behind, lacing my fingers together to squeeze him tight. The heart link warmed my wrist and Diego clasped both my hands to his heart. It beat in one fast, but rhythmic motion.

"She wanted me to find you," Desmond said.

"She did?"

"Yes, she wanted you to be happy."

The words shot through Diego, hitting him so hard that he would have staggered if I wasn't holding onto him. He walked automatically, not paying attention to anything in particular. I felt him zoning out, pushing himself away from the surface of his mind, burying himself deep in the safety of himself.

"I'm here, I'm not going anywhere," I spoke with magic, and he answered with the hint of a smile.

DIEGO

The garden bloomed right beside Desmond's room. Up a couple of stories, but he could look down upon the gardens. He was next to Mother every day of his life here in Chilijan.

And I had to ask him to leave all of this to return to a desolate, crumbling castle to fix my mistakes. Bitterness flooded my mouth, the emotion so visceral that I tasted it.

He led us down a spiral staircase, and I thought of her. Mother loved them; she would run down the spiral stairs of her room as fast as she could; her dresses and skirts and capes trailing after her. The people in Trellis loved watching Queen Orainia dance and spin. She lived in motion, dancing to music or dancing to magic or twirling in the arms of my father.

I wondered who Desmond's father was. What he was like and if he would hold my Mother, spinning her to whatever music she found? The sound of each step carried through the thin hallway as we walked down. Jack boxed me in, staying a few steps behind on the stairs.

When Desmond opened the large, glistening door, my knees locked. The garden was full of Trellian blooms. Goddess star flowers. Queen roses. Sweet lilies. Pink and yellow Trellian irises.

It mirrored her garden at our castle, where she would sit with Snapdragon as they chatted. Where I'd wrap Snapdragon in my arms, pulling in her for a kiss while she would push me away, scolding that the guards were *right there!* I remembered them both playing with my hair or tugging my feathers if I wasn't paying attention. Mother would sing lullabies and hold me like I was a little faun, playing with my toes and pinching them. She was so full of love; I prayed that Desmond had that too. I prayed that I didn't break her spirit when the rest of the world crumbled so she could give that love to him.

There was a small altar with her painting on it. Some feathers and bells hung around the frame, fresh cut flowers at the base of the altar.

The man with the blue braids and blue-toned skin settled near the altar, kneeling in a soft prayer. He cast a spell meant just to be pretty, little sparkling flecks shining over the altar. He stood when he heard us approach, and his eyes went soft when he saw Desmond. They immediately narrowed and turned to ice when he saw Jack, then they filled with dread when he saw me.

Atam claimed Desmond's hand and raised a challenging eyebrow. Jack waved and it was clear that he didn't know how to react. Atam took a step closer to Desmond, still silent.

"Atam, this is Priestess Jack. She's the one whose magic you felt. And this is Deign, my... brother," Desmond quickly finished and moved so Atam could see us.

"Hi, Atam," Jack said.

I bowed, fully and deeply. Atam was the heir of Chilijan. As Sereia's oldest child, he would one day be the Emperor. So I bowed, even though he barely held back a sneer. His lip started to curl but years at the Empress's court taught his mouth to behave.

"High Prince Atam, it's an honor."

"You're back," he said, the venom dripping from each syllable.

"I am."

"You came back willingly?"

"I came back for her," I said, looking in Jack's direction. Her cheeks were pink. Would Atam understand how precious she was to me? Would he care? Or would he just see us as a problem for Desmond to solve?

"And what about for Desmond? Are you here for him too?"

"I am now," I said, trying to hold Desmond's eyes, trying to show that maybe one day we could see eye to eye as family.

"Diego—Deign—is trying to make things right," Jack said.

Shame ricocheted around my chest; Jack shouldn't have to defend me. My actions were indefensible. Shame was all I should allow myself to feel.

"He's saying goodbye to Mum. He never got to–" Desmond stopped talking and Atam nodded.

"Of course. She died after his actions. No matter how vile, everyone deserves to say goodbye to their mother. We will take our leave," Atam said.

Desmond took a second to react to Atam's declaration, but he nodded and trailed after him. Atam's long, finned tail glittered in the sun like the rest of his scales, but the swish of it as he walked away caught my eye. Jack's cat had the same predatory flick but I had hope that she would warm up to me one day. The only way I'd warm Atam's heart was if I was lit on fire to knock the chill from him.

Jack touched the side of my face; her knuckles brushing against my cheek. Those all-knowing eyes searched for answers I couldn't give and asked questions I'd never know to respond to. The hazel that I adored on Earth seemed overshadowed by the green of the Seer's magic. There was a ring of green around the outside of her eyes that seemed to be getting larger and larger.

How much longer until the hazel would be gone?

How much longer until Jack was lost to the magic too?

"I'm right here, Diego," she said, warmth filling her voice. She tugged on a feather and I wondered if she saw my memories as I remembered them too.

"I see you," I said, taking in the details of her face. The freckles on her cheeks and across her nose. The slight curl of her hair from sweat and humidity. She was breathtaking.

"I see you," she said to me, and I knew that she truly did. She saw every tiny, ugly part that I tried to hide from the worlds.

"Tell me about her," Jack said. She was behind me still, her voice like a spell all its own, and I leaned into her. Jack wrapped her arms around my waist and squeezed. Did I need to say the words out loud? Would she care?

"She loved to dance" my voice was already breaking, "and she would sing lullabies in her garden. It was a lot like this." I picked one of the sweet lilies and gave it to Jack. My mother loved all flowers, but she always smelled like sweet lilies. The lilies on Earth were similar, but dulled, like the Creator ran out of magic before She finished making the Earth.

"She was full of life. Vivacious. That's how you would describe her in your world. But here, everyone said that she was in full bloom. My father would laugh whenever she would get a certain look in her eyes; she loved a reason for a party, and she would think of any reason to have them. My father—he was a pixie so he had wings—would fly just out of her range so she would chase him, and have a reason to run through the courtyards. Not that they needed a reason, but my mother liked to blame her energy on him. He died when I was young. She didn't dance as much after he died, but I would still take her hands and spin her to music."

Jack wiped tears off of my cheeks before I realized that they had fallen. "They sound like fun parents. I don't really know my dad either. Peony sort of remembers him, but he was more of a repeated summer fling than anything else to Mama."

"My mother was a lot like Jazzy, I think. Except louder, but she had that same quality that Jazzy does; she filled the spaces she entered, and everyone was the better for it."

I kneeled at her altar, placing a few more sweet lilies under her painting. She was smiling, wearing a blue gown with her feathers on display. She had bracelets and fine golden chains running down her arms and across her chest; she loved the shimmer of jewels.

Grief came cascading down all at once, wave after wave until I was face down in the garden surrounding her. I knew that was her face, but in my mind the details were different. Her smile was broader than I remembered and her eyes were bluer, deeper. Maybe it was just the painting that altered her but I didn't think so. This felt like the truth of her soul, and maybe I was remembering wrong.

Maybe I just couldn't remember at all.

I picked up each of her three Goddess stones and held them to my heart, praying over each one. I kissed the jagged stone of creation, and the smooth, rounded stone of fate, and the thin, oval stone of justice. I knew she wasn't in Sanctum, resting where she should be. I knew she was trapped somewhere in Obius, likely all of her spirit in that crystal around Desmond's neck.

I knew she wasn't *here*.

Jack sat in the grass with me, running her hands through my hair, trailing them down my horns, smoothing out whatever knot or wrinkle she came across.

"Were you listening?" I asked, and she smiled.

"No, I sensed that you needed those moments of silence. I've been tuning into the souls in Harold. The shaft of the staff feels kinda wobbly. Like it's trying to break free."

The staff laid across her lap, and Jack's eyes were solid green. She scried while I wept, allowing my grief to play out privately.

It was enough to start the tears again.

Jack nudged my head into her lap and laid down in the grass. We stayed there until the suns started to set.

When Desmond and Atam came back, worried that we were still here, Desmond sat down in the grass with me.

"She wanted you to have this," Desmond said, handing me a small envelope sealed with the Trellian crest in dark blue wax. She kept her marker. Father made it for her.

I didn't want to open the letter. I didn't want to break the seal, watching another piece of them crumble because of me. Desmond handed me his knife, and I peeled the seal off as carefully as I could, only cracking the edges that weren't branded.

There was a sunstone wrapped in velvet, tied with a decaying vine. She always used vines. *Bring Trellis with you, and there is nothing more Trellian than tripping over a thousand vines!*

The sunstone glinted in the waning sunlight and I felt the connection immediately.

My feathers fanned out and my skin prickled from a chill that awakened my nerves. My heart, still fractured and broken but healing, thundered in my chest.

Jack beamed, the magic still shining in her eyes and weaving its way through her, tying itself to us in the heart links.

"It's another piece of my heart," I said as I held it like it was the last bit of air in my lungs.

"She said that you would come back one day and that you would need it. I've kept it in my rooms ever since. It was with her music box," Desmond said.

I hugged him with all of the strength that I could muster. I needed the contact, the connection to my brother, my family. I squeezed him tighter and tighter until he groaned. My body strained from the weight of the day, and Desmond sat there rigid, awkward. I hugged him tighter.

"Thank you, Desmond. Thank you for holding onto this," I said.

He patted my back awkwardly, and I laughed, remembering how Falcon would call me a robot or an alien for being so *stiff*. Is this what I was like? I laughed again.

"You're welcome," he said.

"Are you ready, Diego?" Jack asked, the magic practically casting itself.

I felt the incantation of the binding spell before the words ever spilled from her mouth, but then they were there. Desmond scooted away, shocked, but still wanting to watch. Waiting. His eyes were too wide to be calm, but Jack didn't notice or care. The spell was already coming alive.

Holy Goddesses,

Creation, Judgment, and Vision,

The brokenness in front of me needs to mend,

To join joyously, righteously, and with precision,

Tie together the ends that frayed,

Tie together the paths mislaid.

Jack floated up along with her staff. It hovered in front of her just like her cat, Puddin, had done back in her magic shop. The crystal ball was blindingly, brilliantly green. The Seer's emerald magic danced around her in ribbons, wrapped around me and the sunstone until I felt the magic working.

"Deign, are you okay–" Desmond's voice was lost to the magic.

Heaviness settled in my bones. I could *feel* my bones and the weight of having a body. My arms felt sluggish but they felt more grounded. Like I was more real, instead of just a painting or a memory.

Energy crackled through my spine, electric and warm. My eyes glowed so vividly gold that I saw the light they cast around me. I was *alive.*

"I'm great," I said.

CHAPTER ELEVEN

**HOLY GODDESS OF VISION AND TIME
MOIRA, THE SEER**

The portal I opened was directly to Trellis. I needed to get back to the castle and see the true state of the havoc that Snapdragon had wrought. How did I *let* that petulant seedling get that strong or stray that far from what I'd written?

My blessing was too much for the child. She crumbled under the weight of the magic and instead of taking root and rising with it, she smothered herself and the King. If there was anything left of her desecrated soul, I'd put it to rest forever. She wasn't evil, just weak, and the weak deserve to rest.

Trellis Castle was in shambles. Trellis was my favorite of the regions; the trees brought more clarity to my visions.

But the trees were gone. They were charred and dying, husks of their former selves. The smell of smoke lingered in the air; this hellscape was worse than I foresaw. Fate was cruel and I hated seeing this chapter of life.

"You! Who are you? Are you with the Fallen Priestess?" a young Trellian guard shouted at me. I was standing in the middle of the throne room, right next to Deign's old throne.

When I turned, the child nearly choked on his tongue. His wings fluttered and he dropped his spear, falling hard to his knees and putting his face on the cool, etched stone floor.

"No, child, I'm not with Snapdragon," I said chuckling. At least they still taught the children the stories of the Goddesses.

Arturo came running in, sword drawn, ready to start swinging. He was old now; the years were not kind to him. He turned white as a sheet and he also fell to his knees. "M-m-my Goddess! You've returned–"

"Yes, child, I have. We have work to do. Put that pig-sticker away before you stab someone. Where is Jack? My new Priestess? And the King?"

"There's no King–"

"The other one. Desmond."

"Who?" he practically shouted until he realized his mistake and lowered his eyes.

"Desmond. Oh my dear, we have *much* to do."

I took another look around the throne room and how it had turned into an aging relic, just like the rest of Trellis. The links were going to be opened again. It was time to set things right. I toed out of my shoes and walked out of the throne room. I needed to plant my feet in the soil of Obius. It had been centuries since I had been back in my realm.

When Deign shattered the links, I was on Earth visiting Candela. We took turns visiting each other; sometimes just standing at the edges of the worlds in our Holy Grounds, but we each liked to *be* in the other realms. Our other sister, Toltune, stayed in Sanctum more. She needed the quiet and the solace that Sanctum brought. She took her work seriously, laying the souls to rest and making sure that everyone was in their proper place.

When the links shattered, Candela and I couldn't reach her. The three of us stood together at the Holy Grounds, screaming in rage and disbelief.

I hadn't *seen* this. I hadn't predicted that King Deign would be so desperate to protect Snapdragon or how deeply the insanity would take root in her.

How could I have been so inattentive to these children? They needed to be reminded of their paths and how to walk them. They needed guidance. They needed to remember what life was supposed to be like before Deign inserted himself in my Fates.

"You can't possibly be–"

"I can't what," I growled, and Arturo lowered his face to the floor, his shoulders trembling.

"I-I-I-I apologize, Your Divine Grace. My Lady of Vision. Oh Blessed Goddess–"

"Best you remember the Goddess part, Arturo. The Fates are written, but that doesn't mean I won't *rewrite* them."

He nodded so ferociously that his forehead scraped the stone floor.

"Rise, child. Admit mistakes and move forward. There has been too much time wasted for anything else."

The other guard stood also, his eyes downcast. What a lovely child; his heart was so pure but filled with so little magic. He'd been born to a dead world, and there was no magic to stir him. I tilted his chin up so he would look at me, and felt the terror in him.

"Peace child, tell me your name." I knew his name; I knew everyone's names but asking always helped the children respond.

"Claude," he said, his voice so small like he'd forgotten the sound of it himself.

"Claude, Arturo, gather the guards. We have much to do," I said, casting a small spell to bring out the magic in their veins. It was there, but it was so weak and dormant. It needed to remember how to live again too. My beautiful gem of Obius needed to be polished. Releasing small spells, I healed the land around me. I let the magic seep into the scorched souls of Trellis for them to remember. I pushed the magic to their fingers so they could feel them, wrapping alchemy around their hearts to make them beat again.

My heart warmed at the smiles on their faces as magic flooded their frail bodies. They'd been cut off from the truth of their beings; it must feel like coming home.

But for now, we had to put their joy aside because there was work to be done.

It was time for Jack and Deign to start playing the parts that were written for them.

PUDDIN

The last time I went through a portal was when the links were falling apart and I jumped through. I was young and dumb and wanted an adventure. It didn't fully register that I'd never go home until the links crumbled completely and there was no way back. I searched. I tried spell after spell. I prayed to all three of the Goddesses and even a few made-up human ones.

This time was just as bad. I felt my body compress and stretch and cave in on itself. My bones were breaking and my organs squeezed until I thought they would pop.

I fell through the sky, through time, through space, through a million different universes, and it took an eternity.

It was probably a few seconds. I couldn't tell.

But then, my eyes were open and I saw two suns in the sky. I saw a real, true blue sky. My senses were overloaded; the smell of flowers and the feel of the grass beneath me, my tail caught awkwardly under me, and my hands digging into the dirt–

My hands.

I held them up. They were hands, not paws. They were fuzzy and soft, my nails longer and curled, but nails instead of claws. When I looked down, I saw my body. My true body, what I looked like as a Catfolk. My tail curled around my body, hugging me, and it was longer, fluffier than on Earth. I was tall, at least the height of a human, at least Jack's size.

I could look her in the eyes here.

I could hug her like she had hugged me so many times before when I was a housecat and could fit in her arms. My cat-face was there, but not as small or compressed as an Earth cat's. I touched my ears, and just took in the strangeness of my body. It had been so long since I was *me*. I stretched out in the grass, letting the feel of it brush against my fur. A breeze picked up and it rustled my whiskers until the scent of the sea reached my nose and I sprang up.

The sea.

Was I in–

Chilijan!

I got to my feet so quickly that I was dizzy, but I ran anyway, diving into Ubbin Lake and swimming. Cats on Earth didn't enjoy water, but not Catfolk. Water was part of our world; we lived in the huts and cabins on stilts and along the water's edges in Chilijan. Everything in Chilijan was tied to the water and I swam through its depths.

The undercurrent of energy was there, just like I remembered. It wrapped around me like the waters were welcoming me home. When I saw another Catfolk, I swam over to them and surfaced to talk.

"Is this truly Chilijan?" I asked.

"Hmm? Yes, of course?" she responded.

"I've been gone a long time," I said, my words all purrs, and the Catfolk woman grinned at me. She was beautiful. Was I that beautiful?

"Yes, sister, I smell something strange on you. But you're home," she said, swimming around me.

We swam together, weaving between each other, tails slapping the water as the game picked up. She was laughing and I was breathless.

"It's Earth, if you can believe it."

"Earth? Like the human world? How could you have come from there? The links–"

"–are waking up. It's a long story." She splashed me, flinging water right so it caught me between my ears.

I told her the story of Jack opening the link and falling through. I told her how the Seer was back, and she laughed like I had told a joke.

"At least you haven't wandered so far that you've forgotten how to swim!" she laughed again. I'd forgotten how easily my people smiled.

"Never," I purred, the smile on my face making my lips sore. "Please, tell me your name."

"Oh, meow, I'm Enid. You?"

"Bastet," I said, remembering my true name. Puddin was lovely, and it was the name that Jack had given me. But here, in the waters of my motherland, I used the name my mother blessed me with.

"Ohh, that does sound old!" Enid splashed and swam away. We played and chased for another hour until all of my limbs were so sore I could barely float. "Ohh, you probably haven't heard."

"Heard what?"

"There's a new Priestess! The one from Trellis finally died or something. Our Priestess, Zarina, died a long time ago, after the Shattering. I wasn't born yet, but my mam says that she was lovely, but without the Seer, we never got another Priestess–"

Tears pricked my eyes. I knew Zarina; well, I knew *of* her. She was the Priestess when I was a kitten, before the Shattering. Priestess Zarina was very kind. She didn't speak much, but she prayed over every soul she met.

"–this one is supposedly from *Earth!* Can you believe that? How crazy is that? First Bastet here says she's from Earth and now suddenly a human Priestess–"

"She's here? Jack? Jack is *here?*" I said, my words tumbling out too fast. Enid cocked her head, ears twitching.

"I think so? I didn't see it, but my friend's brother said that she was traveling with two guys. They both had horns, but one of them had *blue feathers!* He must be some kinda crazy, right? A human and a Trellian royal? Those are all long dead."

"And they came here?" I asked again, my heart thundering in my chest. *Please say yes, please say yes, please, please, please–*

"Yeah, they were heading to the palace. Apparently, this so-called Priestess wanted to meet the Empress."

"Is, um, is Empress Sereia still reigning?"

"Of course she is!" Enid laughed, splashing me again.

Relief flooded through me. The Empress was still around. Some things stayed the same, after all.

"Her Grace is still on the throne. The palace isn't far. Have you ever been? She still keeps the gates open. She didn't want Chilijan to be like Trellis, so we never stopped living. There's just not much magic, but who needs it? When we have the waters and the sky and the fruits of home, who needs magic?"

Enid floated happily, without a care in the world next to me. She clearly didn't know about the fire. Or how horrible life was having your magic ripped from you, or weakened to a pitiful state. Or how terrifying it was to be trapped in an alien world that didn't care if you lived or died. I never turned into a human, like Diego. I turned into a feline because that's what my body was closest to on Earth.

"Mm," I purred, blinking and staring up at the sky.

The suns had moved and the light changed. The sky was a darker shade of blue and my chest tightened. I could see in colors here, all of them, not the limited view I had on Earth.

"If you want to go to the palace today, you need to go before sunset. The Empress closes the gates at night, but opens them at first light."

I heard a howl in the distance and Enid's ears perked up. "Oh no, that's my mam! I hafta go. Bye, Bastet! Welcome home!"

Enid dove under the water to spring herself forward with the practiced speed of a Catfolk that spent every day of her life in these waters. I sucked in a deep breath, paddling through the water and letting the magic seep into me. I took a long, deep drink too, until my thirst was gone. The water was sweeter in Obius like it was always mixed with honey.

I had no landmarks around me that I knew. When I was a kitten, the lake was filled with more houses. Or maybe, I was in a different part of the lake. The palace would be in the center unless the Empress somehow moved the entire thing.

I swam in that direction, deeper into Ubbin Lake when I felt a wave of energy ripple through the lake. The waves it left in its wake nearly shoved me under the surface, but I stayed afloat.

Green magic misted through the air, and I swam faster.

Moira was here. She was here and she was *awake*.

The green of the Seer's magic settled in the lake, and I was overwhelmed with magic. I hadn't been tapped into Obius's lifeline of energy since I was a kitten.

It was too much.

My eyes burned and my lungs burned–was I swallowing water?–and I couldn't get my legs to keep me going. When I opened my eyes under the water, there were other Catfolk struggling, and we all kicked our way to the surface.

"Get to the bridge!" someone shouted, and at least twenty Catfolk swam to the right, and I followed. We needed to get out of the water so we could *breathe* again–

Another wave of magic hit, bringing another actual wave. It shoved me down into the depths of the lake. Water sprites were struggling to swim, but they came to our aid, helping get the Catfolk out of the water.

Before I fully blacked out, I was tossed up on a bridge and someone was pulling me away from the edge.

"What was that!"

"Where did that come from!"

"Is the Empress okay?"

"What if it's that human? Aren't they evil?

The chatter picked up all around me, but my eyes were dropping. Whatever spell that was, it had overloaded me, and I was quickly passing out.

"Bastet! Hey, stay awake, it's okay! It's me, Enid! We can get you to a healer, and everything will be okay–"

Enid's face was the last thing I saw but the taste of Chilijan's waters were on my lips, so I let myself go.

JACK

I knew the magic was coming before I saw the waves of green filtering across the land. Diego grabbed my hand like the spell would drag me away. His shoulders were hunched and a ring of gold hovered just above his skin. His magic was more alive than I'd ever seen, and he was radiating energy. The mixture of the green, green magic, and Diego's golden aura overwhelmed me for a moment. I couldn't tell where the alchemy started and ended, and I was mashed squarely in the middle.

His heart was only halfway together.

"What was–" Desmond was cut off by another wave of magic. It knocked the wind out of him, while Diego and I stood still. Atam was kneeling next to Desmond, with protective arms and accusing eyes.

"It's not me," I said.

"No, I know this magic–" Diego started.

"It's the Seer," we said in unison. The heart links thrummed back to life, pulsing and linking our magic further together. Atam laughed, somehow shrill but breathless.

"The Seer hasn't been in Obius since before the Shattering. She couldn't just–"

"When the link shattered, the Goddesses said that they couldn't rebuild them, but since you've started to–" Desmond's thoughts raced away, and I wanted to follow him. I wanted to know.

My crystal ball, Harold, floated up and shone green. The souls in there rocketed around like they were desperately looking for a way to escape. There wasn't one; the crystal was a perfectly round vessel. The color of the crystal matched the color of my eyes; it laced through me, twisting and weaving with every fiber of my body. The Seer's magic took over, and I let myself flow into it. I needed to *see*.

"Jack, please, my Blossom, don't go, don't listen to that spell. Close your ears. Close your mind. Jack, stay here, stay with *me*," Diego's hands were on my face. I knew the sensation of his skin, how warm they were, the texture of his hands. I felt every year of isolation in his palms; the memories lodged in every whorl and loop. But the pull of the Blessing was too much to ignore, and I didn't know if I *wanted* to ignore it.

I didn't want to walk away from whoever I was supposed to be, and as the magic called, the more certain I was that I was going to find out.

Too many images came for me to sort them all out. I saw a glimpse of every living soul in Obius. Just a flash; a couple milliseconds of their lives and how the fabric of their collective existence wove together to create

Obius. It was a rainbow—of course it would be—and I tried to touch each of the colors. Just like the details of Diego's hands, I saw all of the little grooves and edges of Obius, all of its secrets and beginnings.

My heart was racing.

I was peeking behind the curtain of the universe. I saw every soul, every collection of star lights, and how they lit up the world of Obius. My eyes burned with tears and I knew this was my purpose, the true reason that life was breathed into me. I was meant to see this.

The further I pushed myself away from the magic, the more I realized that Obius reminded me of a wave. The shape of the star lights crested like a wave, and it was like their stars created the soul of Obius itself.

My body expanded through the magic and I stretched out until I felt connected to each set of stars.

Vision and time,
Vision and time,
Gaze forward,
Smile in hindsight,
Vision and time,
Vision and time,
Beautiful, beautiful is this blessing of mine.

A woman's voice rang out through the magic, rocking me back, and I retreated back to my human body. I felt compressed, like now that I had been opened, I'd never fit back into my original packaging.

The voice played over and over in my mind. My hands were sweating and Diego was staring right into my eyes, but I couldn't *see* him.

All I could see was the voice. All I could hear. All I could feel and smell—

Vision and time,
Vision and time,
Gaze forward,
Smile in hindsight,

Vision and time,
Vision and time,
Beautiful, beautiful is this blessing of mine.

"Jack! Please, answer me–" He looked so human, but I knew he wasn't. Why wasn't I seeing his horns? His feathers? There should be gold in his eyes but they were only brown now.

The voice echoed through him too and his head whipped around, looking for it. The alarm that sounded through Diego's body pulsed through me too, radiating from the heart links to remind me of where I was. His thoughts came to me as fast as my own, and it was hard to remember whose was whose now.

"Diego, I saw–"

"I know," he said. "The Seer. It's Nana."

"Abuela," I said. The name on his lips made it real. Desmond and Atam just watched, and I clung to Diego.

The Seer was Mari's adoptive grandmother. The Seer *gave* us the heart links. The Seer was in Obius and it was Abuela.

"She's in Trellis," I declared. Rightness buzzed through me. I saw her standing at the edge of the castle, smiling sweetly. Sickly sweet.

"We're leaving," Diego said, nodding to me. He turned to Desmond, looking for an answer. A fire was lit in him. Desmond prayed for an end to this magicless world, and now he had it. He knew what he had to do. Desmond grabbed his satchel and looped it over his head, turning to place a quick kiss on Atam's hands and lips.

I turned to Diego, making sure that he also knew what needed to be done.

He grinned, wild and wolfish. The dark brown of his eyes on Earth seemed to come back, tinting the magical gold and making them sparkle. I saw his star lights flash around him, glimmering with magic and shining on the parts of him that were still trying to come alive.

"Anywhere with you, my Blossom."

Warmth filled my chest. Things were going to be okay.

"Trellis Castle, here we come."

Chapter Twelve

JACK

We made it out of Aquarine Palace in record time. Desmond had everything ready before the next crazy wave of Seer magic settled across the land. I watched him become more animated than I had ever seen him as he talked logistics with the palace crew, and Atam's fondness shone through as he tutted and tsked around him. He had the bags packed and found some more clothes for all of us. Food. Water canisters. And rides.

I didn't know all of the etiquette in Obius, but something told me that horses were a no-go when there were people with hooves and tails walking around.

I was wrong.

The horses were chatty. They had opinions about everything, and were not thrilled that their contract was *so long, how could you possibly expect us to run for that long?* Their thoughts were just as busy, and I needed to set up some mental boundaries before I lost it.

Diego bumped against my shoulder.

"A flower for your thoughts?"

"There's too many damn thoughts, you'd run out of flowers."

"Lucky for me that we're here, where flowers are plentiful."

I smiled despite myself. It would still take a day or even two to reach Trellis Castle. Aquarine was in the heart of Chilijan, and we had to get back to the border before facing another day to reach the castle itself.

"Desmond seems to be settling into himself," Diego said when it was clear that I couldn't carry on with my side of the conversation.

"He does, doesn't he? He seems like he's more at peace with himself now."

"Everyone needs to say their goodbyes," Diego said softly, and flashes of his tear-marked face came to me.

"Did it help? To see her grave?"

"I'm not sure, really. It made it real. And maybe that's what I needed more than anything. It's hard to believe I'm even back in Obius. Seeing her altar was, ah, what would you call it in human? Here, I'd say stone making."

"A reality check?" I laughed as he struggled to find the human words and Diego smiled, but it didn't reach his eyes. A shadow of the broken man he was on Earth came back then, and it took everything in me not to knock us both off these horses for a hug.

"Yes, but also... humbling to see another outcome from the Shattering. Of course, she would die without magic. Everyone would. But until I saw the altar, it was just too blurry to imagine?" Diego raked his hands through his hair, again bumping his horns and cursing under his breath.

The horses kept chatting, but I had gotten better about tuning it out.

"Did you see the feathers? Blue! Crazy. They better pay well."

Sorta better, anyway.

"It feels like everyone is staring," he mumbled as he picked at the reins. He didn't seem to hear the horses' gossip, so I tried to reassure him. The reins were old and well-worn, and Diego rubbed the leather-like material to give himself something to do.

Diego seemed natural in a saddle. I saw more flashes of his life on Earth, wearing older clothes from eras past. I saw him riding on a beach. I saw him shouting at Falcon with that too-rare smile on his face. He had happy moments on Earth. Knowing that eased the wedge in my chest.

"They have questions. I think that everyone who sees you likely has a few," I said.

"I'm not that interesting," Diego scoffed, straightening his back, more and more aware of the eyes on him as we passed through a small town.

"You're kinda like a unicorn," I said.

"Angry and territorial?" Diego said, the confusion etched so deeply on his face I was worried it would freeze.

"No... like a legend. A myth or a bedtime story. What do you mean 'angry and territorial?'"

"You've clearly never met a unicorn." This time the smile reached his eyes and I watched as he relaxed.

"Why are we talking about unicorns? It's not the right season for them, we should be safe crossing," Desmond said, forcing his horse to trot faster to catch up to us.

"You know, on Earth, unicorns are fuzzy and cute. Rainbow colored. Not evil," I laughed. The brothers stared at me like I had grown an extra head.

"Why would *anyone* willingly meet a unicorn?" Desmond's horror was comical.

"It is true, I have noticed the fascination with them on Earth. Especially with children," Diego said with a shutter.

"Children!" Desmond screeched and nearly fell off his horse. Diego's hand was lightning fast and steadied him.

"Okay, maybe we stop talking about them before Desmond has a panic attack," I said, raising a hand in surrender. Unlike them, I was not steady on a horse, and I wasn't about to let go for any reason.

Harold flashed gold, and I turned to study the orb. Alchemy swirled inside the globe, and I connected to it. The crystal held so many souls, and I felt the presence of each one. Snapdragon's green spark shone in the middle, glimmering a little brighter.

"That crystal… is it alive? It responds to you like a servant," Desmond said. He poked it and Harold floated to my other side.

"It's not alive, but there's a ton of magic in there. I've been layering magic into it for years. Plus the layers my sister and my best friend have added, and then all of the souls–"

"There are souls in there!" Desmond screeched again.

You know, for a psychic–one blessed by an actual goddess–I didn't get surprised often. Rarely, really. But every time Desmond *squealed*, it truly caught me off guard. He was not the type of man you'd expect to *squeal* like that.

"Please tell me I've never made a noise like that. I know we're blood and we both favor my mother, but please tell me I don't sound like that." Diego's voice pleaded in my mind and I bit my lip to keep from laughing.

"I've never heard you squeal, no. Maybe one day," I winked at him and Diego flushed pink. Sometimes Diego made it too easy to tease him.

"You're wicked!" Diego rode a little ahead to give himself some space to calm the blush. His ears were still pink.

"Do you see that?" Desmond asked, pointing ahead.

I leaned forward so I could get a better look, but I couldn't tell what I was seeing. Harold floated in front of me and green magic flooded the sphere. When it cleared, I saw a lot of people. They had cat-like faces, with pointed ears and whiskers. They stood on two legs with feet that ended in large, feet-like paws, and had long tails that moved frantically. They all moved frantically. Weak wisps of magic flew between them, but they didn't have the magic they were searching for.

That blast from the Seer injured some of their people. Desmond moved toward the horizon, hand blocking the sunlight so he could see further.

"There's Fae folk heading this way," he said.

"We need to help, they're hurt," I said.

Desmond nodded once, and the horses picked up the pace, practically flying forward.

"I need to go a little faster but I don't want to fall," I said, more to myself than the horse.

"Dontcha worry, Priestess, I won't let you fall. Hang on tight," my horse said. He galloped and I held on for dear life, as we strode across the swampy lands. The area we made it to was mostly marshland. The lake kept the ground soggy, but no one seemed to mind—my horse included.

"Deign, go help people pull the injured out of the waters. The magic there isn't enough. I can cast a few healing spells to help, but it would be easier if everyone was closer," Desmond said. He gave more directions, and Diego watched earnestly.

"Understood," he said and strode away.

"What can I do?" I asked.

"Can you heal at all?"

"Some," I said. Harold glowed bright, and I knew I could help. When I glanced inside the crystal though, it showed me one particular Catfolk. A woman. White fur with gray spots on her sides and back. A long, white, fluffy tail.

No, it couldn't be—

When she opened her eyes, blinking the lovely blue I knew so well from Earth.

"Puddin!" I screamed, racing toward her. The magic guided my feet, and I knew she was here. My shoes were sopping wet; the lake water seeping through and sending chills through me.

"Jack, where are you–" Desmond's words were cut off. I had to find her. I paused, letting my mind catch up to the magic, and listened. I was going to find her. She was just waking up. She was confused. She was lost.

"Oh my girl, I'm going to find you," her cat-like voice purred. I heard it clear as day. Puddin was here.

Harold's staff zipped off to the right and I had to pivot quickly to follow, stumbling through the reeds at the shoreline until I saw a hut with several people standing on the porch. I pushed my way through and climbed up on the damaged bridge. It didn't look like it should be able to hold two people, much less the crowd that was there. A younger Catfolk knelt next to Puddin, helping her up.

"Bastet, can you hear me? You're okay, just take it easy getting up–"

"Puddin," I said, breathless from the run. Her head snapped up and she searched the crowd. She heard my voice.

"J-Jack?" she said. Her words were clearer here than they were on Earth. She only sounded like this when she was concentrating really hard. I pushed my way through as gently and quickly as I could to get to her.

When I finally got through, she was sitting up. One leg stretched out, the other pulled up so she could rest her arms on her knee. I'd seen Mari sit like that a thousand times, and seeing Puddin here filled me with so much homesickness I was dizzy.

"I'm here," I said and I opened my arms. Puddin got up to meet me for a hug, and it felt like I was being hugged by Peony. Her nails lightly scratched the back of my hair, likely messing up my already mussed hair.

It was odd to hold my cat with all of my body. She was so much smaller on Earth–truly the size of an overweight house cat–but here she was just another person. Taller and leaner. Her tail whipped back and forth in a way I knew meant she was happy.

"I found you," she said, forcing a purr into the words.

"I think you mean *I* found *you*," I said, and she batted at my shoulder. When I finally let go of her to see her real face, all of the pieces clicked into place. I remembered her on Earth and really looked at her Obius face. They were the same, just like Diego was the same, but just more himself.

"Are you hurt?" I asked, already knowing that she was fine. I felt her energy, and everything was fine. She was safe.

"No complaints, surprisingly. You look..." she paused, cocking her head to study me, "different." She twitched her whiskers.

"So do you."

I smoothed the fur on her forehead like I'd done every day before I came to Obius. I wanted to curl up on my couch with my blanket and my cat and watch a lame reality TV show. The loss of all that hit me again. So much had happened that I didn't even think about how if I got out of Obius, I'd be homeless. The fire had destroyed my home, and when we finally left this place, I'd return to nothing.

"Stay with me, Jack," she said, purring loudly just for me, as she pressed her forehead to mine. Her fur was just as soft as always. She put one clawed hand on my shoulder, the nails just lightly pricking me to bring me back.

"How are you here?" I said as my voice cracked. Puddin wrapped her tail around me in a hug.

"I jumped through a portal. Abuela–*Moira*–opened a portal and I just went after her. I had to do something. And Jack, you have to know, she's–"

"The Seer. Yep. That one came to me loud and clear when she started that spell."

Diego took that moment to come over, bobbing and weaving through the crowd to find me. He looked between the two of us, before he asked, "Puddin? Is that you?"

"It's Bastet here, but yes, it's me. I see Obius brought you back to yourself too," she said, arching an eyebrow. No matter the form, Puddin was elegant.

"I've never felt less like myself, actually," his thoughts screamed, but his mouth said, "Yes, it's good to be back." His overly polite smile took over his face, and it changed the energy around him. Tightly coiled but hiding in plain sight. The heart link warmed when he noticed my staring.

Puddin smiled, exposing her canines. "Liar."

DIEGO

We lost a day stopping to help the injured Catfolk. All of the magic from the Seer's spells made the air feel thick in my lungs. Every breath was a struggle, as it both filled my lungs too shallowly and left me breathless. I was drowning in magic. Jack's heady, green magic mixed with the acrid magic from the Seer. It was ancient, grand–it reminded me of every mistake that I had ever made and I swallowed hard to push down my emotions.

Jack insisted that we stay the night in the village. She wasn't ready to leave, and Desmond wasn't either. He thrived in a catastrophe; Desmond wore a real smile as he knelt from person to person, casting a healing spell. His magic never seemed to run out or weaken.

Desmond and Puddin–Bastet, I reminded myself–secured some housing for us for the night. Bastet was thrilled to see Jack safe, but she pulled me aside and asked me to keep an eye on her. Guilt was tangled in her words, asking me to watch over Jack so she could be with her people for a night. She blinked long and slow, before smiling and leaving to join arms with another Catfolk woman. They were healing and helping, but the joy that came from them, from being together with their people, made the weight of the destruction lighter. I wondered if that weight would ever lift from my shoulders. Perhaps one day I'd walk through the forests and feel only sunlight instead of shadows on my face.

This village was in ruins from whatever spell the Seer had cast, but the people were alive, mostly unharmed, and happy to rebuild together.

This was the unity that I missed when I was on Earth, but now it seemed strange. The village of Arrow Gate would need to be completely rebuilt. The Catfolk worked with water sprites as they cleared the debris or dove for things buried in the lake.

The small hut they placed us in was undamaged and on land. It had been mostly abandoned; even the Catfolk wanted to be on the water. I cleaned to have something to occupy my hands. It helped to be useful. Jack needed a clean place to rest; I could give that to her. My chest ached from all the magic, and I plopped down on the bed to try to catch my breath. Everyone seemed to have a purpose except for me. I searched for some way to be useful, to contribute, but there was little to be done from the one that caused the trauma.

Jack's hair dripped down on her feet when she came in. The droplets clung to her legs and rolled down as she tried to towel it away. She'd showered and been given a light green dress that made her auburn hair stand out further. There were bags under her eyes and a sadness there that I hadn't seen before. She plopped down on the bed next to me and shook her hair out to comb her fingers through it.

"Let me," I said, sitting up and scooting her body closer to mine. Her back was to me and I grabbed a towel to dab the ends of her hair. She smelled like sweet lilies and cool water. I tugged gently on the knots, combing them out.

"Thanks," she said, her voice dreamy and faraway. The staff glowed green and I knew she was floating away from me.

"Are you here with me? Or having a vision?" I tossed the towel on a chair and listened to Jack's breathing, slow and even.

"I'm here. Just happy."

I worked through a few more knots until her hair was drying and massaged her scalp. She sighed and leaned against me, pulling my arms around her waist.

"I wasn't expecting to see Puddin here," I said.

"Me either, and I'm a psychic," she laughed. She was so warm, and my heart felt like it was beating in sync with hers. Soft, slow, steady. The air around her was clearer too, and I didn't feel as suffocated. I squeezed, hugging her a little tighter to me.

Jack pulled my hand to her heart, resting at the top of her breast. The beat thrummed in my hand, in the heart link, and down my arm. She turned so she could face me, threading her arms around my neck. Jack rubbed her nose against mine and I felt the smile on her lips. The weight of her pressed against me, chest to chest, her breath warm against my skin; I wanted nothing more than to kiss her.

"I'm glad you found her," I said.

"I'm glad I found *you*," she said. Her eyes were shiny, darker than her normal hazel, and her pupils were blown out. Her thoughts came through loud and clear even without the heart link to amplify them. ***Kiss me,*** her magic whispered.

She straddled my lap, and I ran my hands up her back. Jack was rarely this bold, and I wanted to keep her close. She watched me expectantly, waiting to see what I would do, how far I would take this moment. I didn't want to take anything from the moment; I just wanted it to stretch out forever. But holding time in my hand wasn't my blessing; it was hers. Every caress healed a little wound in my heart. Jack asserted herself here, and I happily ceded to her. I'd give her anything.

"I can practically hear the gears turning," she said, leaning back to look at me fully. I saw the scan of concern, checking me over for whatever subtle tells she saw in the lines of my face.

"You're beautiful," I said.

She was. She always was beautiful, but Obius amplified the essence of things. Inner beauty radiated outwardly, and Jack shone like another sun. It was the tenderness in her eyes or how pink her lips were or how the freckles played around her cheeks that made her so beautiful. It was all of those things and more. She was *more*. Every time I looked at her, I saw another reason to love her.

"You're stalling," she said, flicking the edge of my horn. It made my ear itch.

The words were too much, so I pulled her hand from my neck and put it on my chest. Her heart link was hot through my shirt, but the magic was working. Words were such fragile things, and I needed her to feel what the sounds couldn't convey.

I love you.

This isn't how I wanted our first time to be.

What will you say if I'm lying above you with my feathers fully out for you to see?

I'm not human, I'm not Fae. I'm half a man, with half a heart.

I'm afraid I'll break everything again.

It's been a really *long time. There hasn't been... anyone since Snapdragon.*

I'm nervous.

Jack sat fully on my thighs, her weight a calming force to my nerves that were on fire. I was still getting used to my body having sensation again. For so long, everything was numb and deadened, but now every caress, every brush blazed through me. Jack's touch was firm but sweet. Her hands made full contact with my arms, my skin, and I felt the fire through me calm. A little. She teased the edges of my feathers and I shivered.

"I don't want–"

"You're not messing anything up. This is everything, Diego," she said, pressing my hand to her heart again and then hers to mine. "You are enough. I'm not asking for anything more. All I want is you."

"There isn't much here," I said and a tear welled up in my eye. I tried to turn away, but she had me pinned.

Jack eased me down, gently pushing until I was lying flat on my back and I felt the blood rush to my cheeks and groin. I shifted, self-conscious under her assessing eyes but they never left me. My body heated up; the flush was all over my face and spreading quickly down my neck and chest and even lower. Her eyes stayed on mine.

"Diego, the weight you are carrying on your shoulders is too much. Let me carry it with you, or help you to set it down, finally. You have been taking responsibility for your actions *and* Snapdragon's for nearly six hundred years. That's long enough. You're here, you're *trying*, it's enough."

"There's no forgiveness for what I've done," I said.

Jack's hands were on my face, and the connection between the heart links and her was heady. She laid herself against me and laced our fingers together.

"I don't know who you need forgiveness from, but if it's me, I forgive you. I see you Diego. I see the parts that are still not healed, and I love them too."

I shifted until I could sit up, needing to say these words out loud. I chewed on my lips, then my fingers, then tucked my hands under my legs to force the fidgeting to stop. The heart links could share emotions I couldn't say, but I still wanted to try. Jack sat up with me, her damp hair now a mess again. My fingers itched to tangle it more just so I could help smooth it out again.

"U-umm, you know when I was on Earth, that I was less than human. I was barely alive. Barely functional. I couldn't do much for any length of time. I was living in stasis, does that make sense?"

She nodded.

"I had periods where I would be more like myself, shifts in the natural energy on Earth, or finding a rare piece of alchemy, or just having a better day. But Jack, until I met Falcon, I was alone. I traveled a lot. I didn't age like a human, and that could only be passed off as lucky for so many years.

It was better that way, easier. Humans are so beautiful, but their lives are so short. I never wanted to find someone I could fall in love with, because I knew another goodbye would break whatever was left of my heart."

"So you were... completely alone?" she asked, finally catching my drift.

My face was burning hot. I swallowed hard, desperately trying not to wriggle under her attention. She was so focused on me, taking in every detail, listening to the words that I wasn't saying as much as the ones I did.

"Yes. Completely alone."

"And you never...?"

"No," I said matter-of-factly, trying to calm the heat in my face. "I never thought about it, to be honest. I was struggling to stay upright some days. Voluntarily lying down with someone and wondering if I'd be able to get back up again was not very high on the priority list."

"But I've seen memories of you dancing. You looked happy," she said when she finally registered that I hadn't taken a woman to bed in six hundred years. I laughed, short and breathy. She tilted her head, waiting for me to continue.

"Dancing is quite tiring, but it is its own kind of magic. Sometimes the music, the liveliness of everyone dancing would trick my body into thinking it was alive again."

Jack played with the edges of my shirt, pulling at the loose threads.

"And when the music would end, you would go home alone." It wasn't pity in her voice, but it was close to it. She wasn't thrilled that I'd spent so much time alone. I knew that it was what I deserved, and solitude was all I had to offer.

"I'm so sorry that you were so alone," she finally said, so quietly I thought I imagined it. She squeezed my hand, digging her nails in my palm. The ache in my chest wasn't from heartbreak, for once. I held my breath, waiting for her to continue, waiting for myself to speak up.

"Please trust me that I'm not saying no to you, to anything that you want. I'll give you my everything. I just need time to figure out what my everything is."

Jack's smile was radiant. How did the Creator make a human so beautiful? It would be cruel if I wasn't allowed to admire all of the details of her face. The twist of her lips and the sparkle in her eyes were so vibrantly human.

"So, if I said that I wanted your shirt, would you give it to me?"

"Yes, although I don't know why you'd want it. It's much too large for you and it's not fresh–"

"It smells like you," she said, the sweetness back in her voice.

I sucked in a breath and tugged the shirt off in one swift motion. Her eyes traveled over my chest, down my stomach, stealing a glance lower, before her eyes snapped back up to mine. When I looked down at myself, the flush had spread from my neck to the skin just under my collarbones.

I gave her the shirt, and Jack hugged it to her chest.

"Thank you," she said, pushing me back again to lie down.

"It's late, will you, um, will you stay here with me? Here?" I said, gesturing to the spot she was lying in just moments ago.

"Considering this is our room, I don't think you have much of a choice," she said, playfully pinching me and I twitched.

My cheeks were on fire. My skin was alive, alive, alive, and every brush of her fingers was electric.

"I'm, ah, sensitive," I said, before wrapping my arms around her waist to make her settle next to me. She ran her hands over my forearms, the feathers fanning out on their own.

"They're sensitive, too." I willed them to go back down, but they didn't. She pulled my arm closer up and rubbed the plumage against her face.

Jack waggled her eyebrows, grinning wide, as she got comfortable. "Noted. Diego?"

"Hmm?"

"Don't let go of me, okay? I'm here, I'm not going anywhere." Jack snuggled into me, taking deep, heaving breaths as she settled.

"I won't," I said, squeezing a little tighter. *"I love you,"* I whispered, and she whispered it back.

JACK

Morning came entirely too quickly. Diego, true to his word, held me all night long. So much so that my shoulder was numb, but I wouldn't complain. I sat up, easing myself out of his grip so I could watch him sleep for a moment. I had his shirt still clutched to my chest, and the fabric smelled of his sandalwood skin.

All of the worry and fear were erased from his face when his eyes finally closed. Diego's eyelashes practically rested on his cheeks. The flush had finally gone down, but I'd never forget the sight of how far it spread down his chest. Or just his chest, in general. He had a few freckles on his collarbone that I traced; as I trailed my fingers over them, I realized it was a tree. Diego had the trees of Trellis painted on his skin too.

He spasmed in his sleep, his hands opening and closing, before he finally woke up. "Jack, where–"

"Here. I just woke up," I said.

The panic eased, and he closed his eyes again. His arm was effectively around my hips and butt, and he dragged me closer. I laid back down and he sighed happily.

"Just a few more minutes," he said.

"Shouldn't we be up already?"

"Probably, but I'm not ready to let go yet."

"Well, how can I *possibly* get up after a line like that?"

He laughed, warm and still full of sleep.

"You can't, obviously. You'll just have to stay here all day," he said, nuzzling the back of my neck, planting kisses there.

The hair on his chest was soft, making the cocoon of his arms more cozy. Diego's body was heated; every place his skin touched mine was electric and I was pleasantly overheated from the contact. I pressed myself against him again, cuddling as close to him as possible. The heart links buzzed with magic, and I knew that I'd drown in this happiness without any regret.

"Don't you at least want your shirt back?"

Diego kissed down my neck to the end of my shoulder.

"I told you I'd give you whatever you asked for. I won't take it back."

"So if I ask for every piece of clothing you own–"

"I'll be a nudist. It could get awkward," he laughed through his words; the real laugh that I felt through his whole body, that lit me up inside from the heart link. Puddin took that moment to come in, us laughing in a heap on the bed, with Diego shirtless and the blankets pooled around his waist.

She blinked at me, at him, and cocked her head. The same deadpan look she had on Earth transferred even better on her Catfolk features. She looked so unamused that it bordered on being offensive.

"I'm clearly interrupting, but we need to get going. Once Diego can find some clothing, we can leave." She flicked her tail, and I could tell she was amused.

Diego's cheeks were pink again, but he didn't react otherwise. He had an adorable grimace that turned into a full-on groan right after Puddin left. He threw an arm over his face, trying and failing to hide the blush. I loved making Diego react; I loved seeing him alive to react, and each blush was a victory. I was going to bring him to life fully again.

"That was embarrassing," he sighed, running a hand through his hair. Being by the water made his hair curl even more. The light waves he had on Earth were turning into ringlets. I pulled one and watched it bounce.

"Imagine if I had asked for your pants," I said with a wink.

He huffed a bit and stood up to search for another shirt.

"If we stay on course we can be back in Trellis by nightfall," Diego said.

Harold floated up and the flash of visions started when I grabbed the staff's hilt. It showed me a few images of Abuela standing in Trellis Castle. I saw Arturo again, on his knees before her. I saw trees sprouting and Diego smiling. I saw a crown.

"How much further until Trellis Castle?"

"Two days. The castle is in the southern part, so we have a lot of ground to cover." He found a plain white shirt and slipped it over his head. His horns got caught on the hem but he worked it down in a relatively smooth motion.

Magic stirred in my chest and I realized that the normal noise from the village was gone. Wave after wave of dread shot through me, making me shiver and my heart race. Harold's staff was in my hand once I held it out, but the crystal only shone with the green magic that I now claimed as my own.

"Diego, I don't like how quiet it is. Something isn't right."

My stomach knotted up and I doubled over, laying practically face down on the bed. I was seeing stars. Not the familiar star lights of my visions, but the kind where I was blacking out. Like when I couldn't control my magic and it would overwhelm all of my senses. The magic summoned me and I responded; it was a call I couldn't ignore as the universe opened for me, waiting.

Diego's hand was on my back, my shoulder, touching my face. I felt it, but I was long gone. I was floating and traveling away.

"Diego," I whispered out, his voice lost to the swirling magic in my mind.

My soul was taking a walk. It was heading for Earth.

It was heading for Mari.

CHAPTER THIRTEEN

MARI

It actually hurt more when I wasn't lighting myself on fire. That seemed to fit the whole allegory that my life had become.

Everything played out in my mind in fits and starts, like I was watching a movie of myself.

On the floor. Flaming out. Falcon and Peony kneeling next to me. Jazzy was squawking around doing something, but the roar of the fire–me, I'm talking about me here–drowned everything out.

It was peaceful, oddly.

Peony Hawthorne was crying so that meant I was well and truly fucked.

Didn't I want the fucking to be Falcon's job?

Laughter shot up through my throat and he had to dodge before I burned him again. He ducked between my flames but kept his gaze steady on me. The fire in my belly wanted those to never drift, never look away. He blinked, eyes darting away for a fraction of a second before they were back to me.

The curtain was on fire. Sherwin was diligently working on putting it out. He was a good egg. I liked him. I made a mental note not to go supernova in his range. Assuming I had any control over that.

Falcon smoothed some hair out of my face; my braids were tangled and gross. My hair was frizzy and messy, and I smelled like charcoal. The charms I diligently weaved into my hair were slowly falling out or melting and with every missing one I felt further from myself. Jack joked she knew how I was feeling from how many bangles and beads I had on, but it wasn't far from the truth. The jingling was appealing; soft and lyrical, the sound of movement soothed me.

Falcon's mouth was moving. He was saying something to me, but I couldn't hear him. His scarred-up hands and arms were red again, likely from the heat that came pouring off of me. His nerves were raw, but he stayed close.

I forced the fire back down, trying to calm it before I exploded and did any more damage. My eyes traveled to where Abuela had been standing just moments ago.

Abuela hopped through that portal like it was nothing. She opened it so easily. She didn't even work up a sweat casting whatever spell she used. Did a goddess even need spellwork? My head went fuzzy. A goddess. My fill-in grandmother was a goddess. She changed her name to suit whatever purpose she needed, but she never told me what her true name was. Moira. Memories filtered through me, back when my mother was still alive. Abuela and her would drink tea, and take turns hugging me. I remember feeling so surrounded by love, but the memory felt tainted now.

Was she just pretending?

"Marigold Groves, I did not craft you to be a child that lays on the floor when the days get tough. You were made from my golden flame, and you will rise just like the fire in you commands. Get up, Mari," a woman's voice called to me. Familiar but not; I couldn't place it.

"Can you hear that?" I asked. I don't know who I directed my words to, but Falcon answered.

"Only thing I'm hearing is you, Mari." Falcon gingerly reached out and touched my face. It was warm. Not like the inferno I currently was, but human warm. Alive and real.

"I think a goddess was talking to me," I said.

"Been there, girl. It didn't end well, remember? Maybe take it with a grain of salt," Falcon laughed between his words.

"The difference this time, my dear Falcon, is that Marigold is actually hearing a goddess. Me." The voice boomed around the room and this time everyone heard it.

Falcon leaped up, standing guard in front of me with a knife that he pulled from somewhere. Peony and Sherwin were ducking, looking around.

Then I saw her. Fair skin, curvy hips with a sway just to be extra, flame bright red hair, and thin braids mixed through it.

"That's rich lady, who are–"

"Candela. You know me as the Creator. You should bow or something. That open-mouth look ruins your pretty face," she said with teeth. Falcon closed his mouth and scowled. She arched an eyebrow at me, the smile on her predatory and fire-filled.

"Candela. And you're the Creator," Falcon repeated

"Yes, dear, keep up. I know I made the humans a little simple, but not that much."

Jazzy took that moment to come back to her senses. She approached Candela slowly, studying her face, head tilting this way and that, until she finally said, "I've seen you at the markets before."

"They're great, aren't they? I love watching the humans go treasure hunting. But we aren't here to talk about how much I love my humans,"

Candela said. She sauntered over to me, hips swaying like a cartoon character, and grabbed my face.

Her eyes were red.

Her eyes were made of fire. *Wildfire.*

"Now you see it. That's my girl."

"Why are you here?" I squeaked out. My voice betrayed me with tininess.

Falcon was solid against me, and I was aware of how still Peony and Sherwin were. His arms shook from what I hoped was just exhaustion, but he didn't let go. He smelled like a charred forest, and I was relieved that the smoke wasn't from me.

Would he hold me like this again? One day when I wasn't on fire? Every wick burned out eventually, right? That's what Puddin used to say when I'd forget to blow the candles out in Jack's kitchen.

Wait. Where was Puddin?

"Ohh, come now, Mari. Why do you think I'm here? Aside from the glorious scenery." Candela waved her hand in the general direction of the windows.

I couldn't look away from the fires in her eyes. Did my eyes sparkle like that now?

Falcon's hands were firm on my arms, holding me in place against him.

His voice didn't betray any anxiety as he spoke, "If I've learned anything over the last few weeks, it's that you being here is probably bad news for us,"

Her smile made my knees weak–how was she that fucking enchanting?–and I nearly vomited.

"Falcon, my blessed child, you are a terrible student. What you *should* have learned is that you were not meant to be subdued easily. It would take the act of... say, a goddess, to slay you," Candela patted his cheek. He didn't flinch but I did. "It would be good for you to remember that."

"What do you want with Mari?" Jazzy spat out, bolder now and standing in front of me.

"I want nothing more than she can willingly give. I'm no monster. But for now, what I want is for her to be back in Obius. My sister is in a mood. She will need some convincing to put down her battleax, so to speak."

"Convincing?" I said. Her eyes were hard to look away from.

Candela traced a finger down my jawline, gently dragging her nails against my skin, and the Wildfire in my chest nearly exploded. I felt like I was erupting from her magic, and it would take all of my restraint to keep it in.

She licked her lips and the fire in her eyes burned brighter. It was blazing through me, hotter than it ever had before, hotter than it was on Obius, and I felt myself turning to ash.

The Goddess of Creation brushed her lips against my ear as she whispered, "Marigold, you were forged from my flame and now my magic is ever-burning in your heart. It's time for you to return to Obius."

Her hair tickled as she moved away and then she raised her hands, two fingers pointed up as she began to dance. There was a beat to her movements that I felt but couldn't hear. The drum of her magic was like a literal drum in my chest, until I couldn't fight its rhythm and began to sway with her as time seemed to slow around us. Candela was strikingly beautiful, and I wanted to touch her face or maybe scream.

"That's it, Mari, feel the magic," she said with her eyes. The words bounced around my brain like a bad idea I didn't want to shake.

"Mari–" Falcon was far away; the heat of his hands not enough to keep the fire burning.

"It's time to open the link, Mari. I'm going to open it. You're going to step through. Falcon too, probably, knowing him. Remind my sister how much she loves her favorites here on Earth."

I stopped dancing, still captivated by the flame but I managed to say, "Abuela loves me?"

"Oh Mari, how could anyone not love you?" Candela's hands were on my face again, and the Wildfire went supernova.

I was going to die, surely.

But I didn't. I felt the flame in me burn hotter and hotter; it changed from a red flame to blue to purple and finally a white, blazing nova. Candela opened the link and I grabbed Falcon's hands, clinging to them like he was the kindling to keep my flames burning. The link was the size of the doorframe and was the same color as the nova in my heart. I saw it and immediately knew it was the same magic. Candela's drum beat magic echoed through me but I didn't move with her–I moved to Falcon who wrapped his arms around me fully. Smoke billowed off of us in waves.

"You can bring him too. My sister has an extra soft spot for this one. Burn bright, Marigold." Candela's eyes were alive with Wildfire and she shoved us through the portal.

And then we were falling, falling, falling.

PEONY

No, no, no, no, no!

Candela, the Creator Goddess, just waltzed right in, charmed and be-guiled Mari into going back to *fucking Obius where we just left*, and then closed the link behind her.

She closed the link.

Mari and Falcon were trapped *again* in Obius. Jack and Diego were still there.

And I was *here*.

Trapped in a small cabin with an angry goddess, my mother, and Sher-win.

And where the hell did Puddin go?

"Peony, calm down. I can practically see the smoke coming out of your ears. All that worrying is going to ruin your stomach. You eat those pills like candy," the goddess scolded. I got scolded by a *goddess*.

"I'm sorry, did you just–" I closed my eyes and sucked in a breath.

Picking a fight with a goddess was literally the *worst* idea I'd ever had. Sherwin seemed to pick up on this also, and he handed me my antacids and bowed to the goddess.

Should I be bowing? What was the protocol for meeting your maker?

"Thank you, King's Shadow Sherwin. You have aged like Trellian wine, I see." Candela trailed her fingers around his jaw the same way she did to Mari. I popped an extra antacid.

Mama took that moment to come alive as if suddenly picking up on my rage, and she thundered around the room, stomping and smashing plates, throwing them against any hard surface she could find. The small cabin was now full of broken plates and dishes.

"Mama, stop! What the hell!"

"Candela. You've taken two of my girls! They're stuck in Obius! How could you–"

"Oh cut the drama, Jazzy. You think we haven't seen what you've been up to for all these years? I think you know your place, and it's frankly out of my way. Your girls will be fine." Candela spared me one more glance before she grabbed my arm, lightning fast, and pulled me close.

"Hey–"

"Peony Hawthorne, Truth Speaker, hear my words clearly and know them as truth. Your sisters by blood and bond will return. One day, you will hear our voices. Listen closely."

Candela drew a sigil on my forehead, and I felt the magic seep into me, thick and heavy, digging its way through my mind and into my body, weighing me down until my knees wanted to buckle.

"Truth Speaker, you will stand strong," Candela's voice boomed again and my knees locked up, forcing my body straight instead of collapsing. She was infuriatingly attractive. Her magic made the glow around her more alluring, and I couldn't look away.

She nodded to me, and I saw the same fire in her eyes that I'd seen in Mari's. It was mesmerizing.

And then she just left.

"What the hell just happened?" Sherwin asked, turning me to him so he could inspect me. I touched my forehead, praying there wasn't an actual mark, and felt nothing.

"She drew a sigil on me."

"What sigil did she write on you? Do you know?"

I touched my forehead again, feeling the magic swell within and the answer came to me: Justice.

In that moment of recognition, I felt a bit like my sister: flashes of things to come passed through me and I shuddered. I couldn't make sense of what I saw—doors, black, black magic, the warmth of my sister's smiling face—and it was gone. The sigil heated my skin, like it had been etched into me forever and I was just noticing.

She drew the sigil for the Judge on me.

ARTURO

"Arturo, I know you have carried the burden of this kingdom for far too long. You've guided the country as much as you could without outright defying the will of the Emerald Priestess. You are not to blame here, child. You've done well, but your work is not done yet," the Seer said. Her holy words were divine and clear. She wore odd, tattered human robes; they looked haphazardly put together, as if someone had poorly sewn scraps of cloth to build her a proper skirt.

I was still kneeling. My knees ached, but She hadn't commanded me to rise, and I'd already disrespected Her once. Another such indiscretion wouldn't be forgiven; as was proper. I'd let everything slide and let my soldiers forget what it meant to be sworn to this family's guard, to the Goddess.

Some of them had never even seen Her face.

I was old; my body was wearing out before its time. I was middle-aged for a Fae, but I had the bones of the elderly. It had been so long since She had graced us with Her presence, that I'd forgotten how comforting the aura of Her was.

"Arturo? I can feel your attention waning, am I boring you?" She said with a playful smile tugging at the corners of her aged face.

"Not at all, my Goddess," I lied. She should kill me for this disgrace, but the Holy Seer was never known for vengeance. She was a Goddess of love, and I currently deserved none of it, even though I only wanted to stare into Her aged face forever.

"Hmm, so as I was saying–"

"Yes, my Goddess, we will find them."

Her staff clacked on the tile in the throne room. Snapdragon had ordered all of the rugs to be removed. Her paranoia told her that the rugs would hide the footsteps of her enemies, but there were so many ghosts in her mind that rug or no rug, she would not have heard them at all. I knew this was true. The Seer crafted a staff from bits and pieces of the broken tree limbs, The staff held no crystal, no gem. In the cage atop the staff sat crushed leaves, feather stems, flower petals, and vines. She pulled the fragments of Wildfire out and placed them at the top of her staff.

"I am so very proud of you Arturo. I know this will not be easy for you. Deign was once your dearest friend and your king. He was the purpose of your life, and now he is the purpose once again."

"Yes, my Goddess," I said, lowering my head so she could not see the tears forming in my eyes, "I will find the former king and the human Priestess. I will bring them to you so you can see their futures."

"Oh child, raise your head. I've seen their futures. Right now I'm concerned with their present actions. Find them," She commanded, and the severity of Her words dug its way into my bones.

They could try to defy the will of the Goddess, but I would not. I bowed my head even further until my forehead touched the cool tile.

"Yes, my Goddess."

FALCON

The irony was not lost on me that I was dragged through a portal to Obius. The same sucking, ripping, tearing apart feeling from when I pushed Jack through was back in full force. Of course, she also dragged me through the portal, but I deserved it that time.

This time I would have jumped even if Mari wasn't holding onto me for dear life.

The Creator Goddess was proud of her little show, twisting Mari's emotions and playing to the weakest parts of her when she was already fragile. Mari's magic burned with the intensity of the sun, but she was crumbling inside, and the Wildfire was going to eat her alive.

Tossing her back into Obius was like pouring gasoline on an explosion.

Mari's arms were around my neck, her legs flailing out behind her as we fell through the sky. We were falling head first, the blood rushing to my ears and making the whipping of the air hit harder. Once my body knit itself back together, I started casting the Cube. With one arm around her, and one to cast, I worked the spell.

If the Cube failed, it would be a moot point—we'd die on impact, but at least I'd be softer for Mari to land on than the ground.

The swell of Mari's magic surrounded us, amplifying my Cube to make another one. The two together had made a diamond around us. Her hugging me tighter was the only indication that she was awake.

"I've got you," I said. My words were probably lost to the noise around us, but I said it anyway. I wouldn't let her crash and burn.

"Brace yourself," she whispered. I felt the impressions of her words more than the words themselves, and I listened. I braced, layering as much of my magic into the Cube as I could.

We hit the ground and I saw stars. It happened too fast for me to be afraid, so I just tried to brace for impact. We bounced, Mari mostly on top of me, at least three times before rolling to a stop against a large tree trunk. I was pinned against the tree with Mari in my arms. She didn't move, but I felt her breathing. She was alive. I was numb, and prayed that was only temporary.

"Mari? Can you move?"

"Are you itching that much for me to get up?"

"No, but it's not gentlemanly to cop a feel," I said, very keenly aware that my hands were on her lower back.

She huffed out a laugh, over-warm and breathy. "Since when are you a gentleman?"

"Hey, I might not be a hero but I'm not that much of an asshole."

"Another tragedy," she said, sliding up and rocking back on her heels. She stretched out her back, the vertebrae popping. The fire had settled in her and she reached a hand out for me, pulling me to my feet. Every touch felt like she transferred the fire to me. Everything hurt but I didn't let go of her hand.

I was not as bouncy as she was; my body was taking hit after hit, and I felt each one. Not quite like getting hit by a truck–been there, done that–but definitely like I had been recently electrocuted and skydived without a parachute. My bones popped and creaked too, but I got no relief from it. I was getting *old*. No wonder D moved so slow.

We landed in a clearing. It looked like where I'd woken up with Jack, but the land was different. Greener. More alive. The sky was still that infinite blue I could get lost in, but now there were more clouds. The suns chased each other across the sky with clouds darting around them. There was glitter in the sky, now that I was really looking. The light made everything shimmer like it was covered in dew, no matter the time of day. I felt like the tan crayon amongst the pack of sparkle ones, being here.

Obius felt like a fairytale instead of a nightmare now.

Which in theory, I should be happy about, but I wasn't. My *things-are-about-to-blow-up-in-your-face* sense was going wild and every ounce of me was rocking forward, leaning in for a fight. Movement caught my eye, and I stilled. My body coiled, ready to strike, and I listened.

"Falcon–"

"*Shh.*" I hissed at her, stepping fully in front of her so Mari's back was to the massive tree trunk.

I worked the Cube again, forcing the walls back up, letting my magic run wild with the open vein of energy that pulsed through the air. Each time I cast, my body lurched. I was too fucked up for this much magic and my bones were less than thrilled that I was gearing up to get my ass beat *again*.

Where the fuck was that energy coming from? Obius was supposedly a dead world but the amount of magic I felt told me otherwise.

"What is it?" she hissed back. A fireball was already burning in her hands–probably *also* her hands–and she swayed with the crackle of her flame.

"Dunno, but I don't like it. It's too…"

"Alive?"

"Yes."

"Yeah, I get that vibe too. Someone jump-started Obius, and I don't think it's Jack. Can Diego do something like this?"

Mari wriggled around me, stepping out to inspect the clearing. There were trees here. Fully grown, large trees, massive, sky-scraper-like, and full of color. The trunks were so vividly red and orange that it looked like the paint was still drying. The leaves were greens and yellows and purples. They all looked freshly painted too. Pine and mint, like every *nature fresh* candle I'd encountered, emanated from the forest.

The worn and ragged banners of Trellis Castle flew overhead in the distance. This *was* the same clearing.

"He's full of surprises, but no, I don't think so."

I couldn't tear my eyes away from the banners. They blew wildly in the wind, but the trees didn't sway. There was a rumbling in the ground and it made me reach for my knife. My arm flew up to wrap around Mari, but she stood her ground.

"Mari–"

"I see it too."

"Bad vibes, girl, we need to move," I said, reaching for her hand and wincing when I put my hand straight into the fire. The banners in the distance were becoming less distant.

"Too late, Falcon," she said, already bounding across the field, setting everything on fire. *Wildfire.*

She leaped, using the fire to propel her up before she slashed through the air, spinning fire all around her. Mari was suspended in flames like they were solid enough to hold her. She summoned more and more fire–they cropped up everywhere, funneling whatever was coming straight to us.

Then I saw them.

The soldiers. More banners. Trellis.

There was an army marching toward us again, and this time there were a lot more soldiers than last time. Even at a distance, I recognized that bitch ass general I'd met in the castle. He carried a shield and a long, thin blade. He was good with that thing, but his magic was lacking.

However, the arrogant set to his shoulders as he sauntered through the forests and fields told me that something had changed.

"Ah, fuck me," I groaned as I took off after Mari.

So much for a warm welcome; Mari was going to make sure everyone felt her blaze. Her columns of fire made me sweat. My hair stuck to my face, my shirt clung to my skin, and my nerves responded by burning enough to match Mari's energy. I pumped my legs faster, forcing myself to move swiftly.

The forest was going to burn again. The trees had to be new growth; they either moved or they had regrown to full size in the few days since we'd been gone. How long was a day on Obius compared to on Earth? Did they match?

Did it matter if Mari was going to destroy everything?

"Mari, stop! The trees!" I shouted, hoping my words carried across the flames to her.

She danced through them, just like Candela had done. When she turned to look at me, her eyes were violet with fire and my heart stuttered. She winked at me and spun through more fire. The columns turned to walls. There was too much fire for me to get through this time. She blocked me out with her magic, and that stung as much as my aching body.

"D, if you can hear me, we need backup. Stat. Lefty, come get your girl. I don't know if I can walk through this one," I said to the air. My hands tingled. The phantom pain from my nerves burning with the Lightning spell seared through me again, a painfully clear reminder that I wasn't ready to take on Wildfire solo. Mari danced through the magic, higher and higher, over the firebox she was creating.

"I'll try to contain her. Get your asses in gear and find us," I said to them again, my words were soft, begging. I prayed that Jack could feel my energy, that she would know that I was here, that Mari was going nuclear. I touched the forest floor, palms down in the new soil, and tried to send my pleas to Jack and Diego.

Time was going to run out for her and the forest if they didn't hear me.

CHAPTER FOURTEEN

JACK

My soul got up and took a little walk, leaving my body behind in Chilijan. I wasn't used to soul-walking anymore. Not that I had really gotten used to it, but in Obius, my soul just seemed to expand and grow every time the magic swelled in me.

But not this time.

I was disconnected from my body. I knew it was there, somewhere back on Obius, but the realm felt lightyears away, like I had been racing across the universe and now I'd forgotten which direction I came from.

This wasn't like the connection to the heart link either. This was dark. This was cold. This was not Earth.

Where had I run to?

My feet were frozen, and I felt stuck in place. There was nothingness around me and it was hard to keep the panic at bay; where had I gone? I couldn't feel my body or where my magic ended or where I ended. Was *I* ending?

"My Blossom," Diego's voice brushed against my face. This was familiar; this I remembered even though I couldn't feel the heart link on my wrist. I couldn't feel my wrist or any other part of my human body.

I tried to speak, to say something back to him, but I was just energy and light, lighting up a spot in this bleak nothingness. I prayed that he could hear the impressions of my voice just like I used to hear his—before he was something more than just light.

"I know that you can hear me, answer me, please. I'll wait until you can find yourself. You know I'm good at waiting."

I tried to stay still and focus on the energy around and within me. The link to Diego was a golden light in my chest, and that much I *could* feel. He was safety and love. I reached for it. For a second I thought I felt the cool metal of the heart link and the coarseness of his fingertips.

"There you are. Where have you wandered to, my Blossom?"

"I don't know," I said, and the words finally came. They echoed around me and I flinched. My energy gathered and I felt more grounded in myself. My hands and feet tingled; I knew that I had them and just the knowledge made me remember how it was to have them.

"I can feel you lingering there, like a little leaf in the wind. I can't hear your sweet voice though, so I'll just keep talking. You can find your way back if you follow my voice. Listen for me, Jack, and I'll guide you home. I'll bring you back to me," he said.

And I did, I listened. I strained to hear every note of his voice.

"It's funny, there's so many things I want to tell you, so many memories for you to hear, but I know you can see them whenever you want. Your magic is brilliant, you know that don't you? I hope you do."

The darkness and nothingness was lessening, a little; I could see the outline of my hands, lit up in star lights and let loose a long, deep exhale.

"Well, maybe I can tell you why I call you my Blossom. It's an old tradition. The Trellians love flowers. Everything about our homeland is laced with flowers because there's nothing more perfect and beautiful than a flower in bloom. You're in bloom, Jack. You're beautiful, and you'll be my everbloom."

"I want you to be my everbloom too," I said, the words floating around me. I knew they didn't reach Diego. I had wandered too far to reach him, but the heart link had us tethered together, and that would not break. The charms clanged together, bringing more awareness to my arm. I tried to remember what each bead and charm looked like, but the details were back with Diego.

"I think I heard you, just then. Maybe. Maybe I'm just hopeful it was you. I don't think I could face being in Obius without you, Jack. For so long, I just wanted to come home, but now that I'm here... nothing is the same, and it no longer feels like home. Seems like I'm adrift now too, hmm?"

The darkness cleared out even more and I realized that I was on Earth. I'd made it back to Earth without a heart link to guide me. It was Mari's apartment, and it was a mess. Peony and Sherwin were there, putting things back in order. Picture frames had rattled off the walls and her furniture was tucked against the walls instead of where it belonged. Mari's ridiculously large DVD collection was a mess on the floor and Mama was there straightening them–

Mama.

She must have sensed me then because she turned, looking around but couldn't find me.

"I'm here," I said, but the words were lost in between the realms, not loud enough for her to hear.

I held my hand up to wave, or maybe to reach for her, but nothing happened. Mama's hair was a frizzy mess. No ribbons or head scarves. No makeup to make her look glamorous. Mama looked like she had been the one trapped in Wildfire instead of the forests, and seeing her so disheveled made my star lights hurt too.

She shook it off and went back to straightening the DVDs.

"I can't believe Mari and Falcon are in Obius. Puddin has to be there too, that's the only thing that makes any damn sense," Peony said as she scooted an end table back in place.

"When the dust finally settles in Trellis, I want to take you to my room." Boyish and shy, Diego's voice broke the tension around me and I leaned into the magic that never failed to connect us.

Sherwin glanced around, looking at something. He likely felt me in the room too. Peony was still ranting; the sound of her voice too far away now, and I realized that I was going back. I shivered; the call of the darkness was so loud and I didn't want to face it alone. I hugged my wrist to my chest. The charms of the heart link glittered with magic, lighting me up inside. I wasn't alone.

"Oh, ah, that was forward. I meant, I just wanted to show you where I grew up. In person. Together. And I wanted to show you all of my things—"

I could practically hear his cheeks turning red. I saw the pink creeping up his cheeks and ears so clearly that he could have been standing next to me. I wished he was.

"Everything I say sounds more dubious than it's meant."

"Do you want me in your bed, Diego?" The nothingness swallowed the words. I wasn't even sure they were thought loudly enough for anyone to hear, much less respond to, but then the heat of Diego's tone shifted. I suddenly remembered in detail how his hands felt when he held me like he was drowning back in my house on Earth.

"Everything you wear makes you beautiful, but having you in my bed with only the bedsheets to cover you would make you divine.

One day, I'll be lying there beside you, and not even a sheet will separate us."

His honeyed words pulled me back to my body too quickly and I jolted awake, fully present in my human body, in the small hut in Chilijan. Puddin had just checked in on us–how much time had passed?

"Diego?" I asked, a hand out to him, but he was already at my side. Diego was on his knees and nearly eye-level.

"I'm here," he said, his eyes still molten gold and shining with more than just magic. The shyness was gone. Diego was relaxed and in control; his eyes never left me. He was still shirtless, and the wide expanse of his chest was more appealing than staring into the universe. He was real and solid, the heat from him being nearby giving me chills.

"Thank you," I said, squeezing his hands.

"For what, Jack?" He tilted his head, the picture of innocence, but I saw the glint in his eye. I saw the hook he had dropped, waiting to see if I would take the bait and the hope that I would.

"For talking to me. I heard you. I was soul-walking; it just happened so fast and then I was gone–"

"You're safe, I promise–"

"I know because you guided me home. You brought me back," I said, opening the sheet and laying down on the bed.

His cheeks were warm, but so were his eyes, and the rest of him. Diego slowly climbed into the small bed and laid down so he was facing me. Our hands tangled together and he snaked an arm under me to hold me close. It took him a minute to settle, to relax again against me, and I snuggled closer.

"So I take it you heard everything then?" Diego's breath tickled my ear sending shivers down my spine. He rubbed the small of my back.

"Everything," I whispered. I didn't want to break this moment by being bold.

Diego was grand and regal but so very shy; I refused to ruin this bout of bravery by cracking a joke or squirming too much, so instead I let my fingers dance across his chest, playing with his freckles and the little bit of hair there. Diego's heartbeat thumped strongly in his chest, solid and in sync.

Diego rolled so he was on top of me as I laid on my back. Time seemed suspended as his eyes roved over me. Diego so rarely gave into his emotions, and I wanted him to keep going. He lowered his mouth to my neck and kissed me just under my ear, leaving my heart pounding. The heart links warmed and pulsed, as I pressed myself even closer to him. The sheet fell away and I arched up into him; my hands fisted the back of his shirt, trying to pull it up to touch his heated skin. Diego let out a soft, featherlight moan right next to my ear.

He leaned back and smiled, wide and full; the smile he seemed to save for me, and brushed a lock of hair out of his eyes. These were the moments where Diego felt truly alive.

"The very next time I get you in a bed, I'm going to take my time to get to know every inch of you," Diego said between kisses.

"I'm sensing a but–"

"But sadly, my Blossom, that moment isn't right now."

He planted them on my neck, my cheeks, the top of my head, my lips, back down my neck. I groaned some kind of noise that was *deeply* attractive, and Diego laughed. The heat of his breath against my skin, as he laughed, lit up the magic in the heart links. He sat up, pulling my wrist to his lips, kissing me there too. I grinned, beaming at him and hoping that he could see the love that was shining in my heart for him. I hoped that he knew that I saw the sunlight in him too.

"Are you sure? Because I could definitely stay here for a few more hours. Days, even."

The playfulness in his eyes gave me butterflies. "I'm sure. I'm also sure I heard Desmond politely not entering our hut. I think he's ready to get going."

I wasn't. Trellis was too far and too close. My visions told me things would be okay, but the nagging feeling of dread in the pit of my stomach told me otherwise. Obius felt too unsettled with the return of the Seer, and losing control of my magic made the uneasiness amplify. I caught a glimpse of Harold gleaming in the low light of our small hut. The hair on my arms stood up, and I knew my gut was right.

Diego buttoned his shirt as he got up. The shirt was a soft white linen piece that let the gold in his skin shine through it. The bravery had faded and he watched me with a timid smile. With every button on the shirt, he closed himself off more. Even with the power to read his mind, Diego felt like a mystery.

"Where did you go, just now?" I asked as I held a hand out for Harold. It churned with green and golden magic. The feel of the wooden staff in my hands was grounding, calming. The staff seemed to have smoothed itself out in the places that I tended to grip. Harold responded to me again.

"Nowhere, just not ready to leave."

"Apologies Priestess, but we need to move," Desmond called from outside the door. "Several of the Catfolk said that they were seeing Trellian banners flying. People are coming."

The door opened and a nervous-looking Puddin came in. "I saw something in the sky, Jack. It looked like two falling stars." Puddin's tail flicked back and forth, the nerves plain as the whiskers on her face. She was beautiful in the way only a cat could be. It was weird not scooping her up to snuggle her.

"Let's check it out," Diego said, clapping Desmond on the arm, and pulling him out the door with him.

"Things heating up with Diego?" Puddin asked once the guys were out of earshot.

"So being nosy isn't just a cat thing, it's a you thing?"

"Not sure why it can't be both," she purred and we both laughed. Puddin's tail curled around me and she pressed her nose to my cheek.

"Things are *warming* up but not heating up. Diego's surprisingly... shy. It's sweet," I said, thinking back to all the times his cheeks pinkened, all the times he pushed through to dare to be brave.

"Whatever he's doing, I approve. Oh my girl, you're glowing. You look so happy." She pawed at my hair, trying to tuck it behind my ears but getting it stuck in her claws.

Happy. I was happy. I was happy here in Obius where my magic seemed to sing and I was happy in Diego's arms. I was happy in a way that I didn't know I'd ever be, and it made the heart link brighten. The charms were shimmering, teeming with magic.

"What's the story with those?" she said, already knowing the answer.

"Heart links. Are they dangerous magic?" I fiddled with the beads, Desmond's words coming back to me.

"Danger is in the eye of the beholder. Heart links are old magic. They were used for weddings, but not everyone has a heart of gold, Jack. The same magic that binds two people together in love can bind them together in anger, hatred. The links can be broken though," she said.

"They can?"

"All magic can be broken, surely you've learned that much by now. The best way to release a heart link is for both parties to agree to it. You can imagine that doesn't happen often," she said. Puddin was already heading out when she turned back to me. "My girl, I've loved you in every moment we've shared and I've seen you become the alchemist you were meant to be. Now it's time to be who you are."

"What if it's too much for Diego?"

"Then you'll need to ask him to release you from the heart link. Oh, but Jack, what if you're not too much? What if you're just what he needs?" She winked at me and left the small hut. Leave it to my cat to stir up all of my emotions and leave them there for me to process alone.

Happy.

That was a choice that I could make, and I knew what I needed to do to keep making it.

But first, we had a kingdom to save.

DIEGO

Desmond was frantic. He paced and picked at his shirtsleeves and his eyes darted up to the sky. I squeezed his shoulder and he nearly jumped out of his skin.

"Peace, Desmond. You're walking holes in the ground." I took several steps back to give him the space that he needed. His breathing was fast, and his pupils were blown. "What's got you so frightened?"

"The Trellian banners marching on the only place I've ever called home? The stars falling from the sky? Aquarine is furlongs away, but to a determined army, I doubt it would take them as long as it took us."

My eyes traced the outline of the banners; they were so tattered, so faded. It was hard to believe that they were even real. They were flown for parades, not marches.

"Nothing is going to happen to Aquarine," I said, trying to believe the words too. I was no seer, but my gut told me the banners were flying for me. They were looking for me, and likely, for Jack.

They'd likely be looking for Snapdragon too, but there wasn't much left of her to be found. The emerald-like gleam that I caught glimpses of in Jack's staff was enough to remind me that she was still around. A wave of affection and protectiveness washed over me as I watched Jack; my heart beat in my chest, strong and solid. Things would be different this time.

Desmond's feathers puffed against his shirt. He'd gone back to wearing long sleeves. I took out a small knife that Falcon had given me and seized an arm. The blade was thin and sharp, but I carefully slit the seams of the shirt until his feathers could breathe.

"What the hell–"

"You need to breathe, Desmond. And you need to let your feathers out. You're going to molt if you don't," I said, gently smoothing down the plumes.

"Mum used to say that all the time," he murmured more to himself than to me.

"She would fuss at me for anything that could ruffle a feather. *'Those feathers should be your pride and joy. They're–"*

"The markings of kings! Of Trellis! That's me on your arm, so don't–"

"Go ruffling my feathers!"

We laughed, sharing a moment separated by centuries that still rang in our hearts like yule bells. The wall that Desmond hid behind was finally showing some cracks, and I wanted to chisel him out of whatever stony cage he'd locked himself in. I was thankful to the Goddesses that he wasn't totally alone, that he had Atam to pass the days with. He was so young and I was only just seeing it. His horns probably still had their faun softness.

"Glad to see you got the lectures just as much as I did," I said.

"Possibly more. Mum loved to tell me, *'Little Horn, you'll make me gray! Your imp of a brother never had me worry this much!'"*

"She was a gem," I said, my voice cracking.

"She was. She is," Desmond said, holding the crystal up that held her spirit.

"May I– can I hold the crystal for a moment?" I regretted asking the second the words left my mouth, but Desmond only smiled fondly and slipped the pendant off.

He handed it to me, and the weight sent me reeling. It was heavy. Much heavier than a sapphire ought to be, and that was because my mother's beautiful, light-filled soul was in it. I held it up to my heart, magic stirring in my chest. At first, I thought it was a binding spell; the kind that my family was known for, the kind that she had taught me.

But it wasn't.

It was just her spirit, reaching through the confines of the crystalline walls of the sapphire, to touch my heart. It felt like a lullaby. She'd sing to me to calm the storm in my heart or the thunder in my mind until the skies of my inner world were blue again.

I kissed the pendant before I handed it back to Desmond. He had been her caretaker when I could not be, and he deserved to continue that honor.

"Thank you," I said, pausing to make sure that Desmond saw how sincere the words were on my lips.

"You're welcome, brother." He nodded before motioning us to get ready.

We needed to ride out and get in front of whatever was coming. Desmond held his hand out, palm up. It was an old, familial greeting in Trellis. Mother must have taught it to him. Placing my hand on his forearm, I squeezed and he squeezed back.

"I've got you," I said, and Desmond smiled.

"I'll be right at your side."

"Diego. Be prepared. It's Arturo. I can see him. And he's got... an army. I didn't think there were that many soldiers in Trellis, but he's got them all with him. I can feel the ground shaking. There are mage hounds too but they feel different. Don't approach them!"

Jack's voice came through loud and clear, before I saw her running off in the opposite direction. She was hurried and panicked.

"Trust me," she pleaded as her steps grew faster. Puddin and the staff bobbled along with her, taking long strides to keep up with her.

"Always, my Blossom. Be safe. I'm here. Call for me and I will come."

"I love you."

"And I you."

"Deign? Let's go," Desmond said.

I cast one final look at the direction that she ran, before turning back. The heart that I always thought was missing and shattered was running across the field, auburn hair soaring behind her, magic lighting her way.

"Jack told me that she saw my former general and things look... bad. We need to be prepared."

"Through the heart links?" Desmond's voice rose, but he shook the anger out, backing himself up. He blinked a couple of times, trying to school his disapproval of the heart links from his face.

Was I truly this bad at hiding my emotions?

"Yes, through the heart links. She's not joining us."

"What? She can't be left to her own devices—"

"She can and she will. She's not foolhardy and her magic will keep her safe. We have to trust her. I do, do you?"

"Do I trust the human Priestess that bewitched my damnable brother and is likely getting lost in the woods of a realm she doesn't know? No, I don't trust her that much."

"Good thing I have enough faith in her for a hundred men." I clapped him on the back and climbed up on a horse.

He blinked at me a few times, before mounting his own horse. "I'm starting to see why you got yourself into so much trouble."

I grinned at him, and Desmond had one for me. This could be something, someday. I hoped that one day the word brother would come from him with ease instead of caution.

"My general, Arturo, he's terrible with magic but excellent with a sword. Stay out of reach."

"Anything else I should know?"

"Apparently, this army is the largest one ever amassed by Trellis and all of my mage hounds are here." I flexed my knuckles, tapping into the magic that flowed in my veins. The magic of Kings. The magic of Trellis, of Obius. I was home. I was standing on Obius land with more of my family than I knew still existed.

"Lovely. I'll send letters to Atam to let him know he can have my brooches."

"Don't be so pessimistic. Two against an army? I'd take those odds."

"This is *definitely* how you got into so much trouble. Why the hell did Mum think you would be a good king?"

"She had faith in me," I said smiling, as I ground my heels to the horse's side to get us moving.

The magic in me was waking up, thanks to the love that was around me. My chest was full and my hands ached to cast. It had been too damn long since I had let loose with magic. Alchemy felt different to everyone, but for me, it was slow and hot. It traveled through me like lava, creeping and singing its way before I let it out to breathe. The binding and breaking spells, my elemental magic of air that I inherited from my father, the ancient, forbidden spells Mother taught me with warning in her eyes.

The winds picked up around us. The currents swirled around me, tiny tunnels of air wrapping around my hands. Pulling the currents together, a tornado formed between my fingers until Desmond jumped. Jack may have controlled the Lightning, but the winds listened and obeyed my commands.

"I don't like that look in your eyes."

"Probably smart. Stay out of my line of sight," I said.

Golden magic crackled in my fingers, and when I spared a glance to Desmond, he did the same. Magic radiated from him, wind and bindings, just like mine.

"Likewise, old man."

We rode like the winds pushed us along and maybe they did. Everything was coming, coming, coming.

MARI

My fingers were going off like each one was a friggin Roman candle. I was all alight and it was glorious, but this realm had already seen enough fire without me reenacting Snapdragon's fiery mess. I tried to focus on my breathing, focus on controlling the fire that raged through me, dying to be free but forcing it back down.

I was in a circle of fire, but it was a controlled burn. It was inward with me as the only kindling. I could let the fire dance without it going wild.

Probably.

Falcon was scouting, doing his best forest ranger impression before he came striding back to me, stopping short of the flames. It wasn't disappointing that he didn't run through the flames because what sane man would do that?

Not that anything about Falcon screamed sanity.

"Mari, you gotta drop the fire," he said.

"Working on it," I lied. I wanted to burn brighter. I needed it. I wasn't trying to stop the fire, just contain it.

"Well, work faster because we have company. There's some banners that I think are Trellian. I didn't get a good look at the symbols, but regardless, there's people coming this way, and we need to not be here causing a scene."

"What scene?"

"Marigold Groves, you are nothing short of a showstopper, and while *I* appreciate the greatness of your magic, locals probably won't. Drop the fire before we're fucked."

I glanced up at the sky, looking for the banners he mentioned. I didn't see anything, but then I smelled something rotten and the fire leaped up. Falcon immediately turned, searching for the threat.

"Not these fuckers again," he mumbled. His words just barely carried over the fire, but his magic soared past it. Falcon started casting the Cube, which was becoming his signature spell in my mind.

"Remember that lost soul in Jack's place?" I asked, hoping he heard me.

"Unfortunately," he said.

"Can't you just do that sci-fi movie shit again?"

"You know, that never even occurred to me," he laughed.

The Cube was up and holding. Here in Obius, land of magic, he didn't need to constantly sustain the spell. Magic took on the life it was supposed to have here, and the Cube was perfect. He had been perfecting it even more so it would knit around my skin, in between my fingers until the spell wrapped around me like a glove.

The wickedness on his face was alarming. Part of my brain had entered panic mode, but the other parts were too excited, too alive to look away.

Falcon winked at me and my stomach dropped. He clenched his fists, and I saw sparks of dark, dark forest green magic spark around them until the color changed to midnight blue. He flung the magic around until it was a tactile thing, whipping it across the ground, sending sparks flying.

"Falcon, what the hell is that?"

"No idea, but it's kinda nifty, right? Same spell, but looks totally different here." He cracked it again, handling it like a whip. Magic bounced off, and it shot through my wall of flames.

"Watch it!"

"Same to you, I'm crispy enough as is." He caught the end of the black, tar-like whip in his hand easily, yanking on both ends of it until it snapped together, vibrating with magic.

A huge, hulking beast broke through the trees. Branches snapped under its feet as it pawed its way over to us. Suddenly a wall of flames did not feel like sufficient coverage. It stood up on its hind legs and it was taller than my fire. The reddish-orange thing slapped its three tails around like it was trying to mimic the magical whip Falcon had made.

"Isn't that one of Diego's things? You said something about them not being evil, right?"

"Mage-hound. They listen to D; he created them."

"Any chance it'll listen to us? His besties? His human friends?" I was rambling, but that happened when I was panicking. And when the beast opened its mouth and I saw the *rows* of teeth, I panicked. "Falcon–"

He cracked the whip near his feet, sending a ripple of energy over the ground. He grinned and it was stunningly awful and brilliant.

"Nope. We're gonna make a run for it, because I'd catch hell for killing one of D's pets, but he can't be too mad about me just subduing it. A lot. Like sorta permanently–"

"That sounds like killing it–"

"Yeah, I realized that as I was saying it. Three, two, one, *run!*"

Falcon swung the whip overhead, spinning with it, and the beast backed up. It was snarling and making some kind of braying noise, but it backed up. Falcon released the whip, letting it singe the ground as much as my fire had and the beast squealed before it jumped. He slapped the ground again, and the magic seized the creature. It stumbled forward and fell, the sticky tar of the whip wrapping around its legs and torso.

"It'll be fine. Intention is important. I definitely was thinking *hold gently but effectively* and nothing death-related. Problem-solving is my jam," he said, and this time he reached through the ring of fire and grabbed my hand.

He was trying not to wince, to scream, but he forced himself through the circle until he was standing in my space, too close. Falcon slapped at his body, trying to stamp out the flames on his clothes.

"You're going to get burnt," I said, trying to back up.

"No, I'm not, because you're going to drop the circle right now. Mari, come back to me. I want to look at *you,* not just your magic. Drop it, please." Falcon's skin was too pink for my liking. He was burning but he didn't move.

"I don't know if I can," I whimpered, and I saw the hope drain from his face and change to resignation. The fire licked up my arms and legs, burning and singing, and it was perfect.

"Then please don't hate me for this," he said, wrapping the whip around my hands and arms and chest. He moved slow, achingly slow–his skin was getting redder by the second–until the flames were quelled. The whip was tied around me but not tightly. He tied it like a bow, and when he let go, the flames went out.

"What did you do?" I asked, trying to ignite my flames but unable to.

"Hold but not kill. Gentle. Effective." He held my hands, and they were normal, human temperature. No smoke came billowing from them, no flakes of charred skin came off. They were just my hands, maybe a little drier and chapped. My hands ached like they did in a cold winter.

"Will you release me?"

"As soon as you ask, but not until I'm sure you won't barbeque me."

"I'd never hurt you on purpose."

"It's the accidental part I'm worried about, Mari," he said, still gripping my hands.

I squeezed back and I felt a spark that was not from the Wildfire in my heart. It was just from him.

"We have to keep moving, can you run okay like this?"

I didn't really do great with running in general, but I'd make it work.

"All good here."

"Good, let's find a place to hide. We need more info before we go charging into a slaughter."

He took the hair tie from his hair and I watched the silky, thick, black strands fan out. Falcon shook his hair before gathering it back to get it out of his face again. His hair was really pretty even though he was drenched in sweat. He had a few strands that he missed and I reached up to tuck them behind his ears. I blew on my fingers, trying to cool them down as much as I could before I touched his face. For a man covered in scars, his face was remarkably unmarred. My hands didn't burn him; I'd forgotten they were safe for now.

"I need you to trust me, Mari," he said, whispering in my ear. His body was practically pressed against me, and I quieted the fire in my heart as much as I could. His magic kept me from igniting, but I felt like I was melting inside.

"I do trust you," I said honestly, and his smile was so soft it made me itch. Falcon was as pointy as I was, and seeing the fondness in his eyes made something in my chest flutter.

"Awesome, try not to scream," he said, as he wrapped his arms around my waist and tackled us off of a small cliff. I hadn't even seen the cliff; I was so wrapped up in my magic that I didn't know where we were. There were cliffs and trees, but I could smell the salt of the ocean.

We were freefalling, and I should have been screaming, but I just wanted to spread my arms wide and feel the air sailing past me. Falcon gripped me like we were going to die, but the Cube would absorb the impact.

I saw soldiers looking over the cliff as we were falling and I shot a small fireball at them. It was really small, like the fire I played with before I swallowed the real thing. Falcon's containment spell worked.

The water came up fast, and I realized then that my hands were literally tied. Falcon seemed to realize that too, and fiddled with the bindings.

"Kick to the surface! I'll be right behind–" Falcon was cut off as we fell into the ocean. We hit the water hard and everything stung like I'd been slapped. I plunged down deep and the water was crisp and cold, waking up every cell in my body.

My wrists were still tied, but I stopped moving, trying to figure out which way was up before I started kicking in earnest. Falcon was under me, swimming close and grabbing me around my waist as he pushed us both up to break the surface. My legs burned from kicking so hard and my lungs were thankful for the air by the time we made it back up.

"You're a helluva swimmer," I said, still struggling to keep myself up with tied hands.

Falcon trod water and ripped the bind. The magic faded and dissolved in the water around us in an inky trail.

"Thanks. Search and rescue is a fun party trick." He pointed to the land that felt miles away and we began to swim. I moved a lot slower than he did; for as easy as he moved in the water, his name should have been Duck.

"How'd you learn to swim so well?"

"Real answer?"

"That's generally what people want when they ask questions, Falcon."

His hair was plastered to his face and he grinned like it was his day job.

"I was a Navy SEAL. Sorta."

"You were in the military? So you do have a last name," I said. Water kept getting in my nose and mouth, but Falcon just glided through the water.

"That's the sorta part. I don't have a last name, that I know of, anyway. Or a social security number. Driver's license. Any of it."

"How–?"

Falcon waggled his eyebrows, waved a hand through the air, and said, *"Magic."* He laughed at his own bad joke and I joined him. I swallowed more salty water.

"So they just let a nameless dude join the SEALs?"

"No, John Doe officially joined the SEALs and then died in action. RIP that identity." Falcon was doing the backstroke now, turned so he could face me and watch me struggle not to drown.

"Couldn't think of a more original name?"

"Made it easy to disappear."

"Is that something you do a lot? Disappear?" My question threw off his stroke and it was the first sign of distress I'd seen in him in what felt like ages.

"Only when I have to," he said, watching me closely. I didn't know what he was looking for, or what I was looking for, really, but he continued to swim.

"We need to have more of these little therapy seshes. Good for the soul," I said. And it was; Wildfire seemed placated, and the urge to boil the ocean with us in it was far from the surface of my thoughts.

"You're next, I feel like I've been emotionally vomiting on everyone and it's a little gross. Too much of this kumbaya stuff and I'll get hives." I let it drop; Peony and I had had this fight so many times over the years that I understood and respected when a line was being drawn in the sand. Falcon had already shared more with me than I expected him to, and every little unexpected tidbit was welcome.

When we finally, finally, *finally* made it to shore, I plopped on the sand and rolled on my back. The sky was the most perfect blue. It was like someone turned up the contrast on a picture, or like I'd been in a dark room and finally brought out into the sunlight. It hurt like I was looking at a memory. I remembered Diego mentioning that everything felt dull to him on Earth, but after being in Obius, I didn't think it was because of his broken heart. Everything *was* dull on Earth compared to this. My eyes didn't know where to focus in the sky: the crispness of the clouds or the endless, sparkling blue sky. There was so much tranquility in the air that it was visceral, forcing you to be the truest, purest essence of yourself.

"I swallowed Wildfire because I wanted to know what magic really felt like," I said, the words coming out garbled and between my ragged breathing. The confession made my heart race, but I was so glad to have said the words out loud, to someone that might understand.

"Mari–"

"No, it's okay. I don't regret it. I just wanted to keep up." Tears pricked in my eyes and I used a sandy hand to wipe them away. The fire lit itself in me again, like my emotions had lit the torch. I'd never felt so free to just lay the burdens of my heart right out in the open.

"Mari!" I turned my head to see Falcon lying flat on his back, his hands up in surrender, with a spear pointed at his cheek. I squirmed, trying to get away but felt a boot connect with my chest, pushing me down.

"Oh *fuck no*," I spat, and I grabbed the guy's leg and let the fire loose. It shot up his leg, rolled over his hips, and crackled up his torso. He screamed, trying to get away from me, but I didn't let go. I saw my body moving in my mind, leaping up and landing on my feet, spinning fire like I was a weaver-woman creating a blanket of flames.

Do not hurt Falcon, I commanded the flames, and they listened mostly. The fire danced across the shore, racing through the throng of soldiers. The crest was Trellian. I remembered that asshole Arturo watching us fight through his crowds under the same banner. The fire hit Falcon's still tender arms and he shook it off because he was back on his feet too. It didn't take long for him to wrestle the spear away and start the elaborate dance with several soldiers to beat them back. He moved with practiced, trained motions, and I saw it in the lines of his body. How his muscles flexed and the strength of his stances. Falcon systematically decimated the field with a spear, using only bursts of magic to keep people from heading in my direction.

I gathered the blaze in my hands and felt the power thrumming to life in my veins. The beat of Wildfire drumming steadily in my core was mirrored in my steps. I moved in time with the magic, in time with the blaze, and I swirled it around myself and down my arms.

A soldier turned to take a swipe at me and I tossed the ball of fire at him. He shouted but the fire took him fast, and I ran over to be with Falcon. Back to back, just like we were in Jack's burning shop, casting and fighting our way through. The sky was still so, so blue, and I wondered if Wildfire would burn enough for it to turn red. The soldiers sloshed in the muddy ground—the muck painting them to look like kindling.

I was made for *war*.

Chapter Fifteen

JACK

Diego and Desmond took off. Puddin stayed behind with me and I was grateful for her company. The air buzzed. I felt too many souls, too many people nearby and it made me antsy. We were still outside of the little hut, and the small village teemed with energy, but I felt something larger. Searching the horizon but not seeing anything that would feel that large, I grabbed Harold to steady myself. My knees were weak and my stomach was in knots. This energy was *wrong*.

"Jack?"

"This is bad, Puddin. We need to move. I don't know what it is but it's bad–"

"Slow down, focus on your magic. You're a Priestess, girl. Use that magic. What's happening?" She had her tail curled around me like a cape. Puddin was so tall in Obius. It was distracting. Everything was distracting. There was just too much energy in the air.

I took a deep breath and grabbed my staff with purpose this time, and then I drew a circle and stepped inside. Puddin smiled and backed up, already knowing the spell. The staff stayed at eye level, and I knew it wouldn't take long for me to get lost in the beauty of the crystal. Snapdragon's green soul glinted as a tiny sparkle, but I saw her and felt her acknowledgment.

The Full Circle spell cast itself as I thought it into existence. The ring shone with my green, green magic and clarity snapped into focus so sharply in my mind, that I flinched. I forced myself to slow down, to ease into the magic, as I took a deep breath in to center the magic.

The visions came in quick, rapid-fire succession. No longer than a second each, shuffling themselves through my mind like I shuffled a deck of cards.

I saw Falcon and Mari. They were fighting, standing back to back and with a challenge in Mari's eyes that I would hate to be on the receiving end of. Falcon twirled a spear, stabbing and slicing with ease. His magic burst from him suddenly and wildly. They stepped in time with each other and I admired how brave Mari felt at that moment. She was fearless, the fire burning in her so bright she could have been a third sun.

The ground around them squelched as they moved across the marshy, sandy terrain. They were on a beach, and I knew that beach; it was the crossing into Chilijan. When I focused more on the background, I saw the bridge.

Then I saw Arturo, standing at the back of the crowd of soldiers that poured over the landscape. It was an army. A legion. There were so many soldiers; too many for them to just be Trellian. I saw wings, horns, tails, and fur. The Trellians were forest dwellers; the scaled people and the watery sprites didn't fit with the people that I had come to know as Trellian.

Abuela's face flashed in my mind and she winked at me.

I dropped the circle and stepped out. Her face did nothing to calm the gut-clenching knots; Abuela knew I was here. She knew my magic and she'd find us. It was just a matter of time.

"What did you see?"

"We need to get to the bridge that leads us out of Chilijan. Falcon and Mari are here. Those weren't falling stars that you saw; it was them. Diego and Desmond need to know what's coming for them."

"Jack, look." Puddin's claws were out and magic swirled around her. Desmond rode furiously back toward us, but he was alone. No Diego in tow. No Diego in sight.

"Priestess Jack, connect to Deign and boost his magic. He's going to try something stupid, I can almost guarantee it. Whatever he's going to do, don't let him do it alone. Please," Snapdragon's soft voice echoed in my mind.

Flashes of Diego came to me. He practically drowned in his magic. I saw him about to summon some feat of magic and the way his arms were trembling. I saw the sweat forming on his brow and how it made his hair curl even more. I saw the look in his eyes and how he seemed to look straight at me, even in the flashes of a vision.

I saw Diego as the King he should have been, instead of the King he was of the past.

"Gravity," Snapdragon whispered. *"Deign is going to cast Gravity. It's too much for him–"*

Then the flashes were gone. I saw Desmond smiling on a balcony at Trellis Castle, just like I saw in visions before during Diego's coronation. But then that faded, melted away from my mind. My insides felt like they were melting too. The flashes were too bright, too hard to look at, like all of the pictures were exposed instead of waiting for them to develop.

The image of Desmond so bright and happy had morphed into something sinister and twisted; the landscape changed, and Trellis was burnt and dead. Everything about Obius was burnt and dead. I could taste the decay on my tongue and felt myself starting to gag–

My magic slipped away from me, and I dropped my staff. Harold rattled around on the top, still connected but the vines holding it to the staff were breaking.

"What's going on?" I asked but not sure who I was addressing. I reached around in the darkness of my mind, looking for the answer, looking for the right path, the *future* as it should be, and I saw nothing but darkness and ruins.

"This is how it started for me," Snapdragon's voice sounded so far away, but I searched for her in the darkness.

"How do I stop it?"

"I don't know, I never figured that out."

I caught a flash of Snapdragon then, hunched up in the corner of her room in Trellis Castle. She hugged herself, shaking her head, willing the visions to *stop* but they didn't. I felt Wildfire surrounding us both, her panicked eyes darting around for an exit she'd never find. Then she was gone too.

Puddin grabbed my arm and it startled me back into my body, back to being with her. Her eyes were cobalt blue. Had they always been this blue? My memories of her seemed to fade; everything about Earth seemed so far away now. I wanted the familiar comfort of her wards and the steady, humming spells that Mari and I had practiced for years. I got lost in the Seer's magic, floating too far from who I was and the realization punched me in the gut hard. I wasn't hiding in my bedroom, but I hid myself in the inky darkness between the worlds, floating between them so I wouldn't be fully trapped in either place. Puddin's hands–not paws, they really weren't paws, just hands with longer nails–supported all of my body weight. She watched me with such intensity that I knew she could tell that I was slipping away again.

"Jack, you need to stop doing whatever you're doing. You need to stay here with me. It's already too late," she said.

"What do you mean?"

"Move slowly, hands up," she said, backing away with her hands in the air.

Then I saw them. The soldiers. Hundreds of them. How did they get here so fast? They were so far away in my visions–

"Priestess!" Desmond's voice, high and panicked, cut through the scene. He ran with all his might. Energy bounced off of him as he slid his way through the crowd of people, easily dodging anything that got too close to him.

"Desmond?"

"Do not harm her!" he shouted, a sword raised high in his hand with wind magic propelling him further.

"Jack, down!" Puddin screeched and she launched magic at a huge, towering man.

He was Fae, but he had to be part giant. Something. He was *massive* and his huge, lumbering arms swung at me. I ducked just in time and Puddin lobbed some kind of watery, angry magic straight at him. The giant took the blow right to the chest and Desmond came flying across the field. The sword planted itself in the giant's chest and he stumbled. Desmond had the sword out, ready for the next fight before I processed the fallen creature. His soul floated up closer to my staff and I nodded, letting it enter the shining globe. The soldiers didn't stop and Desmond flung wind magic at anyone that approached us. He tried to keep a barrier around us, but there were still more coming.

Harold came to life then, the magic shifting from a soft glow of gold to the emerald green I've come to know as the Seer's Blessing. I saw them all sparkling in the orb, waiting for me to do what this magic was made for.

But I couldn't.

With no link to Sanctum, no place to send them, and so another soul took up residence in there with the rest.

"My Blossom. Desmond is coming for you. He's going to help you find your way to me. I can't leave. Arturo is here."

Diego's voice boomed through my chest and I held the citrine pendant around my neck to steady myself. His voice boomed so much louder than what I was used to.

"Diego, what are you doing?"

"I'm going to end this nonsense with Arturo. Stay with Desmond."

"What? No! I'm coming–"

"No, Jack, you aren't. This is something I need to do. Stay with Desmond. I'll be back soon, my Blossom."

I don't know how or what he did, but I felt the heart links disconnect. I felt the magic fading like a slow leak from a water balloon. The magic left me feeling hollow and alone in a way that I didn't know I could feel. I saw his star lights fading; the outline of his face became blurry, and I tried to grab at him, but my hands passed right through the dimming light.

"Diego!" I shouted, when did my voice get so loud? Was that all in my head?

"Jack–"

He broke the link. *Our* link. He shattered the heart link and I sank to my knees.

Diego was gone, and I couldn't sense him anywhere near me in the sea of souls around me.

DIEGO

Desmond's words had come back to haunt me. *How could you bind a Priestess? What monster would do such a thing?*

It replayed over and over in my mind.

I didn't create the magic that linked us, but I would be damned if I'd kept her tied to me as I readied myself to cast Gravity.

Gravity was all-encompassing. It sucked and ripped apart everything in its grasp, and I couldn't let her be a part of that. I wouldn't. The spell formed in my chest like a bubble desperate to pop. The blackness of the spell felt like a poison that I'd injected. It clung and stuck to me, trying to pull me apart with its power. Unlike the lightness of the winds or the holiness of the bindings, Gravity was nothingness. It boiled and roiled under my skin, and I simmered in the bleakness of it. I stood at the edge of something terrible, and I knew it, but I wasn't turning back.

Gravity was the last trick in my book–and the time came for me to bring it out and let it go.

My mother had warned me against casting it; similar to the binding magic that we were known for, Gravity had the opposite effect. It didn't shatter things, so much as force them to cease to be. A black hole opened itself in my chest and I breathed it through my whole being. The spell was coming and I prepared myself for it to come into the world as best as I could. Gravity had only been cast once before that I'd known in history, and the Queen that cast it had her name banished. I was already banished once–once more couldn't be any worse.

Arturo's troops were endless; they sprung up all over the horizon. I needed a way to stop them, to stop *everything* before anyone else got hurt. I needed more time to cast, so I built my circles. I drew lines in the marshy ground, adding the sigils of the Goddesses, of my family, of the intricacies tying magic to the life that pulsed in the ground.

The heart links were ancient magic, but they couldn't stand up to Gravity. I shattered the link between us, and it felt like I'd smashed through the worlds again except this time it was the universe in my heart. The fractured thing kept beating, even though I wanted Gravity to take me down with it.

"Fallen King! What do you think you're doing?"

I knew the voice, but I couldn't place it. It sounded like a memory, and I'd lost too many of those. Searching the horizon for the voice, none seemed out of place. Nothing stood out amongst the crowd of soldiers, moving and marching to a forced drum beat. They weren't the people of Trellis, but the ugliest side of Seer magic: taking control over souls and working them as their welder required.

It didn't matter. Gravity wouldn't care if there was one soldier or a thousand. It would keep consuming and consuming until I forced it to stop.

Assuming I could stop it.

No, you will stop it. If you don't then you've broken your link to Jack for no reason. Don't do that to her. Don't let this beast of alchemy hurt her.

Gravity had a heaviness that I could only explain as wet and sticky. It enveloped me, pulling at every crevice in my heart, and the new one I just made from breaking the heart link. I had to cast it and let it go.

The spell came forward easily. Desperate to consume, to breathe, but I forced it to stay within my control. The magic *would* submit or I would shut it down. Like all great alchemy, it had a life of its own.

It started so small; the blackness of it felt too difficult to look at. Gravity was truly the absence of light. It was the absence of *life*, cold and starving, waiting for me to drop it. The spell pulsed with energy, filling my hands until I realized that it had doubled in size just in the few seconds that I watched it.

The words of the incantation were stuck in my throat, waiting and begging to be released, so Gravity could be what it needed to be.

Holy Darkness,

There was no stopping now—

Come forth from the blood of kings,

I said a prayer to whoever was listening, praying for this to work, so I could end this before Jack would meet her end at the tip of a blade or a spell I couldn't stop.

Let the Gravity of existence be removed,

Let the Gravity of light fall away,

Let the Gravity of life be consumed in your Darkness,

Listen as I call your name,

Holy Darkness,

Please don't let this be a mistake, please don't let this be a mistake, please—

Gravity

The black orb in my hands turned liquid; it seeped between my fingers, dripping on the ground until it reformed itself. I saw the galaxies burning inside it. Stars bright as suns dancing through its ending, all-consuming darkness. My heart dropped. I saw the star lights of the banished Queen, shame etched on her face.

Then it spread.

Each drop that hit the dirt opened up, gaining mass by the second.

"Listen as I call your name," I said. My words were so feeble that my knees locked and I felt the world getting darker and darker. My eyes were heavy like Gravity had seeped back into me instead of the land, and I sank into the ground. Gravity pulled but didn't reach too much for me.

"Listen as I call your name," I said and the spell slowed, trying to obey the comment.

"Listen as I call your name." It slowed again, still surging across the land. It inched forward like a lava flow; molten, liquid destruction.

Movement caught my eye and my focus got consumed by the spell. I knew the magic instantly as I tried to hold the spell but Gravity wanted more. It demanded more. It was no longer listening.

Falcon and Mari were running through the hills between Trellis and Chilijan. Mari bristled as a red-hot flame and Falcon trailed behind her, soldiers right on their heels. They were running directly toward the path of Gravity. I shouted for them—as loud and as powerfully as I could, reaching and reaching for whatever magic I still had in me to warn them.

"Listen as I call your name," I said again, shouting the words. My chest ached, the void of the magic that Gravity took with it.

The inky, horrid blackness shifted, slowing enough to pause like it considered my request, before I felt the snap of the magic between us breaking. Gravity had answered, and it said, *no.*

I fingered the charms of the heart link, hoping that there was still something there, some thread of magic hidden within it to reach Jack. The charms moved with lifeless energy.

There wasn't. Of course there wasn't.

Falcon and Mari stopped running. They turned to see the mass of magic coming for them, and I stared at Falcon. Mari lobbed fire at it, but the flames just fell away like everything else in its path. The land was black. Where Wildfire had scorched and burned, Gravity removed. It predated Wildfire; Gravity was the opposite of creation—it was a blank, black canvas. It wanted to clean the slate of Obius until there was nothing left for it to consume.

"Listen as I call your name," I tried again. Gravity was already out of my grasp.

"Falcon, please, just run."

He didn't hear those words. Mari slung more fire, trying to get the spell to stop advancing. It didn't.

The soldiers pursuing them seemed to realize that the danger was no longer the humans but the weight of the magic before them. Some tossed their spears or shot their arrows. Gravity welcomed them all, taking each lance and bolt greedily.

"I'm sorry," I whispered to no one.

Chapter Sixteen

FALCON

Mari and I were an efficient team. She spun fire like it was her day job, and I got to swing a big ass spear around, lobbing magic when I needed to. My muscles burned with energy, and I felt myself getting fueled by it. Pain spiked through me in lovely, vibrant waves. My body wasn't going to let me forget how fucked it was, but I kept going. As another soldier approached, I didn't aim to kill, just to incapacitate. I wasn't a killer unless I really had to be, and this wasn't a dire, *need-to-kill-all-the-things* situation yet.

Yet.

I knew better than to think or speak things into existence.

I *knew* better.

And yet...

I felt it before I saw it, nearly crashing into Mari when she abruptly stopped. Magic spread across the land like a disease, attacking every blade of grass, flower, and being that it touched, pulling them in and compacting them in the blackness. It looked like a fucking black hole, but that didn't make sense because we weren't floating up in space.

And *yet...*

"Mari–"

"I see it."

"We need to bounce. Come on–"

"There's no escaping that, Falcon. You think we can burn it down?" Her eyes glimmered with the intensity of an inferno, a galaxy exploding inside of her. She was so fucking magnificent it made my chest ache.

"Unlikely, but I don't have a better idea."

"Let's see how hot I can go," she said, rubbing her hands together and flakes of charred skin fell away. Mari cracked her knuckles and shook out her limbs. Her shoes were long gone; I couldn't remember if she took them off or burned them away, but she stood barefoot on the muddy ground with her feet firmly planted.

I felt the magic rising in her like she turned up the temperature of the entire realm around her. She sparkled and gleamed and I wondered how anything could ever compare to her again.

"You should probably stand behind me." She laughed as the molten, flaming magic dripped from her fingers. It was the same consistency as the blackness that seeped into the land, breaking it down. Every drop of magic that hit the ground around her caught fire until it melted.

The soldiers had stopped advancing. They were loyal but they weren't stupid–a lost cause if I'd ever seen one. I saw the moment when that dawned on their faces: fire closing in, me in their path, their commanders standing back and watching like they just flipped the channel to some boring ass baseball game.

And *yet...*

While Mari cranked up the heat, I cranked up the Cube. She positioned herself to unleash a hellscape and I needed her to be as protected as I could make her. Wildfire was ancient, holy magic and even though Mari might be a force of nature, Wildfire would only truly obey a Goddess. So I stepped through the spell, dancing through the steps like I had been born solely to perfect this spell, to keep this woman safe. Alchemy and casting were fine arts; they responded better to precision and practice, cloaking themselves in ceremony to intensify their presence. So I danced–practiced, precise, prayerful.

The Cube grew brighter and brighter as I built layers between the outer rim of the Cube and Mari's body. I tried to do the same for myself, but I couldn't stay focused. The spell was weighty; I could hold it for others but holding it against me made my arms too heavy, my mind too sluggish.

Mari resonated as a green beacon in the fire and a blazing dot against the blackness in front of her.

I begged the Judge for this to work, enough that she survived; I'd follow whatever path was written for me, but this couldn't be the end for her. Candela mentioned that I'd meet my end at the hand of a Goddess, and while I considered Mari to be one, I doubted that was her meaning. Mari's head snapped up, gazing in the distance.

I saw Arturo at the top of a hill, head held high, a sword glinting the twin suns. A man on the bottom of the hill with his back to Arturo stood motionless. I couldn't make out any details except some blue specks.

Feathers.

Mari's control gave way, losing herself to the magic now; fire came from her eyes, out of her ears and mouth, smoke and sparks flying from her nose. Her hands were just fireballs, but I could still *see* her hands, so the spell was working. She was only burning up, not being fully consumed.

"Mari! I have to go! Diego–"

She waved me away, a wild grin splitting her face in a way that made her look demonic, and she nodded.

"I've got this," I heard her shout from the center of her personal inferno. The fire wrapped itself around her arms and down her legs, covering her torso and chest until she twisted into the dancing flame of a human candle.

I believed her. She did have this. If anyone here could burn their way through a black hole, it was Marigold Groves. Her feral laughter echoed through the land and I took off, sprinting as fast as I could. Diego was too far away for me to reach him with a Cube spell to take the brunt of the sword in Arturo's hands, but I had more tricks up my sleeve.

Summoning the mountains, reaching through the soil to ground myself in its weighty, solid presence, I called the boulders. I hated using this magic because I felt every iota of the boulders that I tossed like pebbles and my body was still running on fumes from my last excursion to Obius. My scarred, fucked up arms trembled, my back twinged, and the broken ribs felt like they were crumbling in my chest, but I held the massive rock with magic. It kept digging itself out when I saw Arturo advancing. He would have that pig-sticker in Diego's back in a matter of seconds, so I forced the magic to *move*, like squeezing a bag to force the stream of energy to flow faster through my body.

It hurt like a bitch. Peony wasn't here to keep me alive this time, and my nerves were very clear about that fact, but the boulder freed itself and sailed through the sky, over the blackness of whatever was killing the world and straight for Arturo.

He saw it, Diego saw it, and they both sprung into action, moving before it connected.

Arturo scanned the land, looking for the boulder's point of origin until his eyes landed on me. I couldn't tell from the distance, but it damn sure looked like he was swearing. I hoped he knew it was me, that I would hound this asshole until his last breath.

Diego stood face to face with him now, and I moved faster. My legs wanted to collapse–all of me wanted to collapse actually–but I forced myself forward. Always forward. I ran through the hoard of troops and they let me pass. They didn't care any longer. Everyone scrambled to get away from the torrent of magic flowing. Panicked screams and shaking figures. The soldiers hauled themselves up, clinging to each other as they ran.

Weapons and gear littered the ground; no one wanted the extra weight to slow down their retreat. Smart, so of course I pilfered everything I could carry. I grabbed a bow and quiver, and a spear. Trellian weaponry appeared so ornate that it looked fragile; the heft of the bow in my hand assured me it wasn't. My body lurched painfully as I drew the bow, and I needed to chill on the magic until my ribs stopped throbbing so much.

Diego shouted—I couldn't make out the words but I heard the anger, the rage. Part of me was proud of him; Diego was a low-simmering pot of feels that was finally, finally, finally boiling. I picked up the pace to get to him faster. The unmistakable crackle of holy, raging fire burst through the air.

Mari's fire finally cut itself loose.

The heat blazed so intensely I nearly retched from the density of it; her magic filled the air and covered the skies, and I'd bet my left arm that the lakes around us would be boiling. It raged around us and every logical part of my mind told me to get the fuck out of the way, but I didn't; logic and me were thready friends at best. I kept pushing forward to Diego.

I stopped short when I realized that the blackness had advanced. It surrounded me; it had moved so fast, retreating and surging through the fire that it covered the ground even faster. Only about a four-foot square area of solid ground remained for me to stand on. All sides covered in the sickening blackness, fire raging overhead.

There was no way out. I'd played all of my cards and I didn't have another hidden trick up my sleeves. The darkness inched closer and closer. I was trapped. Fully, completely trapped. *So this is how it ends*, I thought, weirdly calm. I thought I'd go out in a blaze of glory, not quietly submitting to something inevitable.

I turned to Mari, watching her ignite the horizon. I saw Diego fighting with Arturo; he took a swing at him, and I smiled. I taught him that. I taught him how to throw a punch, how to be a brawler instead of a kingly, gentlemanly dueler.

"Lead with your left, D. You've got this," I said, taking a seat on the ever-smaller patch of marsh. I welcomed the cool, wet soil that chilled my aching body. My knees groaned as I settled down; the fatigue overwhelmed me all at once, hitting harder than most of the punches I'd taken recently. My bones ached until they were numb, until everything was numb.

It wouldn't be long now.

"Burn bright, Mari, be safe."

I cast the Cube around myself, tightening its grasp to me as much as I could, and closed my eyes. Maybe it wasn't brave, but I didn't want to watch the alchemy consume me, so I kept my eyes closed.

The magic covered my feet and legs like a cold, clinging blanket and it worked its way up until the pain in my ribs was gone because they were gone too.

It wrapped me in a cold, dark embrace until there was nothing left.

JACK

Emotion laced through all of the flashes of visions that unsettled me. Nothing made *sense*. Black, black, black magic. Diego fighting Arturo, screaming and throwing punches. Mari igniting herself. Desmond smiling and waving at a crowd of Trellians, his Prince on his arm. Peony and Sherwin playing cards and throwing popcorn at each other. Mama singing while she did the dishes in a home that I didn't recognize. Falcon unraveling to nothingness. Puddin waving goodbye with her humanish hands and blowing kisses.

What was real? Why couldn't I tell anymore? Half of my body felt physical, and the other half felt like it was disintegrating

I felt it the moment that the magic arose. Ancient and slumbering. This was not a spell meant to be woken: created only for the purpose of endings.

Desmond and Puddin pulled me along, forcing me to keep up with them even though my mind was far away, searching through the flashes of visions that didn't make sense and didn't connect.

Endings and darkness. Beginnings and crowns. Goodbyes and welcome homes. What was real? What was real?

"Stop this Priestess. Stop looking for certainties, and start looking at what is happening before you," Snapdragon whispered. My staff came to me but I couldn't remember when I called for it.

"I feel like I'm losing control."

"No Priestess, you're losing confidence. You know how this ends. It's time," she said, and the soft green in Harold's globe turned electric, lighting everything around us. Desmond and Puddin stopped pulling me and stared at the woman in my path.

I stared at Abuela.

She towered in front of me. She didn't have the odd patchwork skirts or flowy blouses. No beads, no gems, no kitschy trinkets. Abuela stood taller than I had ever seen before, at eye level with the straight back that came from youth and arrogance. Her dark brown eyes were emerald green with red, ruby magic twisting through her old, bony fingers.

"You know how this ends, Priestess," Snapdragon whispered again. I pushed myself in front of Desmond and Puddin until Abuela watched me with a smirk. The wrinkles had left her face too, and I stared into the eyes of a woman closer to my own age.

"It's time, Jack," Abuela said.

"Time for what?"

"Oh child, you should know by now. Blessed with my magic and you still can't see what's in front of you?"

She gestured to the land behind me and my stomach dropped. It was black. Inky. Dark and void. Obius felt like a collapsing star and I stood in the center of the destruction.

"What is this?" I knew my mouth must be hanging open.

"This is the end. Every story has an ending, child, only Snapdragon couldn't seem to figure that out." There was no humor, no mirth, no hint that this was some kind of cruel, strange joke. She watched me with an even, clear gaze, waiting for me to catch on to what she said.

The visions came back again, but this time each flash felt like a blow to the head. The first images were the absolute lack of everything. It was overly dark, the kind that meant there wasn't just an absence of light. It was the darkness that lingered in Diego's shattered heart that tried to drag every ounce of life from him. Lost in this hazy void, I reached for my magic to show me anything else.

The next vision was Diego. He was golden from a singular sun, not from magic, lying in a bed with a light green blanket. It was woven and soft, and even in the vision I could feel the delicate, cottony threads. He was shirtless and warm with a thin, gold chain around his neck, a citrine pendant just resting against his heart. He smiled more contentedly than I'd ever seen before and his watchful, shy eyes were fixed on me. The constellation of freckles on his collarbone stood out so brilliantly from the sunlight. My throat tightened and I hugged the heart link to my chest.

He faded from my mind's eye so quickly that I flinched and realized I was reaching for him, searching for him back in the darkness that I had flung myself into.

"Jack Hawthorne, darling Priestess of this ruined world, I am speaking to you," Abuela declared, each syllable ringing out in the darkness.

"Where am I?"

I disconnected from my body again; I couldn't remember where I'd left it or how long it had been. Diego felt so far away and I remembered the shattering of the heart links. He broke them so quickly that it left me shaking. I thought back through the days, trying to remember anything that seemed important. I was unraveling; Abuela seemed far away now too. I'd found a pocket of the universe that was quiet, where my magic wasn't shouting from the rooftops, where no one was left to see me. The void that I descended into was peaceful. It wanted to bring me peace.

Didn't it?

Everything was dull and sleepy. My head was full of storm clouds, but in the nothingness, I felt the hard, wooden handle of my staff. My crystal ball gleamed in the shadow, sparkling emerald green but this time it was laced with gold. The same color as Diego's true eyes, the color of his magic, and the tones of his love that he had so freely given to me.

I focused on the crystal. I studied every sparkling light inside it, feeling and touching the fallen souls that needed to rest. Snapdragon's green spirit faded, growing a softer and softer green, until it seemed to blend fully in with the others.

The staff was solid, real. The wood was real. It had weight here in this void, and I hugged it to my chest. The citrine pendant that Mari gave me glimmered alive with magic. I felt her there, now that I remembered her. The friend that never left my side, that so desperately wanted to stand in the light she thought she didn't deserve. The layers and layers of magic in the citrine spoke to me; Peony, Mama, and Puddin each wrapping their love and magic in the small, yellow gem. It was golden, I realized, just like Diego.

The chill of the blackness tried to wrap its sticky, clingy alchemy around me but I shook it off. I grabbed the center of my staff, and swung it like a scythe. Lightning raced through the air around me, lighting up this horrid void and I swung it again and again.

"You know how this ends," Snapdragon said again, and I smiled down at the crystal. She was right; I *did* know exactly how this ended.

Abuela's face came back into view.

The moss-laden meadows between Chilijan and Trellis came alive—what was left of them—and I felt the soul of every Fae around me. Thousands and thousands of souls, all waiting for an end they weren't ready for.

"Do you see now, child? It's time for everyone to start playing the roles that were written for them. Sometimes, not every soul has a happy ending." She gestured to the land and stood there for a moment, smiling at the scene. She watched the spell claiming more and more of the land. The Trellian soldiers were fleeing. The Chilijan people were running across the bridges and diving in Ubbin Lake's glass-like waters.

My eyes were emerald green, bright enough that the glare reflected in my crystal ball, and I nodded. Lightning churned within it and I smiled. I felt the bolts tingling in my fingers, gently stinging as they begged to come to life. *Rightness.* This was the path forward. I knew it to be the truth. The Goddess's path was wrong.

Desmond and Puddin were at my sides, and I turned to face them. I saw the confusion etched on their faces, the wariness that normally made me feel safe with Puddin was so heavy it made her hard to look at.

"Stand back," I said. Harold was alive with magic and I swung the staff. The sense of rightness that guided my steps through this realm of magic ignited in me fully and my heart was steady.

"What do you think you're doing!" Abuela screeched. The humanness of her voice faded until it was strained and animalistic. I saw the edges of her eyes narrow and splinter with rage. She searched my face, looking for what spell I would cast, but of course, she knew. She knew every play in my playbook because they were once hers. Only now she had forgotten them.

Abuela sounded like a wounded, frenzied beast trying to lash out at anything and everything in her grasp. At me. I smiled, wide and full, not letting her take another breath without seeing how deeply her magic had taken root in me.

I saw the flashes of her ending–letting Snapdragon's twisted, sad prophecies play out as the final swan song for Obius.

"I know how this ends," I said and swung my staff again, letting loose the Lightning.

CHAPTER SEVENTEEN

DIEGO

The boulder seemed to come out of nowhere, but then again, so did Arturo. I knew that he would be here; he couldn't pass up a chance to swing a sword or pretend to be a leader. He had always been like that; he wanted to lead all of our childhood games. He said over and over how all he wanted to do was serve the Trellian royal family, how that was what he was born to do, destined to be, and I went along with it.

Sherwin was my closest friend and thus he became the King's Shadow; he stayed with me night and day, my constant and ever-present friend kept me sane on the days when I thought I was drowning. I gave Arturo the reins of the Royal Guard, thinking it would be the best place for him. He would be happy, in charge of something, feeling seen in the way that he always wanted to be seen.

What part of my reign wasn't a mistake? How did I miss the malice in his heart?

Arturo circled me, sword in one hand with a smaller, twin dagger in his other, in a stance I'd seen a thousand times. He readied himself to attack at any second, sizing me up and waiting for a place to strike. I wielded no weapon and didn't intend to. Arturo took a careful step forward, the wind catching the cape my mother had made for him. It moved and I remembered days past, when she was still alive and making better choices than I ever had.

"Your Majesty," he said.

"Arturo."

"I'm afraid that I can no longer be your sword arm. The Seer has commanded–"

I barked out a laugh that sounded so cruel even I wanted to flinch. The Seer. Everything started because the Goddess broke Snapdragon's mind; the burden of her "blessing" breaking and ripping her apart until she was lost completely. I remembered how her spirit collapsed and faded in my arms as Jack tried to lay her to rest. I remembered the vision she showed me of Snapdragon's true, final moments, and how it was the same fucking blade in his hand that he *dared* to raise against me.

Arturo sensed the shift in my mood and rolled his wrist, loosening his stance to strike. He knew my emotions even after all these years had passed.

"You killed Snapdragon," I spat. My throat closed, choking on the word *kill*, and my heart thudded painfully in my chest. Her death played out again and again in my mind, and I wanted to rip him limb from limb.

"No, I ended the madness, or tried to. She was long gone by then, Deign. After *you* shattered our worlds, what did you think would happen here? Your mother was gone. Trellis had no ruler! The people were clambering for Snapdragon to help, to do something, and she was put on the throne. *Your* throne, where that heinous little nymph always wanted to be! Except she had *lost* you, and she was mad. She wasn't Snapdragon, the Emerald Priestess, beloved by all. She was Snapdragon, the deranged and grieving tyrant. She was cruel. She closed the gates and let Trellis starve. She burned the Rainbow Forest! How can you possibly defend her?" Arturo shouted;

it was the first time I'd ever heard him raise his voice in anger. The first time he'd ever raised his voice to me.

"Because she was lost just like the rest of you! How could you abandon her?"

It was his turn to laugh, and it made me want to run him through with that blade. "Deign, no one could reach her even if they tried. And they did. Everyone did. Sherwin disappeared too. She had no one."

"She had *you*."

"And I chose mercy. For her, for everyone."

I leaped, swinging wildly and reaching for his throat. He tried to swipe at me with the sword but I palmed the blade, ripping it out of his hand. It sliced my palm but I couldn't feel anything other than fury. My hands were wet and red; blood hit the ground and each drop resonated in my ears. It should hurt. I should feel it, but I felt nothing. He backed up, holding the dagger so I could see the details and I stopped cold. The handle was covered in green and gold gems with specks of tarnished red.

"Deign–"

"Is that her blood?" I asked, pointing to the dagger. He glanced down, adjusting his grip to cover the flecks of it. That was all the answer I needed. How many years had her blood stained that wretched blade?

"I did what needed to be done."

Another wave of Gravity pooled in my chest. The weight of this spell sickened me, making everything about my movements feel weak and I rejected it. I pushed it down–magic would not be his end. He didn't deserve the ease of Gravity seeping over him and breaking him down to nothing but forgotten molecules.

"You're a murderer," I said through gritted teeth.

"So are you," he sneered.

My hands were on his throat again; I moved faster than I thought possible, and I squeezed. He couldn't keep a grip on the dagger's hilt, and it fell into the mud beside us. I squeezed tighter and tighter until he was gasping.

"You're right." Arturo's eyes went wide and he started to struggle in earnest. I didn't let him go; I wasn't going to.

"Deign–"

He struggled, clawing at my hands. Blood ran down my arm from the cut on my palm. There were long, thick scratches on my arms that I couldn't feel.

"Deign!"

"That name is dead now, too. I'm just Diego."

Arturo pointed at the ground and saw Gravity coming closer to us. It was going to cover everything. Shame prickled up through my chest; I knew I was going to get Jack hurt in the end. I knew it. No matter what I did, it ended in tragedy.

A flash of red caught my attention and I lost my grip. Arturo stumbled, and we both ducked in time to miss the fire that shot overhead. He coughed and sputtered, reaching blindly for his dagger. It clattered across the dirt, landing next to me.

"She died terrified and her spirit twisted beyond recognition that she never let go," I said, my voice shaking from rage.

"She was a power-hungry demon. My only regret is not slaying her sooner before the madness warped whatever was left of her soul." He spat on the ground, never breaking eye contact.

My body moved of its own volition, exploding up and at Arturo. I hoisted him up until I saw the dagger planted in his chest, and the bloom of red that seeped down his Trellian tunic brought me no joy, no cry of victory. The chapter closed, and the reign of the Shattered King came fully to a close. Arturo stumbled back, holding the dagger in his chest until he sank to his knees.

Arturo collapsed and he stared straight at me. "I-I-I regret not killing J-Jack too." He closed his eyes, and I kicked his body as hard as I could so it would roll down the hill into the mass of Gravity. I wanted to feel regret. I wanted to be remorseful.

But I wasn't.

I felt like I had rid Trellis of one more monster, and even if this was the end of my beloved forest kingdom, at least it would come without Arturo's bloodstained hands at the helm.

Fire danced all around me, over the blackness of Gravity and I watched as Mari lit up the world. She twirled and spun, moving across the nothingness like she was weightless herself. She blazed the horizon until she got closer and closer to me. Mari was alight from head to foot, and she shot fire as Gravity inched toward me.

"Strap in bro, we got work to do," she said.

"Where's Falcon? I thought I saw–"

"Rescue mission time. Then we go for Jack."

MARI

Falcon got himself boxed in by the black crap that devoured the land. He moved calmly, and I told myself he'd be fine, he was safe. I didn't believe it, and my magic reacted to my panic, ratcheting up its intensity more.

This spell was heinous. It slowly destroyed everything it touched, leaving the world with gaping holes in it as it moved and claimed more and more.

I saw it.

I saw Falcon trying to save Diego, then gently gazing back at me. I saw resignation on his face that his fate was cast in stone, as he quietly laid himself to rest in this horrible vacuum of magic.

I spun my flames until they were pointed arrows, barbed and poisonous, and shot them at the void-creating spell. My fear tangled with the magic–I couldn't lose him here, not like this. It didn't like it. It didn't like it *at all*. I shot more and more of them; the flame infused with my intentions, and I wanted that spell to die. The flames did the best they could to obey my desire for destruction. I shot more arrows as I danced through the fire until the spell spit some flowers back up. They were crumpled and the petals were worse for wear, but they were intact.

Come hell or high water–or me–Falcon would walk out of this shit even if I had to smoke him out.

Diego brawled with Arturo as the blackened alchemy continued its march. He needed this. I didn't know all of the gory details but for Diego to be moving with that level of fury, he *needed* this. I hoped it gave him the closure that he craved. I hoped it would lay his heart to rest.

He came along with me with little protest and I watched as Arturo's lifeless body was consumed by the spellwork.

"What is this?" I asked.

"It's Gravity," he said, his voice so quiet I almost didn't hear it.

"So it's like, what? Creating a void? Did you do this?"

"Yes, it's essentially a black hole."

More fire came from me, still desperate to give life to my emotions and frustrations. I felt like I was going to burn the rest of the world down, assuming Diego's magic didn't get there first. "I dropped the spell. I... I never should have cast it," Diego muttered out.

"Yeah, I'm picking up on that. Where's Jack? She's not–"

"No, she's not here. She's with my brother, Desmond."

"The facts just keep coming," I mumbled and Diego gave me a weak smile.

Gravity sputtered against the flames but didn't fully stop. I lobbed more fire at it just for the hell of it.

"Where is she then? Can't you communicate with her?" I must have said the wrong thing because tears welled up in his eyes and he turned to collect himself.

After he cleared his throat, he said, "I broke the heart links."

"How did you even– You know what? Doesn't matter. We need to get to Falcon."

"Mari–"

"Don't you say that he's gone. He would not just tap out like that. He wouldn't. You know that about him." I couldn't control the tone or how violently I let the fire blaze around me, but Diego took several steps back to avoid the flames.

"Nothing escapes from Gravity." He looked around at yet another mess that he created with those sad, sad eyes.

I slapped the shit out of him, as hard as I could but with as little heat. The sound echoed in this void-like canyon and he stared at me wide-eyed.

"You are going to fix this. I don't care how, but you are going to fix this. And I know you will because Jack believes in you. Falcon believes in you. And that's enough for me. Now get your ass up because we have shit to do. Falcon isn't going to save himself this time. Are you ready to clean up your mess?"

I cooled the fire as much as I could; my body wasn't actively on fire and that was a start. His eyes were hard and cold, I liked that look much better. This was a man ready to work.

"I know you've got a bum heart, but *we* are not going to let Gravity destroy Obius. My fire seems to help. I'm going to burn this spell down. I need you to grab Falcon when we see him."

"If he was taken by Gravity, he's gone, Mari."

The inferno of Wildfire built in my hand and I placed it on the ground. The black goopy magic practically evaporated and Diego's mouth hung open.

"Holy magic versus kingly magic. Checkmate. Now be ready to go get your man."

Diego nodded, the spark of life coming back to his eyes, and the spark of his magic coming back too.

FALCON

Being lost in a void, full of literally nothing, was a lot colder and danker than I expected. I wasn't really expecting to feel anything, considering being pulled into a vacuum of non-existence seemed a lot like death. I was ready for it; I said my prayers, I made my peace, but I should have known better than to expect things to be that straightforward for me, even my own death.

Time seemed like a very nebulous thing on Earth, but here it was worse. I had no idea how long I'd been here or how long I would be conscious. My body didn't feel like it existed, but I was able to *think* about it, and that was equal parts terrifying and nice. At least I couldn't feel my damn ribs anymore.

But then there was *heat*. Everything–nothing?–around me heated up like I was suddenly tossed in boiling water. I still couldn't feel my body but I felt the heat creeping through my thoughts like I was suddenly too aware that my thoughts were sweating.

The absence of light faded and light flooded in. My eyes–physical ones, I was pretty sure–burned from the intensity until there was nothing but light to look at.

That's when I realized that I still had a physical body, and all of the pain came rushing back like someone had broken the dam on physicality. No bueno feels there.

A man's head came into focus. Dark, curly hair that desperately needed to be brushed. The charcoal scent of a world on fire.

I saw her eyes before I could see anything else. Mari's eyes were full of flames, burning purple and white, blazing with Wildfire. Diego's head and mass of hair was right next to her. They both threw their arms around me and I winced. It hurt. My body was fucked up, and I was not excited about standing. I wasn't sure I *could* stand, which meant that they were either going to: A. use a shitty healing spell on me because both of them sucked at it, or B. Diego was going to *carry me*, and dying might actually be preferential to both of those.

"I've got you," Diego said, helping me to my feet. I could feel them, and that was definitely not an improvement.

"Nice to see you too, buddy."

"Falcon, can you walk?" Mari asked. It was hard to judge how she felt when her eyes were full of fire, but I heard the care in her voice.

"We're about to find out." Diego looped his arm around my shoulders and hoisted me up. He let go for a second to see if I was steady enough to stand. I wobbled but didn't fall.

"We need to keep moving," Mari said.

Lightning crackled through the sky and my blood ran cold. I don't know if I'd ever be able to look at lightning without panicking, but today wasn't the day. It was Jack's magic, beyond a shadow of a doubt. The waning sunlight was replaced by the flashes of her magic. It cracked like a whip; lacing through the sky like the veins of a leaf and spreading out endlessly, just like it had on my arms and chest.

"What the hell is that?" Mari asked.

"Lightning," Diego and I said in unison.

He turned to me and glanced at my arms. They were still covered in my own leafy, veiny scars from tangling with Lightning. Without the haze of his magic, my nerves were buzzing back to life, pain searing through each nerve ending.

"That can't be good," I said, and Mari took off running again.

I held my side, prayed that I wouldn't puncture a lung, and took off after her. Diego loomed right next to me, eyes hard and sad. He had, undoubtedly, fucked up again. The bolts raced across the sky like she frantically sought for something. Even the air was electric, and it made me *jumpy*. My body responded to every demand of movement too quickly and with too much strength, like a foal learning to walk. I was clumsy but fast, my legs jerking under me instead of propelling me forward with grace.

"You okay?" he asked.

"Absolutely not, but that doesn't matter now."

Diego nodded once, watching the Lightning. It was mesmerizing in a terrifying way. I felt sick watching the bolts scatter.

Diego watched the world turning black, the sky lighting up with electricity, and everything else covered in fire. I watched the planes of his face and studied the sadness that overwhelmed my friend.

"You aren't facing this alone this time, D. I feel like you haven't realized that these women can move mountains and rewrite history." I clapped his shoulder and pointed at Mari as she cascaded fire all around her like she was made of napalm.

His eyes were glistening and teary; so I stopped running. My ribs needed the break, and Diego was about to break. I wrapped him in my arms, hugging him as tight to me as I could without blacking out from pain.

"You're not alone, D. Not anymore."

"I really messed up this time. I never should have used Gravity," he whispered.

I rubbed the back of his head, trying to straighten the mess of curls that hung from his head.

"Not your best work, that's for sure. Like, top-notch magic though–this shit is positively terrifying."

"You're the worst," he said, a tiny, almost laugh forming.

"Yep, which means you can't be. So now you gotta go see her. You gotta make this right," I said, vaguely gesturing at everything.

"I will."

Another crack of Lightning made us pick up the pace. Mari stopped at the edge of a lake, with Jack not fifty feet away. The blaze slowed and the Lightning lit up the sky; Jack fully on display. She trembled as she worked her magic. The Lightning made me break out into a cold sweat. It was too close, too soon to be near it. Every fiber of my being rejected being this close to Lightning. It raged in the sky and I tried my best not to collapse.

Diego stood at the top of the small hill to watch the scene—his body trembled too, but his fear wasn't the terrifying magic of his lover, but what would happen to her.

Gravity slowly encased the land. Jack held a Full Circle with her staff, Lightning storming and threatening to strike at will. My hands were clammy and I rooted myself in place. She was lost to the magic, I could tell from here; her eyes were neon green, so bright I could hardly look in her direction. Another man with the same blue feathers that Diego had nearby with a cat-like woman watched her too. Their eyes were glued to Jack, just like the rest of us.

I knew what Diego was about to do—the same stupid thing I'd be doing.

Diego broke into a run, charging right at the circle, right for her. I'd never been so proud of him. Broken heart or not, he was complete and alive and I shouted for him to run faster.

Nana hovered over the Gravity-filled ground, staring Jack down like there was nothing else in the world for her to look at. My heart dropped when I realized Mari wasn't looking at Jack, she was looking *through* her, right at Nana. And Nana didn't even notice her.

I was left alone at the top of the hill, watching Gravity, Lightning, and Wildfire threaten to tear the world apart just from the sheer amount of power coming from them. I slipped my shoes off, letting my feet feel the dampness of the dew and mud, grounding myself in the earthiness of Obius.

Nana picked up my presence then; she spared a glance my way and I held up a pair of deuces. I saw the toothless-granny smile that I'd come to know as home, even in the distance.

Then I lifted a boulder, as much as my strained shoulders could tolerate, and lobbed it right at her.

CHAPTER EIGHTEEN

JACK

I felt the link between Diego and me crumble like it was made of dust instead of iron-clad magic. It wasn't the same spell he used to shatter the link between the realms. I knew what that felt like, and how it seemed to make every seam in your body start to quake. This was different. This magic unraveled the knot like it was a slipknot, it faded. The charm bracelet on my wrist moved too freely, up and down because it was no longer bound in place.

But now wasn't the time to grieve–and what was I grieving, exactly? Was he saying goodbye? Letting go of me? Doing something stupid because he thought he was being valiant? He still owed me an explanation. He needed to speak the words into existence and explain why he broke another link.

But now wasn't the time for that conversation.

My staff rocked back and forth, Lightning building and building in the crystal. Harold already had a Full Circle erected, and its magic embraced me like a hug. It felt like Mari was standing with me, like I wasn't fully alone in this circle with no link to Diego or anyone else.

I was untethered, and the pull of the Seer's magic was calling me to give in.

Abuela–*the Seer*–stood in front of me, everything about her horribly, intensely neutral. Her words called for me to give in to the current of magic.

It was tempting–the release of the magic, letting it follow directions eons older than I'd ever be. . I could just give in, let the magic sweep me and everything else away, but I knew that wasn't how this ended.

The blackness, the nothingness of an eternal void was one option.

Life, restoring the forest, and putting a King back on the throne of Trellis was the other.

"Child, it's time to end this nonsense. It's time that you listened to the magic in your blood and listened to what I've written for you," Abuela said. She gave me a tiny, pitying smile, and I reached for her thoughts. I could never read her properly on Earth, but here in Obius, my magic expanded so much farther and was braver than it ever dared to be back home.

Her thoughts were a dark, old book with pages flipping so quickly that they were falling out. I tried to read them, but I knew what they all said. This was the end. Hard reset. Rest and death for everything living in Obius and Earth alike, with Sanctum opening its doors to find places of rest for every soul in existence.

Abuela's green magic grew thick in the air, making everything acrid and sour. Her magic manhandled the energy around her, trying to force the souls around her into submission. The pages of her great book were scattered in her mind, like she had torn the book apart and tossed the pages in the wind.

That's when I noticed the spell that was seeping into the land of Obius like an inky poison. It lurched forward inch by inch. I didn't want to look away from it, like if I averted my gaze it would swallow me up whole too.

The hair raised on my arms and a familiar aura washed over me, stepping through my circle with ease. His golden magic and golden eyes were laser-focused on me despite the scene playing out, and I opened my arms to Diego. His breathing was ragged. His skin smelled of sweat and magic. Diego always smelled like the forest he came from, like sandalwood. I breathed him in and we stood there together for a beat. He pressed his forehead to mine and our skin stuck together.

I didn't need the heart link now to see the love in his eyes, the ask for forgiveness. His thoughts were loud too and I couldn't shut them off even if I tried.

They came through too quickly, some not even in a language I knew. Our fingers brushed until we had woven them together, the heat of his palm running through my entire arm.

"I'm sorry," he started but I shushed him.

"Later," I said.

A Lightning storm spilled from Harold, and I lost my grip on the staff as it crumbled in my hands. The crystal bounced in the dirt until the thread-like ties that kept it in place were shattered too. Diego bent to pick it up but then stopped short.

The Lightning reacted to the closeness of his hand, arcing and racing toward the edges of the crystal, wanting to get a better look at the Fallen King. He slowly, *slowly* picked up the crystal. Nothing happened to him. No magic, no blast of energy, nothing.

"This is yours, my Blossom."

It shone the gold of his magic back at me until I saw it lighting Diego up like a spotlight. He looked like a king then: regal and noble, like he had been taken right out of a fairy tale. Like he was meant to save the world instead of break it.

Harold floated over to me, resting in the air between us. There were thousands of souls in my hands but the only soul I wanted to see was

Diego's. He was so close in my circle, wrapped in my magic, with his eyes down.

"What do you need?" he asked, before taking a step back to allow my magic to breathe. The Lightning broke free from the crystal again but this time it just shimmered in a light show for whoever was left in Obius to see.

"You," I said, honestly leaving me breathless.

"YOU!" Abuela screamed, her magic another wave of rage to buffer against us, but Diego held his arms out trying to shield me from it.

"I'm here, I'm not leaving again," he whispered as the magic flew around us.

"Promise?"

"Try to keep me away," he said, tucking my hair behind my ears. It was a mess, flying around with the magic whipping it around. I saw the green of my eyes reflecting on him. Magic was pouring out of me in waterfalls, rushing and spilling everywhere.

"Of course, the Shatterer would return to stir up more chaos," Abuela said. She looked around at the spell devouring the world and tsked. Her lip curled as she looked at him, at us standing together in my circle.

"I didn't–"

"–mean to. You never do, Deign. Innocence dipped in blood, that's you, Deign, the great Fallen King of Trellis. You have the *gall* to challenge the Goddesses not once, but twice? You knew what falling in love with another Priestess would bring. Are you truly surprised by this? Everything started with your arrogance and now it ends with it."

Diego clenched his fists and held his tongue, but I couldn't. I wouldn't.

I got more and more flashes of the future and I knew that those were real. Diego in my home. Making coffee. Making the bed. Laughing with Mari; the kind of laugh that soaked through the room and lit it up. I saw Peony smiling and Mari glowing with the energy of a newborn star. I saw Falcon off to the side, trying to convince Diego to take one more job, it'll be a piece of cake, I swear. Sherwin making flower arrangements for Peony. Puddin bathing in the sunlight. I saw the years unfolding in front of us and it didn't feel like a wish but a promise.

"But it doesn't, Abuela. It doesn't end here," I said. I stepped outside of the protection of my circle and the wave of Diego's dark magic hit like a slap across the face. I didn't react. I wouldn't.

"Do you see what he's done yet again?"

The rage that flared in her made my stomach drop, but I stood my ground. I held the crystal in my hands, and I saw Snapdragon coming up to the edge. She was cheering me on, telling me to keep going.

"Nothing that can't be fixed."

"He's going to let Gravity have the ruins of the world that he destroyed. How could you *possibly* not see that with the magic I've given you?" Her anger took on a red, bloody aura. The air around her charged and full of wrath, waiting for a reason to unleash it.

"But Abuela, that's why I can see it. The visions I've seen aren't of endings." I glanced back at Diego and he gave me the barest hint of a smile. It reminded me of the day when he strolled into my shop, when my world changed forever. "All I see are beginnings."

"You're seeing what you want to see, because this damn king won't play the part he was born to! Always the special one, always standing apart from the crowd. We didn't bless him with the magic he has just for him to destroy everything!"

She lashed out then. Her magic was thick, red, and moving like a whip. She cracked it a few times on the ground, the lashings sending streams of magic across the ground. Diego was protected within my circle, but who knew for how long.

That's when I saw Mari, an incandescent and charging flame. She leaped in front of me, her eyes never leaving Abuela.

Abuela cracked the magical whip again, but Mari didn't move.

"Mari, stop, no—"

"How fucking dare you," she spat at Abuela. Fire leaked out of every pore. She was molten. Abuela lowered the spell but didn't look away.

"Marigold, this is not your time. You need to step aside."

"Never," she seethed. Mari's magic was going to explode; suddenly the fear of Gravity consuming the world seemed less of a threat than Mari blowing it up.

There was no ground left between us and Abuela. Gravity was tearing the land apart, and Abuela floated above, just out of reach. I stole a glance at Diego and even without our heart links, he seemed to know what I was going to do, and he shook his head, yelling *no*. Horror and fear blended into something repulsive on his face. Diego's golden eyes were dull from fear as his lips trembled trying to find the words to talk me out of it.

I took half a second to ground myself with Harold, my perfect, captivating crystal ball. "Keep me alive, okay?" I whispered and I stepped into Gravity.

For a second, my foot fell through, but I pulled myself back up. I hovered above it, just like Abuela was doing. She was shocked, genuinely shocked for about three seconds. I used that time to really look at what was becoming of Obius.

The lake was draining into Gravity like someone had pulled the plug in a swimming pool. There were water sprites there, swimming and struggling to get out of the reach of the magic. I saw Cat-folk climbing trees. I saw Trellian soldiers fleeing as quickly as they could.

I saw Diego suspended in my Full Circle, safe. Mari ready to explode on command. I saw Desmond and Puddin looking for a place to retreat. Desmond was casting a circle of some sort; something I'd never seen before; maybe one day, he could show me.

Then I felt the air shift and turned in time to see Falcon throwing the largest rock I'd ever seen. It was the size of a mountain. He tossed it like he was throwing away a balled-up receipt. Just as quickly as the boulder came flying at us, we all dodged.

It thudded against Gravity, large enough for the spell to need time to consume it, and until it had, Falcon had given me a firm place to stand on. He was on his knees, but I felt his energy surge; Falcon was okay. He would be okay.

"Never should have let that one out of his cage. Too much of my sisters in him. Falcon always needed a firmer hand," Abuela said. I thought back to his memories and how the undercurrent of every single one was loneliness. His sad, soft eyes that he had as a child grew into a hardened, fearless stare. Falcon marched toward death without so much as a grimace.

"How can you say that about him?" I asked. My heart broke for her, for him. How far had she fallen away from the people who loved her, even without knowing she was a Goddess?

"How can you defend him? He's the reason you're here."

I centered myself again with my crystal. I needed to remember the futures that I saw, not what she was saying.

"Falcon is easy to forgive. His heart is so full of love, I couldn't hold onto that hatred. I don't believe that fate is written in stone," I said. She blinked at me a couple of times without responding.

Her magic burned my lungs. Mari was cooling herself down, looking more like the woman I knew as my bestie instead of a pillar of fire.

"It's not, but it is written. And this," Abuela gestured to all of us, resignation draining what little emotion was left in her away, "was not written. This was not what I had written and it's time you all learned how to submit to your Goddesses."

Her magic was so frenzied on her sad, despondent face that I didn't even realize she was casting until I saw the sigils forming on the boulder and extending over Gravity's reach.

"What are you doing?"

"Jack, you would have been the best Priestess I'd ever called, but you chose not to follow the path that I gave you. You turned your back on who you were meant to be. And you were meant to close the doors on his ruined world, not try to open them again."

When she dropped another spell, it was a black arrow that had a red tip. She flung the bolt, turning away so she wouldn't have to watch the spell do its bidding. Magic dripped like acid off of the tip and she fired it right at Mari.

I didn't think. I didn't stop. I just jumped, pushing Mari out of the way, putting myself in the line of fire. The moment stretched out forever like when I was reaching through time, reaching through the worlds. Harold flew with me, absorbing the impact first.

The arrow hit my crystal, cracking its perfect sheen. The sound was deafening, and I didn't know if it was Harold or me that was breaking.

Some of the emerald magic leaked out; I scooped it up and held it to my chest. I cradled the broken pieces, still suspended in the magic. I thought of the souls caught in there and prayed that they were still safe.

"What–"

"Abuela, this isn't who you are. I know it isn't. Life isn't set in stone. We aren't made of stone. Your magic taught me that."

She paused. Diego had left the safety of my circle, leaping for the boulder that was slowly succumbing to Gravity. He threw his arms around me, checking for damage when he saw the crack in the crystal.

"Things can be rewritten. You said that the king and the priestess were destined to fall in love but couldn't be together. That happened. Diego and Snapdragon–" I looked at Diego before I continued, holding him in my gaze instead of Abuela. "But he isn't a king anymore."

Diego swallowed hard but didn't respond. It didn't look like he was even breathing. I touched his face and he remembered to take a breath. "Stay with me," I mouthed and he nodded. The saddest truth of them all was finally laid bare: Snapdragon saw the fall, saw the end of Deign's reign in Trellis, saw a world consumed with fire. She just didn't know that she was the one holding all the matches.

"Of course, he's a king. He will always be a king," Abuela said, but the heat of her words faded as her eyes landed on him. The more she studied Diego, the more she realized it. Diego wasn't a king. He was just a man who'd made every mistake possible and likely a few more.

"He was, once, but that was a long time ago." I prayed that Diego felt the gentleness in my words, that he saw what I was really trying to say. I prayed that *Diego* heard me instead of *Deign*.

"What say you, Deign? Shattered King?" Abuela's voice wavered–not even a full second, but it was *there*, she was hearing me. The crack in her resolve widened as she watched us. Abuela took in each of us, before gazing back at Diego. All at once she seemed like a tired, old woman. I wanted to comfort her just then–and she sensed something in me changing. The energy surrounding her shifted slowly, morphing from righteous fury to something softer. Something a lot like understanding.

"I say... My name is Diego Ortiz. I am no one's king." His shoulders drooped, but not from sadness. There was so much relief in his voice that my knees went weak. He ran a hand through his hair, bumping his horns again and Abuela took a few steps closer to him. His eyes were so golden, but more human than they had been before.

She grabbed his face, waved a sheen of magic across him, and I saw the tiny, frail light of his soul. It was fractured, but steady. It didn't flicker or fade. And then, she smiled.

"It's a lie and a truth. Diego. Deign. Whatever name you chose, you have the heart of a king, but now I can see the rest of your story unfolding. There is no place for you here, child. And you know that, don't you?"

He nodded once, silent.

"But he does have a place somewhere," I said, and they both looked at me.

"I do?" Diego asked, his voice barely a whisper.

"Of course you do, you dumbass. No wonder you and Falcon get along so well," Mari said, fighting down a smile. She angled herself toward me, forcing herself not to look in Abuela's direction. Her resolve was as strong as her flames, and I gave her a tiny smile. She had been quiet, focusing on keeping her flames down to a low ember. Abuela watched her too, like she was suddenly seeing Mari for who she was becoming.

"With me, on Earth," I said.

"But child, your place isn't there, either," she said to me.

The rightness of that flowed through me. I knew this wasn't my last time in Obius. I'd see the outline of every land, the halls of every castle, and knew the name of every soul that graced these magical plains.

"It's not, but luckily, I think we're getting better at building the links back."

Abuela laughed and it sounded like a memory, like when Mari would drag me to the crystal markets to look for her next greatest find, only for it to be a basket of empanadas. Mari felt it too, and she moved closer to me. The weight seemed to sag from Abuela too. She was softer, older, more like the grandmother we knew instead of the fierce Goddess she was. I felt the energy between Abuela and Mari, and I held Mari's overheated hands. She was sweating, clinging to me, and I didn't let her go.

"Oh Marigold," Abuela said, her voice finally, finally cracking. It was the first hint of remorse we'd seen, and Mari couldn't bear to look at her. I kept holding her hand like I'd been doing all our lives.

"She doesn't really look like a Marigold to me, but hey, who am I to talk? My mother thought Falcon would be a good name," he said. Falcon had hobbled his way over, using a trail of much smaller boulders as stepping stones through the field of Gravity.

"You two were the greatest blessings I ever had," Abuela said.

"How could you?" Mari sobbed, and Abuela moved lightning-fast, wrapping her in a hug.

"Because I wasn't looking for a story for you, my Marigold. I was just looking for an ending. Your mother would be so fiercely proud of you, don't you ever forget that."

Mari clung to Abuela and cried. The tears turned to steam before they truly fell, and Abuela rocked her in her arms, gently shushing her until Mari had cried herself out. Emotion was heavy in my throat, and I took in the scene. Mari hugged Abuela like she was saying goodbye.

"And you," Abuela said to Falcon, holding a hand out for him to take. "I asked my sister a thousand times what she was doing when she crafted you, and all she said was that she was making my greatest joy and my greatest challenge. Let me tell you, she was right."

"I'm not good at sappy moments," he said, blinking away a tear.

"Because your heart is too big. You always had that problem. Too much heart."

"So, what do you think? Is this how Obius ends?" I asked.

Gravity seeped closer and closer to us. It would be a matter of minutes before the safety of the boulder Falcon tossed would be completely enveloped.

"I think we need to clean this up and see what that baby brother of yours is capable of," she said, snapping her fingers causing Desmond and Puddin to appear next to Diego.

"How did–" Mari said before she was cut off with more laughter.

"Oh child, you don't think I've used every trick up my sleeve, have you?"

My crystal ball lowered itself in my hands, and I held it tight. The crack went deep, and I needed to convince all of the souls in there to stay put.

"Don't move," she said, and Abuela started to cast. Her eyes changed from brown to green to red to white, and she held up a hand.

Everything that Gravity touched was folding itself up, over and over again until the land was back to normal. Gravity kept folding and folding until it was the size of a hardback book. Rectangular and heavy instead of the liquidy mess that it had been. She wrapped another spell around it–some kind of binding spell, it felt just like Diego's magic–and a green ribbon was wrapped around it.

"Was that the same spell you used on the twisted soul back on Earth?" Mari asked.

"Yep," Falcon said.

"What the hell," Mari said.

"Containment ain't pretty," he replied.

"Will that hold?" Diego asked. It was the loudest he'd spoken in ages.

"Of course it will, I'm a Goddess. Do you think magic won't bend to my will?" She winked at him and held the black book easily. It made my skin crawl to look at it too closely.

I took a moment to look at the crew around me, and my heart lurched that Peony wasn't here. She should have been here to see this.

"Thank you," I said, and I bowed my head. I didn't know what the protocol was for talking to a Goddess, but I didn't have a barb at the ready. I didn't want to be thorny. My heart yearned for peace, and she seemed to sense that.

"Jack Hawthorne, Holy Priestess of Earth and Obius, hear me. You *are* my greatest Priestess, and I'm glad that I got out of my own way enough to see that. It turns out that even a Goddess's eyes can be clouded."

"What will you do now?" I asked.

Obius looked just as it did before Diego had cast Gravity. The Seer's Blessing came alive again, and I waded through to see the beauty of this land again. The shores of Chilijan were blue and sandy. Lake Ubbin sparkled with magic, and I saw Catfolk swimming. Trees were growing in Trellis, flowers sprouting. The world was surrounded by color, painted fresh and bright like an artist inspired by sunlight.

"I think it's time that I read the stories that I've written. Might need to add a few things here and there," Abuela laughed. She shook her head, our eyes meeting and she winked. Her green magic swirled at her feet, weaving together the tender threads of life and wrapping them in sigils of peace. She swayed her hips side to side, the magic rocking with her, enveloping everything around her in a tight embrace of magic.

"Will you go back to Earth?" Mari asked quickly.

"Perhaps eventually, but for now, no."

"I'll miss you," she said.

"Oh Marigold, your story is just beginning. I can see it now. You were crafted from my sister's eternal flame. There is much for you to do."

Diego kneeled before Abuela, head bowed as he spoke, "Thank you, my Goddess. I'm glad to see the teachings my mother instilled in me about the Goddess's grace were true."

"They weren't always true, and you know that better than anyone, Diego. Eyes up, child, eyes up. It should be me thanking all of you, not the other way around. Sometimes, even a Goddess can forget how the tides of time can change."

Falcon hugged her again, and she hugged him back. He had to let go first because she wasn't going to deny him now. Mari did the same. Both of them had their arms around her neck, their fingers interlocking as Abuela's powerful alchemy washed over them. Abuela used some healing spell to get Falcon back up on his feet, fully upright and healed the broken bones. I watched as the spell worked into his body, stitching and lacing through every wound. Falcon was so battered, and Abuela held him like he was made of glass. She left the scars on his arms, though.

"Sometimes, you're hard-headed and you need to remember who you are. I love you all," she said, and with that, she left.

DIEGO

The Goddess of Vision and Time boxed up all of my messes and took them with her. She left quickly, saying kind goodbyes to Jack, Mari, and Falcon. She had no kind words left for me, and I thought that was for the best. I bowed until I was on my knees as she took her leave with Desmond and Puddin kneeling with me. The Obius born knew to kneel before a Goddess.

Jack watched me, still kneeling, and I stayed there. She wasn't a Goddess, but I still owed her my respect. My eyes downcast, still bowed, still asking silently for her absolution. I'd broken yet another thing, and she needed to see that I was willing to atone.

"Diego?" she said, sitting in the dirt with me. Her dark green jumpsuit was going to be ruined. She didn't notice or seem to care. I desperately wanted to hold her, but I didn't. Not until she granted her permission.

"I feel like I'm constantly at your feet begging for forgiveness. Maybe one day I'll stop breaking things," I said.

There was the widest grin on her face before she laughed. Her magic was calming some, and the hazel of her eyes was returning. I missed seeing them that color.

"Then maybe, you should come *talk to me* before you do something drastic."

"D? Not dramatic? Not likely," Falcon said, also grinning.

"Yeah, I don't see that happening. He's had like literally a thousand years to outgrow that shit," Mari said.

"Agreed, brother. We haven't known each other long, but you don't really seem to be... excellent with your communication," Desmond chimed in. He stood and stretched, about a foot away from us. Looking at him was like looking in the mirror of my past self. He had so much life in his eyes. Desmond looked like the future, and that was exactly what we all needed.

"Eyes up, child, eyes up. Eyes on her," the Seer's words replayed in my head.

"I shouldn't have broken the heart links, Jack. I didn't want you to see what I was going to do. I didn't want you to hear in my thoughts, or feel it as I cast Gravity. I didn't want it to get out of my control, but–"

"–it did," she said. The sweetness in her stemmed from who she was and not who the magic made her be.

My throat tightened just looking at her. I pushed a lock of hair behind her ear just to have an excuse to caress her face. Her skin was silky soft, and I wrapped my hands around her face fully. My thumbs smoothed over the angled planes of her face, across the smattering of freckles there.

"I didn't want you to be bound to me without your permission, either. I know that wasn't the intent when we put them on, but a heart link should be given in love. The next heart links we have will be made by my own hands."

"Maybe we can make them together," she said, pulling my hands to her lips. Jack pressed a kiss to each of my knuckles, and the tension seeped out of me. The heart link was shattered, but *this* wasn't. Whatever the future held for us, it would be for *us* together. Puddin touched her shoulder and wrapped her tail around Jack, bringing her back to everyone.

"Oh, Mari and Falcon haven't met Desmond. And this is Puddin. I mean, Bastet. That's her name in Obius," Jack said, quickly making introductions.

"Never would have guessed you two were related," Falcon deadpanned. Everyone laughed. There was a lightness to these people and I loved every one of them. My heart was full of love, and that was itself its own kind of magic.

"Puddin? You look a little different," Mari said.

"Perceptive, that one," she purred, and before Mari could say anything else, Puddin had her in a hug, tail wrapped around them like she had with Jack just moments ago.

Jack stood up and opened her hand for me to take. The crystal ball floated up even though it was cracked and she palmed it. Those hazel eyes were locked on me and I felt the blush staining my cheeks. She never looked away, and neither did I. I drank this moment in, bound by love instead of magic. Jack placed her hand on my chest, feeling the awkward heartbeat.

"I never meant to pry, Diego. The magic is hard to turn off, and I knew I was digging too deep through your thoughts. Just because I am a psychic doesn't mean I have to tap into that magic flow all the time. I took your privacy from you, and I'm sorry."

"Thank you, my Blossom, but you don't need to apologize."

"Yes, I do, but I'm glad you're so forgiving," she said, leaning against my chest.

"I'm glad you are too, I seem to mess up quite often."

Jack leaned back, a smirk forming on her lips, Lightning dancing in her eyes, "Who says you're forgiven?"

"Ah, I see, I overstepped. Please forgive me, my Blossom," I said, bowing deep at the waist until I heard the laughter bubble up in her chest. I seized her by the hips and lifted, until she was giggling, beaming back at me.

With Jack gathered in my arms, my friends at my side, and a future laid out for Trellis, peace settled in my heart until it spread out through all of my limbs. There was a heaviness to it, like my body had forgotten what it meant to be at ease instead of holding the world's burdens again. She patted my shoulder for me to put her down, but I lingered. I held her in the air like a victory cry until she beamed.

"He really is quite dramatic," Desmond whispered to Falcon who barked out a laugh.

"Oh, I like this one. He's literally a younger you," Falcon clapped Desmond on the back, and no one missed the half-second of shock on his face before he schooled it. Mother taught him well.

"To Trellis!" he cried, pumping a fist in the air, and that's when I saw him as the King he would be. Proud and strong, but not quite so bullheaded. He listened. I watched him as he spoke with the people of Chilijan, how he hung on every word that Jack said, and seeing him now with victory on his lips, this was exactly who Trellis needed.

There were Trellian banners still flying around us, battered and old, likely not brought out since before the Shattering. Trellis Castle and the city center of Treis were still a few days out. We could really push it and get back in two days, but the travel would be exhausting. The outer borders of Chilijan were a mess, but at least the bridges still stood. When the Seer removed Gravity, she put most things back to how they were before. The big things. Bridges. Houses. Lives.

"You okay?" Jack asked. She bumped my shoulder and I wrapped my arm around her.

"I'm great, actually."

"Is that so?"

"Well, I know one thing that would make this moment better," I said as I tipped her chin back to kiss her.

She still smelled like jasmine and mint, the soft scent of the sweet lilies mixed with sweat in her hair. Her breath hitched as she wrapped her arms around my neck. Jack closed the gap between us as she deepened the kiss, and this time I was breathless. Our foreheads pressed together and love reflected in her eyes as much as brilliantly as the Seer's Blessing ever had.

Falcon whooped in the background behind us, with the rest of our friends–our *family*–cheering with him.

I had the universe in my arms, and I was never letting go.

Chapter Nineteen

PEONY

I wasn't normally one to brag, but let me just say, *brilliant* was the only word to really captivate what I was in that moment. Totally fucking brilliant.

Mama alternated between sobbing and screaming, hanging on me, then Sherwin, then back again, until I had to de-escalate the situation before I killed her. Metaphorically. So I gave her a sedative.

But that was only the first part of my brilliance.

Figuring out what the sigils carved in every open surface of the log cabin that Abuela was holed up in? That was the second part.

The third part, the *best* part, was that I realized Sherwin could read them. Which meant that I had a spellbook. I had the directions and the magical mojo to open a link to Obius.

"You really think this is going to work?" Sherwin said. He was drawing a circle made of salt.

I didn't usually draw physical circles, and using salt was a little tacky, but we needed something tried and true, solid. Salt was both.

"Of course, it's going to work," I said, assuring myself. I was on my fourth antacid in the last hour, but that didn't matter, because I was going to bring everyone home, even if I have to drag each of them by their ears.

"I feel ridiculous," Sherwin muttered but didn't say anything else. In all fairness, he did look ridiculous. I covered him in leaves, taping each one to his body until he looked enough like he was "made of the Earth." Because he wasn't, he was made of Obius, but I needed an anchor that wasn't a sobbing mess.

So, Earth anchor: check.

Salt circle: check.

Freshwater pearl necklace imbued with years of magic and now traces of Goddess blood: check.

Abuela really shouldn't leave her bloody scrying bowls out and about. It had to be Goddess blood; it was green. Emerald green. Nothing on Earth bleeds that color.

The necklace was too *wet* against my skin, but I didn't focus on that. I focused on fusing this portal open. I focused on opening a link. I focused on Jack and Mari, who were absolutely getting into shit they shouldn't be.

It was going to work. It *had* to work. Sherwin read the words and they were the same ones that Jack had cast before in her shop before things all went to hell in a handbasket. She could do the spell because she was a Priestess, but I was just a human covered in Goddess blood. That had to count for something.

And then I read the words of the spell.

Holy Goddesses,

Creation, Judgment, and Vision,

The brokenness in front of me needs to mend,

To join joyously, righteously, and with precision,

Tie together the ends that frayed,

Tie together the paths mislaid.

The room began to shake, but the salt circle stayed in place. Sherwin quickly stepped out of the circle and next to me.

The light in the circle was blinding. Green, gold, and silver all mixed together, weaving together like the threads on a loom inside the circle. They were tying themselves together, working and weaving until each seam was flawless.

A doorway formed where the threads once were and my pulse picked up so much, I thought I was going to have a heart attack right there. Sherwin and I squeezed each other's hands, practically bouncing in place.

"Is that–"

"A doorway," I shouted, jumping up and down. It worked! It worked! *It worked!* The door was solid, the link was rebuilt. It was one tiny thread but it was a *start*.

Mama came to at that point, probably from all the shouting, and stood there, mouth open. "How did you–"

"It's amazing what can happen when someone actually reads the damn instructions," I said, victory and antacids sweet yet chalky on my lips.

"Peony Hawthorne, you are a force to be reckoned with. You're brilliant," Sherwin said.

I winked at him and said, "Damn right I am. Let's bring them home. Mama, are you coming this time?"

She grabbed my hand, then reached for Sherwin's. Her magic was back, surging and reacting to the force of the doorway as she beamed, bright eyes, alchemy swirling in the air around her.

"Lead the way, darling."

The handle was wooden and ancient. The door was something that should have been in a castle or a museum. There were sigils around the perimeter with the crest of each Goddess in the center of it.

I turned the carved handle and opened the door.

Chapter Twenty

JACK

It took us more than a week to get back to Trellis proper. Desmond and Diego needed to stop and chat with every person we met along the way. I saw them spending more time together now too. Diego and Desmond would pass the afternoons together, sitting under a tree, talking and laughing. They both laughed so easily now. It warmed me to think of all the memories and wisdom and moments they got to share. The road to Trellis would never be a trail laced with sadness for them now, and it gave Desmond more fortitude to take up the mantle of being king.

Diego seemed lighter than he ever had been, even in the visions of his past. The burden of Obius had been lifted from him and even with a fractured heart, he was more alive than ever. Diego and Desmond played together, verbally sparring and sometimes with magic. Desmond smiled a lot easier now; maybe he needed to hear Diego give up his claim to Obius too.

Falcon and Mari walked side by side, the sparks coming from them all from chemistry, and none from magic. I politely tried to keep their thoughts to myself, but I heard tidbits flying between them.

Puddin wanted to stay another night in Chilijan, with the Catfolk, to make sure that the bridges from Trellis to Chilijan were structurally sound. She frolicked in the water, jumped off the bridges, and climbed the trees. It had been too long since she got to be her true self and I didn't want to rush a second of it.

I wasn't ready to go back to Earth, to the world that I knew, any sooner than I had to. It would be easy to just disappear into the forests of Trellis or the waters of Chilijan, or the lands beyond, but Earth was my home. It was home for all of us now, even Puddin. But in my heart of hearts, in the secret parts that I'd kept for only me, I knew that I would miss Obius fiercely. I'd miss the smell of the forest and the flow of magic, but mostly I'd miss walking through a world that I felt was made for me.

Mari found a small tote bag for me to carry Harold in. The crack hadn't gotten any worse, but I wrapped it in a silk scarf from one of the many people we met along the way.

Maybe it was just the tranquility in the air that settled everyone's nerves except mine.

I knew we were approaching the Rainbow Forest. It was still going to be in ruins and the camaraderie that we had here couldn't last walking through it. Diego would break all over again, and knowing that hurt as much as knowing what destruction lay ahead.

"Priestess, can you still hear me?" Snapdragon's voice was sweet, timid. Very different from the raging woman I'd met. The sound of her voice was featherlight in my mind, and I listened to her carefully.

"Yes," I responded silently. She didn't need to hear me speak to hear my words.

"You know that it's a Priestess' calling to lay souls to rest, yes?"

"Yes, but the links to Sanctum are still broken. I can't–"

"This forest needs rest too, Priestess. Wildfire was so beastly. I... I can't believe I did this." The sorrow in her words made my chest ache. All that was left of her was regret.

"You weren't exactly yourself when this happened," I said, trying to comfort her.

"No, Priestess, I think I was exactly who I was when I unleashed it."

Diego took that moment to grasp my hand and stand in front of me, concern etched in his warm features. Everything about him was warmer now. The weight of no longer having to wear a crown made every step and breath of us lighter. Being just a man, just a person, was what Diego needed more than fixing the rest of his heart.

He pulled me close, trying to be a physical barrier between me and the forest. When his hand brushed the bare skin of my arms or hands, or even when he reached for my face, I felt safe in a way that no magic could contend with. I'd held a Full Circle on my own, alight with the Seer's Blessing to guide my steps, but standing in the circle of his arms was where I knew no harm would ever come to me.

"Jack, the forest is just up ahead."

"I know." I held the citrine pendant and reached for the comfort of home, of Earth. I felt the despair from the forest soak in and took a step closer to Diego. He tightened his grip, holding me steady. Maybe it was my heart that would break this time.

"The castle is at the edge of the forest," he said. The tree sentinels that guarded us when I finally faced Snapdragon were back, slowly moving through the desecrated woods. Even that seemed like ages ago. They followed us, forming two barriers between us and the worst of the destruction.

Priessstessss, Priessstessss, Priessstessss
We will protect you
Priessstessss, Priessstessss, Priessstessss

Bring the King home

Priessstessss, Priessstessss, Priessstessss

Lay your regretssss to ressst too

"What's going on with these trees?" Falcon asked.

"They're the tree sentinels of Trellis. Armored guards for the kingdom. I used to play at their roots when I was a kitten," Puddin said. She climbed up on one of the sentinel's trunks and it changed its shape to allow her a place to lay. I caught little flashes of her as a child; the fur on her ears was still cottony and fuzzy. She batted at the leaves and the sentinels would move their branches for her to chase.

"They love the people of Obius." Puddin's words were all purrs.

We love all peoplessss

"I've heard the stories of the tree sentinels, but I've never met them," Desmond said. He reached, touching the bark of the sentinel closest to him, and the bark changed from its reddish-orange to a dark, cerulean blue.

Hello your Majesssty

We have waited for you

Welcome, welcome

The King issss home

You're home

Their soft sighs breezed through the winds and their branches, making their voices twist in the wind. Each word caressed the sides of my face like a mother soothing their babies.

"Yes, he's home," Diego said, the light in his eyes shining as he looked at Desmond.

Desmond had finally agreed to stop wearing long-sleeved shirts. Diego talked him into it, explaining how it was bad for his feathers and how the people would love to see them. It made him a King, and it made their connection more real. Desmond changed the next day after that chat.

Mari looped her arm through mine. She'd gotten the fire to calm enough that standing next to her didn't make me sweat, so that was progress. Wildfire was still trapped in her body, but that was going to be a problem for another day. She was in no rush, and as long she wasn't hurting or blowing anything up, I didn't have the stamina to fight it.

"You holding up?" she asked.

"Yes. No? Something isn't right, Mari. I feel like I need to do something, and I'm just not sure what it is," I said. Being surrounded by the tree sentinels made that nagging feeling itch inside my head and I couldn't shake it.

"Jack?" Diego said when he noticed that I wasn't present with them. The Seer's Blessing stirred in my chest; the magic spread out through my body, and I waited. The magic would guide me. I just had to listen.

"Trees, show me the forest. Please," I said, resting my head against the trunk of another sentinel.

It'ssss not easssy to look at, Priessssstessss

"No, it's not, but I need to see it."

The tree sentinels sighed their agreement, uprooting themselves and moving quickly to form a protective semi-circle behind us.

The Rainbow Forest stood in front of us, burned and charred, just as I remembered. Thick clouds of smoke still hung in the air, trapped here just like the charred remains of the trees. The color was drained completely so everything was dark brown, black, and ashen. I watched as branches broke upon themselves, the weight of the dead limbs finally forcing them to snap. The life that echoed through Chilijan and the idyllic peace of River Glades was nowhere to be found. The Rainbow Forest looked like death. It looked like an ending, and I knew that it wasn't the *right* ending.

"It never gets easier to look at," Falcon murmured.

Green, green magic flared up in me and I breathed it in. Harold had floated out of my bag, hovering at eye level, and for a second I saw Snapdragon's face before the Shattering. She was leafy green and smiling.

The crack in the crystal was getting larger as I got flashes of the spell. The words came back to me like a song I'd never forget, the beat and the lyrics etched into me when I was first crafted.

I slipped off my shoes, needing to touch the forest floor. I needed to connect with it as much as I could, drinking in the sorrow of the forest.

I heard the cries of the forest as it burned, felt the leaves as they went up in flames, and as the bark turned to ash. I felt the trunks cracking from the dead weight of their canopies and I let it all wash over me.

"Stand back," I said as Mari tried to come to me.

"Jackie, what're you doing?"

"What I should have done when I got here."

My staff had shattered when Abuela was casting her angry magic, and Harold took a bad hit. The crack was rough to the touch, and even though it was alive with the Seer magic, I saw the fracture deepening.

I called the magic to my four directions, letting small globes of green light form around me. Rightness, fullness, magic all hummed through me. I felt it from the crown of my head down through my fingertips, to my toes that were buried in the ashen soil. Harold floated right in front of me, and I smiled at Snapdragon's image. She looked so young, so innocent. It was a time before the Seer's magic had weighed her down and crushed her so completely.

A circle snapped into place around me, connecting through my green globes. Diego caught my eye and nodded. He'd seen this spell many, many times before.

I danced through it, letting the ceremony of this ancient alchemy shine. This was a time for tradition.

I was going to lay the entire forest to rest, starting with Snapdragon.

Palms up, eyes up, heart open, I let the words flow through me.

"Rest, be at peace."

Snapdragon's fragile spirit came out of the broken crystal. Emerald green and beautiful. I held her in my hands and motioned for Diego to come closer.

"Return to the forest to be born again."

Diego stepped into the circle and the magic welcomed him, wrapping around him like a hug, holding him steady as I laid Snapdragon to rest.

Her green soul buried itself in the dirt, and a green stem bloomed in the ashes. She would be born again, here in Obius, and get a fresh start. A new life. One without the Seer's Blessing on her shoulders.

"Jack–"

"She's going to be okay," I said.

Diego hugged me and knelt at the small stem. It was so small, so vividly green. Diego barely touched the tender plant and it wiggled from the contact. The stem poked out of the ground a little more, and I heard Diego leaning in to whisper goodbye. I heard the prayer on his lips, praying for her to have a full, beautiful life filled with simple, easy joys and no storm clouds. I added my own *amen*.

"Will she remember anything?"

Snapdragon's child-like face shone brightly in my mind and I watched as she ran through a fully blooming forest. Flowers hung off of all of the branches and she plucked a few sweet lilies for her vines.

"No, she won't. She won't know who she was, and no one else will know either. I can't lay her to rest in Sanctum, but I can do this."

Priessstessss, Priessstessss, Priessstessss

You are so kind

Our foresssst livessss becaussse of you

Diego kissed my forehead, holding me close to him as the words tumbled out, hushed and reverent. "Keep going, my Blossom."

He retreated from the circle, giving me the space I needed to work. I ground myself in the dirt again, saying my goodbyes to the soft stem of what would become Snapdragon before I continued.

I swirled through the magic, kicking it up, raising all of the souls from my crystal ball until they floated around me. There were over a thousand of them, and I saw flashes of each soul that had perished in Wildfire. The world was fully green around me; magic shimmering the light from the souls. They were rainbow, just like the forest, and I tried to touch each and every one that surrounded me. They pooled in my hands, around my arms, embracing me like a hug. Harold floated with me, and as I moved, I ascended with the magic. Harold joined my dance, the crack getting deeper and deeper until it split open completely. The halves of the crystal started to fall, but the souls cradled it until I held both halves. As I moved with Harold, I made sure I drew out each and every soul in there.

"Rest, be at peace. Return to the forest to be born again."

My magic wrapped around every soul orb as they floated like star lights around us. I dropped the circle, letting them fan out and flow through the forest, finding a place for them to take root and grow again.

The land slowly changed from bleak grayness to joyful green. It was the color of life. Trunks started to sprout along with little stems and flower blooms. Crops of sprites and pixies rolled in the warmed-up soil, steadily waking and rising. The charred remains of the trees were enveloped by the souls reincarnating around them; the Rainbow Forest was glowing with color again, as more and more of the souls reminded them how they should be. The magic filled every lifeless cranny until all evidence of Wildfire had been erased.

The forest was small, but it was alive again. Green.

"Priestess, how did you..." Desmond's words trailed off. Everyone walked through the fledgling forest, but I kept the magic going.

Color slowly came back to each of the trees, until the rainbow was reflected through them again. Red, orange, and yellow trunks. Greens and blues and purples racing through the branches and down the leaves. The trees glittered. Energy crackled and buzzed in the air as more and more Fae folk came out of their homes, looking at the trees.

I kept dancing through the magic. There were still more souls to be laid to rest, so I didn't stop. "Rest, be at peace. Return to the forest to be born again," I cast again, and more magic poured out of me.

Thousands of flashes came to me. I saw the trees growing like skyscrapers and children playing. I saw families being born and coming together. Festivals. Desmond walked through the forest and people cheered. I saw the markets in Treis, full of energy.

My muscles burned from exertion but I kept going.

This was what I was born to do. As I moved through the resting spell, I saw my own life being written out, listening to the Goddesses as they bickered, deciding what to put where. I saw Abuela closing the book and winking at me in my mind's eye.

So I danced more until the crystal cracked into four pieces now.

The suns had set, but today they set on a newborn forest, instead of a dead one.

"You're exquisite," Diego said to me as I finally stopped the spell.

The forest was blooming, trees had risen from the ashes, and there was life all around us.

"Just doing my job," I said, smiling. I was exhausted but too amped to rest.

"Your crystal isn't doing so hot," Falcon said. He scooped up one of the pieces and handed it to me. Harold had shattered into several pieces, some of the crystal crushed and powdery from the magic.

"Yeah," I said, allowing a quiet moment for it. I'd bought this thing online so many years ago and layered it with the magic of everyone I loved.

It was a part of me. I placed all of the pieces I could find in my bag, laying the silk scarf with it. It wouldn't be much use to me as a crystal ball back in my shop, *Visions and Trinkets*, when I finally made it home, but I refused to leave it here.

"Jack, look, the castle is just up ahead," Puddin said.

"You guys go ahead. I'm sure Desmond is going to have to sweet talk his way in and through the halls."

"You aren't coming?" Mari asked.

"I am, I just need a minute?"

"I'll stay with her," Diego said.

It took a while to convince everyone that it was okay to keep going, that we would be right there, but finally, they left. I wanted to stay in the forest and breathe it in. The smoky, burnt smell was gone. Everything smelled of greenery and pine.

"Are you okay, my Blossom?"

"Yeah, I just," a lump formed in my throat and I tried to swallow it down. I couldn't. "I'm not ready to say goodbye."

"My love, you aren't going to say goodbye. Obius flows in your veins now. This is your home as much as Earth is. You don't have to say goodbye."

"Are you coming back with me? You're not going to stay in Obius are you?" I was clinging to him; for every future that I could see, my own was still a mystery.

"Obius was once my home, but it is no longer."

"It's not?" I looked at the forest around me, wondering how he could say that, with the beauty of the forest coming back to life. He placed his hands on my face, playfulness in the corners of his lips.

"Jack, *you* are my home. Wherever you go, I'll follow. For as long as you'll have me. You brought me to life just like this forest. You showed me what living could be like again. I love you in every realm, every universe. I love you to the depth of your star lights and beyond. You're my home."

"I love you too," I said and threw myself into his arms.

His feathers splayed out, fanning over me and tickling my skin. My heart raced as he held me, and I let the tears finally come. Diego smoothed the back of my hair, comfort seeping in through every touch.

"I want to show you my rooms in the castle. I want you to take you to bed and keep you warm." He nuzzled the side of my face, my ear, my hair, until he managed his way back to my lips. Soft, sweet, tender–Diego kissed me like there had never been a dark day in his life, like every sunset was the promise of a sweeter tomorrow. His lips were full and warm, and I knew that I was home too.

"Lead the way."

Diego scooped me up and held me to his chest. Being off of my feet made me realize how much the magic had taken out of me, and I heard my stomach growl. I covered my face in my hands, groaning and laughing. Diego nipped at my lips, making me laugh more.

"Let's feed you first," he laughed as he carried me out of the forest and through the castle gates of Trellis.

DIEGO

Sunlight filtered through the windows of my old bedroom and splashed across Jack's bare form. She was tangled up in my bedding, hair down and splayed across the pillows. The sheet just barely covered the curve of her breast, and I stayed as still as I could so I didn't disturb her. We'd spent the night together, but this was different. The battles were done. The forest was healed. I was healed.

I spent the night making good on my promise to get to know every inch of her intimately. I replayed the image of her lifting her hair for me as I undid the laces of her gown, watching as it fell to the floor. The memory of how we connected first at the lips, then the hands, then deeper, closer than we'd ever been before was still fresh. She writhed and came alive under my touch and when we were both spent, I wrapped her tight in my arms, against my chest until her breathing slowed to sleep.

After she fell asleep and I could move without waking her, I went to work. Jack's crystal ball, Harold, wasn't the perfect globe that it was before, but it was back together. I used a few gold bangles from my mother's collection to fuse the pieces of the crystal. Now it had streams of gold lining its way through the crystal, but it was in one piece again. I loved the alchemy of jewelry making. It was an old art in Trellis, but it was my favorite. Usually a trade for the common folks, but I was determined to learn it. I wanted to craft gifts for my mother. Then for Snapdragon. Then the kingdom. Now finally for Jack. It was something I was good at, and instead of destroying things, I could create.

Jack stretched, reaching for me, and I rolled over in bed to accept her. She played with my feathers in her half-asleep state, scratching at the base until I trembled at the touch. The smile she tried to hide let me know she was actually awake.

"Good morning, my Blossom."

"Morning," she said sleepily, burying her face in the crook of my shoulder.

"Today's the day," I said, pulling the sheets up to cover her bare shoulders.

"Little late to be protecting my modesty, don't you think?" she said, stretching again and the sheet fell. I stole a glance and she laughed.

"You look... a tad cold," I said.

"You're here to keep me warm," she said sitting up. The sheets pooled around her waist and I rubbed my hands down her arms, my eyes staying locked on her face. Jack shook her head, smiling wide as the sunlight made her look radiant. I stole another glance at her chest, letting my eyes travel down to her waist and a little lower–

"Come here then," I said, opening my arms. Jack cuddled back down, her skin coming in full contact with mine. She mussed my hair before settling. She smelled like sleep and comfort, and I stayed very still, needing to memorize this moment too. Jack trailed her fingers across my chest, leaving goosebumps in their wake.

"Today is the day," she said.

"Do you think it'll go okay?"

"I think everyone is going to be excited that Desmond is here, and assuming he doesn't freak out, it'll go great."

The coronation was in a few hours, and the entire castle, the entire *kingdom* was buzzing. There was going to be a grand party with the gates thrown open, and people were already pouring in. The buzz of the castle was what woke me.

"I have a gift for you," I said. I was going to wait to give it to her later, but I couldn't.

Jack cocked her head, surprised. Being able to surprise a psychic felt like a feat. I padded out of bed and across the room to grab the package. I wrapped it up for her. Jack whistled and my cheeks turned pink, so I grabbed a pair of pants.

"Spoilsport," she laughed as I tugged them on.

"Open this," I said and handed her the gift. She pulled the sheets so they were tucked under her arms, and I immediately regretted putting my pants on. She winked at me, my thoughts clearly on display for her.

"What is it?"

"Aren't you supposed to be some kind of amazing psychic?" I said and she tossed the paper at me.

"Oh, he's got jokes now. I see how it is," Jack said as she opened the box. I saw the moment when she realized that it was Harold in the box, and I beamed at her. She picked up the crystal ball and examined it. Her eyes shone with tears but a grin spread across her face.

"Is this? How did you—"

"Alchemy," I said easily and she hugged it to her chest.

"It's perfect."

"It's not, but it's in one piece. You don't have to keep using it, but I didn't want it to stay shattered. This was something I could fix."

Jack's magic immediately responded to the crystal ball, and her eyes lit up emerald green before they returned to her perfect shade of hazel.

"I don't think I'll ever be able to thank you for this, Diego. Really."

"You don't need to thank me. I feel the same for how you've helped with my sunstones." My heart was pounding in my chest, reminding me that it was still broken but functional.

"Actually, I have something for you too," she said.

She unhooked the citrine pendant from her neck and came over to me. The pendant was pretty but not beautiful; the stone itself long and thin, with unsmoothed edges. She wore it all the time, and the heat from her body still clung to the gem. My heart thundered in my chest, excited for the magical boost and to have a piece of Jack with me again.

"I want you to have this. It's not the same as a heart link, but—"

I pulled Jack into my lap and kissed her. She fit in my arms, in my lap, against my chest like we were two halves of the same soul. She looped the necklace around my neck, and the pendant rested at the base of my throat.

"We might need to get you a longer chain," she said.

"I love it. I love you. I've made every mistake in the book and somehow the Goddesses still thought I deserved you."

"I think we made the choice. Fate isn't written in stone."

I kissed her again before she slid off my lap. "Come on, we need to get dressed. Somehow I think showing up to Desmond's coronation naked would not be appreciated."

"To each their own, I suppose."

She tossed a shirt at me and went into the connected bathing room to get ready.

I sat on my bed and looked at my quarters. I hadn't been back here in more than six hundred years, and everything was the same. It was my childhood room, not the one I moved into when I became a king. The paintings and tapestries on the walls were worn but still there. It took us a couple of days to get the castle cleaned back up, but with a little gumption and a lot of magic, it was back to its former glory. Magic was flowing freely in Obius. The links weren't open, but there was enough of Jack's magic in the forest for people to feel it again.

I got myself dressed too. My old robes still fit, but the weight of them felt awkward. No one wore capes and robes on Earth. I found myself missing my cashmere sweaters and jeans. Falcon always laughed at the cashmere, but it was the closest texture on Earth to the way that fabrics felt in Obius. How quickly feelings can change.

I felt like I was wearing a costume for a play instead of the robes of royalty. I studied all of the elaborate stitching and the fine details; vines and flowers and trees were stitched on the lapels of the robes. I saw Jack-in-the-pulpit flowers and it made my heart skip a beat. Jack had been with me all along.

I played with my shirt, adjusting the buttons as Jack came out of the bathing room. She wore an emerald green gown with gold filigree all over it that enhanced the natural color of Jack's eyes and set off the reds in her hair. Some of the air sprites made it for her, and it fit her perfectly. Her neck was bare without her citrine.

"I feel ridiculous," she said.

"You look gorgeous."

Jack had fully stepped into her own power, her own skin. All of the parts of her that reminded me of Snapdragon had faded; their eyes once seemed so similar now were worlds apart. I'd memorize every fleck in Jack's hazel eyes, and see her fully as herself.

"Really? It's not too much? It feels like a lot."

"No, it's perfect. Very fitting for a Priestess."

"Mari is going to be in a dress too, right?"

"She should be, yes."

"I feel less ridiculous then."

I snorted. "Maybe don't mention that to her. Last thing we need is for her to set the coronation party on fire."

"Fair," Jack laughed.

I adjusted the final few buttons, making sure the frilly shirt was appropriately fluffed. I felt ridiculous too. Trellian finery was always a bit much, but after being away from it for so long, it was a lot. I touched the Jack-in-the-pulpit again, smiling to myself, trying to remember how many times I'd worn these clothes and never noticed it there.

I took Jack's hand and placed another kiss on the back of it. I counted my blessings again that I got to do this, freely take hold of her and lay kisses on her for the world to see. I wasn't a king anymore. I didn't have to stay at an arm's distance and keep my heart under lock and key. I gave it all to her, and the world could watch.

"Ready for the party?" she asked.

"Yes," I said as we walked hand in hand, out into the Great Hall. The music picked up as we got closer and Jack's smile grew wider. I was free.

JACK

The coronation party was a *party*. People in Obius knew how to have fun, and as soon as Diego placed the gold and green crown on Desmond's head, settling it between his horns, the entire kingdom erupted into cheers.

Desmond was glowing. He couldn't stop smiling and neither could Atam. Atam had arrived the night before the coronation and stayed glued to Desmond's side. They were never far apart, and seeing how Desmond doted on him made me realize that the depths of love these Trellian men felt must have been genetic. Diego had the same look when he saw me, and it gave me goosebumps.

I also learned that Trellians loved a good party. The ceremony after the coronation was an introduction to the new royal family and soon-to-be Prince Below of Trellis, High Prince of Chilijan, Atam. Only time would tell how that would work out for the lines of succession, but something told me that Desmond and Atam would take it one day at a time and make decisions based on love. If only the Earth could be so lucky.

Diego snaked his hands around my waist, whispering the words of a Trellian love song in my ear, but translated.

"If the suns could shine so bright, you'd still be the only star I'd see, if the moon could smile on us, I'd still be the luckiest because I had you, I had you, I had you." His low, baritone hum sent a shiver down my spine. "In any realm, in any time, even if I broke into a thousand pieces, I'd be the luckiest if you held onto but a single one."

"Was this song written for you?" I asked.

"No, it was popular when I was a child. My father used to sing it to my mother. She hated it, actually. Too sappy, if you could believe it, coming from the woman that sang lullabies to grown men."

"I wish I had met her."

"I do too, but I'm sure she is here. I feel like she would have loved you."

"I hope so."

"Perhaps one day, I'll win your mother over."

"She's a softie. Don't let the threats fool you."

Diego laughed in my ear, placing a kiss at the top of it. "Ah, so Peony really is just like her."

"Too much so, but don't ever let her hear that."

"Let me hear what, exactly?" Peony was standing there, not three feet away, an arched eyebrow and a challenge on her lips. I was already turning to launch myself at her but Mari beat me to it, a healed Falcon trailing behind her.

"Peony! How– When did you– But the link–" I stammered.

"Yes, the link. It's open. Works great," I saw the sparkle in her eyes she got every time she won an argument. It was often.

"How the hell did you get it to work?" Falcon asked. He was a little drunk. Atam, it turns out, was quite the healer. Abuela got him up and functional, but Atam did something to make him feel a few years younger. Routine maintenance, he called it, before wondering how humans survived at all.

"It turns out, if you just *read the instructions*, it helps. A lot," she laughed.

Sherwin materialized behind her, placing a drink in her hand. She didn't flinch at the contact, and that made me smile. Peony's default was flinch, attack, or cast. With Sherwin, she just stood taller, standing in praise he saved for her. I caught flashes of him gushing over her and saw it light her up inside.

"Sherwin!"

"Deign. Diego. Sorry, old habits."

Diego threw his arms around him and they laughed. Diego turned, his thoughts loud and clear even without the heart links, ***Be right back, my Blossom. Sherwin needs Trellian wine.***

I winked at him as he sailed away with Sherwin, and Falcon hot on their heels. They laughed and jostled each other like they were all old friends. Diego's energy spoke of a man joyously fulfilled, and I smiled knowing I had a part in that. The sorrow that tried to tear him apart was such a distant memory these days that it didn't feel real.

"Am I late to the party? Look what the cat dragged in. Figuratively, I didn't do this," Puddin purred as she gathered Peony in her arms. As Puddin shuffled her, I saw Mama come into view.

My heart stopped. The world stopped.

She was hugging me, and I thought I might cry. The tears were there, but they wouldn't fall, so I just squeezed her tighter.

"I'm so thankful that you're safe. Puddin told me what you've done. Jack, my darling, I am so proud of you. I knew you were destined for greatness, I just didn't know you would write your own destiny."

"How long is the portal open? Can we stay for the party? Diego is just so happy, and we've only just really gotten to know Desmond–"

"The portal is a door. It opens and closes like a door should, so yes, we can stay, but this time we're going home *together*," Peony said.

She held my hand along with Mari's and it felt like I was already home. We stood in a little circle, like we'd done a thousand times before, and I felt the harmony shift between us, settling the magic in our hearts. I saw their auras differently now: Mari's was red like Wildfire, and Peony was purple like an amethyst.

The guys, this time including Desmond, came back together. Diego couldn't stop smiling, couldn't hold back the joy, and it rolled off him in waves. Even Peony was charmed. He held my gaze, taking my hand and twirling us back to the dance floor. The people of Trellis and Chilijan whooped and hollered, shouting, "Long live the Fallen King! Long live the Reviver! Long live our Priestess. Long live King Desmond!"

The band picked up and I let myself be swept away. The stained glass windows I saw in visions past glowed with light and magic. The Great Hall lived up to its name with flowers hanging from every possible surface. I saw the flowers Diego taught me about in Chilijan. I saw large, gorgeous Jack-in-the-pulpits surrounded by marigolds and peonies and knew that

Diego had the arrangement made for me. Snapdragon flowers tied the bouquets together, and I was grateful that she wasn't already forgotten.

Flower sprites and air sprites danced in the air, making trails of magic that glittered in the air. The wine flowed and so did the laughter.

Trellis was healing. The Rainbow Forest would return to its former glory, and the people would forgive and forget Diego. He would fade again to another story, another memory, while he moved on with his life. On Earth, with me.

As the music crested, Diego drank it all in.

"You know what that means, right Jack?"

"No?"

"Let me show you," he said as he pulled me close. Diego made a show of stepping back and bowing, and the crowd went wild. His eyes were wild with golden, gleaming magic.

"Diego?" When he stood up, a wave of magic rippled through the Great Hall. He pulled out two bracelets made of green and golden charms.

"Jack Hawthorne, the everbloom of my heart and shining star in every piece scattered in three realms, you are my home. I wanted to give you a heart link when the time was right, but every moment I'm blessed with you is the right time, so here I am. I bind myself to you, and I'll follow through every realm you walk."

Diego offered me the heart link and I couldn't blink back any tears. He smoothed away each one with his thumbs. I held my wrist up to him where the other bracelet still rested. He fastened it and the clasp disappeared. I closed the other around his wrist and our hands laced together for what felt like the thousandth time. I saw flashes of our life and the years that spread out in front of us, but I forced them down. Why ruin the surprise of your life?

I didn't want to spoil one moment with him.

The crowd cheered again, and Diego lifted me in the air, spinning us around before he settled me to his chest. He placed feather-light kisses on my forehead and cheeks, finally closing in on my lips.

"I love you," I said.

"I love you, my Blossom."

The party picked up and I watched as every person I loved in every realm was in this castle, dancing in time to the beat of the music. The door would be waiting for us, but tonight, tonight we were in Obius, the land of magic.

Tonight the rest of our lives were beginning.

JACK HAWTHORNE
HOLY PRIESTESS OF THE SEER
THE END

EPILOGUE

SIX WEEKS LATER

MARI

Life was finally starting to feel normal again. Jack's home was still in ruins, but the construction crew was finally here and Peony was on top of getting things running smoothly. The current ETA of *Visions and Trinkets* being up and running again was sometime in the late spring, and until then, Jack decided that the insurance money would be enough for her to take a much-needed break.

She was different now that we were back on Earth. Happier, more planted. She walked barefoot through every garden and patch of grass that she could find, connecting to each and every blade of grass to feel the life of the Earth. Seeing her find herself gave me hope that I'd figure it out one day too.

Diego was a new constant in our world. He was never a chatty Cathy, but he was talking more. Smiling. Emoting. Not acting like a weird-ass robot.

Peony found an open apartment in the building that I lived in and secured the place for Jack and Diego. They were quietly building a life together, and part of me was green with envy. A tiny part. Mostly though, I couldn't hold back love for them both.

Sherwin was around here and there, mostly when Peony was in town or when Diego called. He was back to his gardens, making and prepping things for when his favorite customer was ready to start buying again.

And then there was Falcon.

He crashed on my couch. In my bed. In my world. He came and went like a summer storm, and I hated that I was excited every time he came back. When we first got back from Obius, Falcon went to Abuela's cabin. He wanted time to process, he said, but mostly I think he needed to grieve what he had lost and didn't need the audience.

But now, he was in my kitchen singing and bopping along to his sixties beach tunes, while he made breakfast. My small apartment smelled like bacon and coffee, and I let myself have this moment.

Wildfire was still trapped in my body, and the days were getting harder. Some days I didn't get out of bed. Some days I spent in the bathtub, covered in ice water to keep the flames at bay.

Some nights when the world was asleep, I'd go to the ocean and let the flames rage and rage, where no one could get hurt.

Sometimes, Falcon would find me charred and burnt, and bring me back home.

Like last night.

He never brought it up, never questioned what I was doing, never asked for an explanation.

It drove me nuts.

"Bacon? Coffee? I'm making a spread today. Waffles are up next. I've got some fresh fruit all chopped and ready. Today we're going to feed you something other than microwaved burritos and take-out pizza."

"I feel judged, Falcon."

"Not judged. I love a solid microwaved burrito as much as the next guy, but you're looking a little thin, Mari. Tired."

He held the words in the air, waiting for me to challenge them. Waiting for an explanation. Waiting for me to admit that I was truly turning to ash.

"I am pretty beat."

"We've been back for like six weeks now, Mari. Are we going to keep not talking about Wildfire? Because I'm starting to think that I'm going to find you one day knocked out from the blaze and you aren't going to wake up."

"Falcon–"

"Tell me I'm wrong." He turned the stove off, taking the bacon out and letting it drain on a paper towel resting on a free burner.

I started to protest, but I couldn't. He was right. We both knew it.

"I don't know how to stop Wildfire. I can't cast here, not like in Obius. There's too many people, too much risk. But if I don't let it out, I feel like I'm going to boil alive."

"We need to find a way to get Wildfire out of your system."

Falcon served me some coffee–he knew exactly how I liked it, and I wasn't mad about that. He piled bacon and fruit on a plate as he started making the waffles. I wasn't a morning eater, but I couldn't refuse.

We both nearly jumped out of our skin when my front door opened. We weren't expecting anyone and Jack always knocked–

Candela, Abuela's sister and *Goddess*, strolled through the doorway. Her long, fiery red hair was in a load of tiny braids, with charms attached to them. A maxi skirt was fitted across her hips and the triangular bandana top screamed a boho vibe that didn't seem to fit in the real world.

"What? You're not going to offer me a cup of coffee too, Falcon?" she said as she took a seat at my little kitchen table.

"Didn't realize you got an invite to breakfast," he growled. I gave him a pointed look that he promptly ignored.

"It's cute you think I need one," she said, the fire igniting in her eyes.

"Candela, what are you doing here?" I asked.

"There's a smart question. You could learn a thing or two from her," she said, grabbing a piece of bacon off my plate.

Falcon huffed out a laugh and turned back to making my waffle. I tossed a pot holder at him and it bounced off without him so much as twitching.

"How're you doing, Mari? How's that Wildfire feeling?"

"Like I'm made of lava and need to explode, mostly."

"Thought so. Wildfire wasn't meant to live in a person, much less a human. You, my dear, are quite interesting."

"I'm not sure I like the sound of that," I said.

Candela grabbed my arm and Wildfire lit up, burning me through and through. She didn't let go, and molten tears leaked from my eyes. I tried to pull away, to let the tears fall back on me so I didn't ruin my counters.

"Let go of her *now*," Falcon said, knife drawn. He was going to fight a Goddess in my kitchen.

"No," she said.

The fire grew until I had to clamp my mouth shut before I burned the whole building down. Falcon yanked me up out of the chair, shoving me behind him. He shook his hand, smoke coming from his fingers.

"Glad to see you two work well as a team. One bomb and one extinguisher. Good. I have work for you."

"You burst into Mari's home, light her on fire, and then demand we work for you? The hell are you smoking?"

"Falcon, maybe don't antagonize the Goddess," I mumbled.

"You should listen to her more." Candela popped a piece of mango in her mouth, eyes locked on me.

"What work?" I asked.

"Like I said, you ask good questions. When the other Hawthorne sister got one of the links open, she did more than that. The links between the realms are not just simple, small doorways. They're like a million tunnels connecting, but Peony started something. My creatures are waking up again. They were dormant for so long, but now they smell the magic coming from Obius. They want to be awake."

"I don't think I like where this is going," Falcon said.

Candela stood and lit a fire in her hand. There were monsters in her flame, things I'd never seen before and never wanted to see again. Fangs and claws. Howling and braying. My skin itched and my stomach dropped through the floor. She flicked her hand and Falcon flew to the other side of my apartment, crashing into the wall where my already-cracked picture frames rattled off again. She grabbed my chin, the fire dancing in her eyes and across her face. I couldn't look away. Wildfire stirred again and it made me feel alive, even as it was killing me.

"Marigold Groves, you have fire in your fingers and ice in your veins. You are a Scion of the Creation Goddess. You have work to do."

...TO BE CONTINUED IN...
CHAOS BORN
THE CREATOR'S FLAME: BOOK 1

DEAR READER

Thank you so much for reading *Visions of Snapdragon*! I sincerely hope that you enjoyed Jack and the rest of the crew learning the depths of their magic and what secrets are waiting for them.

If you enjoyed it, please consider leaving a review and spreading the word! This helps other readers to find this book; chatting and posting about it on social media, blogs, and forums is an absolute blessing for indie writers. This is how we connect with our readers, and every review is so appreciated!

Also, if you'd like some exclusive content and teasers for the next books in Jack's world, you can always sign up for my **NEWSLETTER** too!

Love,

Jana

Acknowledgments

I cried writing the ending chapters. Is that silly to admit? Oh well, because here we are. *Visions of Kings* is everything I wanted Jack's story to end with. Jack, Diego, and Falcon have been living in my heart for a very long time now. They've had several settings before landing in Jack's shop and Trellis.

My loving husband, Glenn, wiped my tears when I wrote "the end." My parents, Shirley and Jim, are still waving the bookish pom-poms. My writing community that kept me going: the Ems (Emma and Emily), The Writer's Guild, my ARC and Street teams on Instagram, and all of my wonderful friends IRL (Joshu, Lena, KK, and Nicolai). And lastly my boys, my wonderful (and infuriating—haha) boys that mostly let me work on my dreams undisturbed.

Then the professionals that got this book to where I wanted it to be: my darling editor, Andrea Davidson, **the Ardent Editor**, whom I can't thank enough for her skills and insights, and Candis Frey-Curry, my **eagle-eyed proofreader** who saved me tons of heartache of digging for typos.

This isn't goodbye forever for Jack and the rest of the crew—Mari's books will be coming up next, and there's a Goddess with Mari in Her crosshairs.

About the Author

Writer. Wife/Mom. Servant to 4lb Chihuahua with a Napoleon complex. Avid coffee drinker. Travel junkie. Book devourer. (Not, *literally*—too much fiber.)

I've been writing most of my life, but my heart has always been drawn to magic. Urban Fantasy--mixing magic with real life--became the perfect genre for me.

Born and raised on the Southeast Coast of Virginia, when I'm not writing or momming, I'm heading for the ocean.

Come join my newsletter called **"The Magic Shop,"** where I'll send you monthly emails to tease upcoming books, provide flower, crystal, and character bios, and *of course,* pictures of His Royal Highness, Prince Babar, my chihuahua.

Feeling social? I'm on Facebook and IG, and I'd love for you to come say hello!

f

facebook.com/profile.php?id=100091558147127

instagram.com/jana_sun_books/

www.ingramcontent.com/pod-product-compliance
Lightning Source LLC
Chambersburg PA
CBHW021143310726
48971CB00002B/465